HEART OF A DEVIL

QUENTIN SECURITY SERIES #5

MORGAN JAMES

CHAPTER
ONE

VINCE

I was seriously not cut out for this shit. The bar crowd had never been my scene, and it was even less so now that I was surrounded by a bunch of immature twenty-somethings who thought they were God's gift to the world.

I fought to keep my expression neutral as I watched the scantily clad bodies dry humping each other on the dance floor. Ripping my eyes away from Gemma, I glanced around the crappy little hole in the wall bar. Louie's was a favorite post-show hangout, but for the life of me, I couldn't figure out why. The place reeked of booze, sweat, and perfume, and a sticky substance that I prayed was alcohol coated the floor in spots.

My boots made a disgusting sound as I shifted, returning my gaze to Gemma. My principle—the woman currently under my protection—was on the dance floor shaking her skinny ass to some country pop song one of her friends had released a few months ago, and the dude behind her was doing his best to get his hand up her short as fuck Daisy Dukes.

Gemma Malone's band members were scattered around the small club, each scouting a new piece of tail to take home for the evening—or the morning, in this case, considering it was past midnight. I'd spent the last ten hours at the venue playing babysitter for her during the final show of her tour. As if that wasn't bad enough, I'd been obligated to accompany her to Louie's when she decided she wanted to come out and unwind with the rest of the band.

It was fairly local, thank God, so I was only about an hour from home. All I wanted to do was herd Gemma out the door, drop her off at her house, then pour myself into bed for a couple of hours before I had to be back at her place. It was already creeping close to one o'clock, and I was supposed to be back over there by eight to take her to the studio.

The guy plastered to Gemma's back was getting bolder, his hand moving between her thighs, and I wondered if she was stupid enough to let him feel her up on the dance floor. Gemma was the chosen poster child for Magnolia Way records and a supposed role model for little girls. I snorted. She wouldn't be much of a role model for long if one of the people standing around the floor waving their cell phones got a picture at just the right angle.

Unfortunately, it was my job to keep her safe, both from the person sending her threatening letters and from herself, so I stomped across the dance floor and wedged myself between them. "Time to go."

Big blue eyes glared up at me. "What the hell, Vince?"

I tipped my head toward the door. "Let's go before you get in trouble."

Her face fell into a petulant expression. "I wasn't doing anything wrong."

"Yeah, come on, man," the drunk kid wheedled. "We was just havin' fun. Right, babe?"

We both ignored the drunken idiot, and I focused on

Gemma. "You were practically fucking him on the dance floor. Unless you want to end up a headline on tomorrow's tabloids, I suggest you get your shit and go."

She rolled her eyes and stomped away, but not in the direction of the front door as I'd hoped. I followed her to the bar where one of her fellow bandmates sat with a beautiful brunette draped over his lap, her tongue currently trailing up the side of his neck. A tumbler of what appeared to be whiskey sat on the bar in front of Brandt, and he lifted a hand, signaling for the bartender to deliver another as he watched Gemma approach.

He slid the glass her way, and she slammed it back, then wiped the back of her wrist across her mouth, all the while glaring at me. Brandt Meacham smirked, his gaze bouncing from me then back to Gemma. "Bodyguard cracking down again?"

Gemma threw back another shot as soon as the bartender placed it in front of her, then turned her attention to Brandt. "I think I'm up for a ride."

He chuckled around the woman trying to suck his face off. "Suit yourself, Gems."

She pinned me with her brilliant blue eyes, one eyebrow lifting toward her hairline. "What about you?"

I clenched my molars together, barely managing to rein in my irritation. "No."

One corner of her mouth kicked up. "What? Don't think you can last eight seconds?"

I stared down at her, unwilling to rise to the bait. A couple silence-filled seconds later, she let out an irritated little huff and spun on her heel, then stomped toward the mechanical bull in the corner. Great. This night just kept getting better and better.

Beside me, Brandt shoved the brunette's head away from

his face and glanced at me. "You can take off, Ink. We're all headed back to my place after this."

Oh, hell no. Bad shit seemed to follow Brandt wherever he went, and the trouble that didn't follow him he brought on himself. He was a borderline alcoholic, and I didn't trust the kid as far as I could throw him. The last time they'd hung out at his place, he decided it was a good idea to pull out a pistol indoors.

One of the other morons in the band had dared him to pull the trigger, and he either hadn't checked to see if it was loaded or he hadn't given a shit. The bullet had passed through two walls before lodging in the drywall of the bedroom where one of his drunken trysts was passed out. There wasn't a snowball's chance in hell that I was letting Gemma hang out with that stupid fuck.

"She's gotta be up early," I said by way of response. "We're taking off as soon as she's done here."

I closed my eyes and released a long exhalation through my nostrils as a loud—and very familiar—"Hey, y'all, watch this!" split the air.

Turning toward the small padded arena, I watched with dismay as Gemma lifted one arm high over her head, the other hand fisted around the reins of the fake bull as it began to rock back and forth. I had to give the girl credit. She was actually pretty coordinated, even half-intoxicated.

A small crowd gathered around, and hoots and hollers filled the air as the bull bucked wildly and Gemma did her best to hold on. Her tiny denim cutoffs bunched up around her hips with each rocking motion, exposing the curve of her ass cheeks. Resigned to let this play out, I folded my arms over my chest. If she wanted to make a spectacle of herself, that was her choice. Her PR person made way more money to put up with her shit than I did.

Almost as soon as the thought crossed my mind, Gemma

was thrown off the bull's back and landed with a giggle on the inflatable floor surrounding the contraption. I pushed off the bar and strode toward her, then hooked one hand around her elbow as she stumbled to her feet. "Fun's over, trouble."

Snatching up the fringed cowgirl boots on the floor, I hauled Gemma across the bar and out the door.

"Hey!" Gemma dug in her heels, trying to pull me to a stop, but I paid her no attention as I pushed out the front door. "What are you doing?"

She pulled against me again, and I ran my tongue over my teeth. Releasing her elbow, I wrapped my arm around her waist and lifted her to my hip like a toddler. My other arm slid under her ass, and I sucked in a breath as my fingers skated over miles of perfectly toned flesh.

She seemed too stunned to speak as I stormed toward my truck, and I was grateful for the temporary reprieve. We crossed the parking lot, and I opened the passenger door, then plunked her ass down on the seat and tossed her boots on the floorboard.

"Hey, asshole, that's—" She abruptly cut off and gave me a funny look.

I settled one hand on her shoulder and dipped my head to look into her eyes. "You good?"

She pressed her lips together and nodded slightly.

"You sure? Because if you feel—Fuck!"

I tried to jump backward as that last shot of whiskey and everything that had preceded it throughout the course of the day splattered across my boots. Keeping one hand on her shoulder to steady her, I closed my eyes and counted to ten. I ground my molars together and glanced up at Gemma's pale face. Perspiration dotted her forehead, and I lightly tapped her cheek to get her attention. "You with me?"

Her eyes opened slowly, sluggishly, and met mine. She gave a listless nod.

"Come on. May as well get the rest of it out." As if my words triggered another bout, she leaned forward and heaved again. This time, I was quick enough to move out of the line of fire. Avoiding the pile of vomit on the pavement, I maneuvered myself between the open door of the cab in an attempt to keep anyone from seeing her.

I was grateful that the parking lot had been packed when we arrived and we'd had to park all the way off to the side. I glanced around but saw nothing, and I prayed that no one had seen. We'd made something of a spectacle leaving the bar, and it wouldn't surprise me in the least if someone tried to capture our little scene on camera.

Turning my attention back to Gemma, I ran my hand in light circles over her back. When she was done, she leaned back against the seat, panting heavily. I opened the back door and hunted around for a bottle of water, then passed it to her. "Drink."

She did as she was told, then moved to hand it back to me. "Keep it. You need to rehydrate." I curled her fingers around it and set it in her lap so she'd have it when she needed it.

Pulling the seatbelt across her torso, I snapped it into place then slammed the door. For the first time ever, I cursed the fact that we weren't at one of her tour stops with a hotel nearby. I could get us a place for the night, but I was already tired as shit, and all I wanted to do was get her ass home then do the same.

I headed around to the driver side, then cranked the engine and pulled out of the lot. On the radio, one song was ending, bleeding right into another, and Gemma roused enough to reach over and crank up the volume. Before I had the chance to brace myself, she belted out the lyrics, and I cringed as her high soprano bounced off my eardrums. "Jesus, woman!"

Gemma took the volume down a couple notches but

continued to sing along with Reba enthusiastically. A few minutes later, she grew quieter and quieter, then finally—blessedly—completely silent. Thank fuck.

Forty-five minutes later, I pulled up in front of her house and cut the engine, then pocketed my keys. "Let's go, sleeping beauty."

Next to me, Gemma snored softly in her seat. I rolled my eyes, then made my way around and pulled her out. Her head lolled back as I lifted her in my arms, and I awkwardly maneuvered her dead weight toward the front door. I punched in the code to the electronic keypad above the door handle that she'd opted to use instead of a physical key. The security system beeped a warning as I stepped inside, and I juggled Gemma as I closed the door and disengaged the alarm.

Gemma blinked up at me as I made my way through the living room and down the hall. "What are you doing?"

"Putting you to bed." I used my elbow to flick on the light as I carried her into her bedroom. She swayed as I stood her on her feet next to the bed. "Your boots are still in my truck. Do you want me to get them?"

She waved my offer away. "No. I need to use the bathroom."

She stumbled in that direction, and I waited awkwardly in the bedroom, trying to ignore the sound of her using the toilet. Water flushed, and I breathed a sigh of relief. Thank Jesus. Now she could go to bed, and I could go home. My hopes went up in smoke when I heard the shower come on.

"Goddamn it, Gemma." Growling in frustration, I stormed toward the bathroom. I stopped dead in my tracks in the doorway, stunned, as I took in Gemma standing under the spray of the shower, fully clothed. Jesus Christ. "What the hell are you doing?"

She turned those giant blue eyes on me. "Washing off. What does it look like?"

I stared at her for a long moment, barely fighting back the urge to tell her exactly what I thought. "Come on, let's just get you to bed."

"Hold on," she complained. "I'm almost done."

I waited for about half a second before I stomped across the room and flicked off the water with a quick turn of my wrist. "Now."

"All right, all right. Jeez." But instead of climbing from the shower, her hands moved toward the button of her shorts, and she shimmied the soaked denim over her hips and down her legs, taking a pair of skimpy pale pink panties with them. I quickly averted my eyes and grabbed a towel from the rack, holding it in front of me like a shield.

God give me strength. I wasn't gonna lie—Gemma without clothes was something else. Not that she'd ever know it, but I'd lusted over her hard for the past twelve days, ever since I'd been hired on. It was my first job since my honorable discharge from the Marines, and I was nervous as hell. I didn't want to screw up. She'd flirted with me a bit over the first couple of days, but hard as it was, I refused to give in to her charm. I wasn't about to risk my job for a pretty face.

Good thing I hadn't tried anything either, because her true colors revealed themselves soon after. For the past week and a half or so, she'd acted like an absolute spoiled little brat who treated me like a servant instead of the man hired to protect her. It irked the hell out of me, but I'd be damned if I let her know she'd gotten under my skin.

I watched over the edge of the towel as her hands moved to the pearl buttons of her pink and blue plaid shirt, and it seemed to take an eternity for her to get them all unsnapped. She pushed the fabric off her shoulders, then let out a little grunt of distress as her arms got trapped inside the sleeves.

"Stupid thing..." She shook one arm, succeeding only in making it worse as the wet fabric clung and tangled together.

"For fuck's sake." I dropped the towel and reached for her. "Turn around."

She wobbled on her feet but managed to turn her back to me, and I peeled the sodden material down her arms and dropped it in the tub.

She gathered her hair, and dragged the damp locks over one shoulder as she glanced back at me. "My bra?"

Jesus. Who had I killed in a past life to deserve this? Clenching my teeth, I released the clasp in the middle of her back and yanked the straps down. As soon as it hit the ground, Gemma let out a little sigh and fell back against me. I caught her around her waist to keep her from falling, and she grasped my arm where it banded just beneath her breasts.

I forced myself to stare straight ahead and not give in to the temptation to look at those gorgeous tits spilling over my forearm. Gemma tipped her head back against my shoulder and wiggled her bottom against me as if trying to get closer.

"Gemma..."

My dick obviously didn't give a shit that she was drunk— maybe even drugged, considering her erratic behavior—and stratospherically out of my league. It thickened at the feel of her and pressed against the front of my jeans, instinctively seeking out her heat.

Gemma reached behind me and grasped the back of my thigh, arching her back like a kitten as she rubbed against me. That in itself told me how out of her mind she was. The girl never looked at me with anything other than complete and utter disdain. For her to touch me, let alone intimately like this, was completely out of character.

I peeled her hand away and spun her in my arms. "Look at me." Her glassy eyes flitted around for a moment before locking on mine. "You good?"

"I could be better." She lifted her hand and cupped my

erection tenting the front of my jeans, then smiled, slow and sultry. "I could make you feel better, too."

I snatched her hand away. "Gemma, stop."

She leaned forward, pressing her breasts against my chest and pouted up at me. "Why don't you like me?"

I swallowed down the urge to comfort her. It was just the alcohol talking. "Let's just get you to bed. You've had too much to drink."

"Whatever." She rolled her eyes and pulled away from me, her lips turning down in a frown. "I don't know why you hate me so much."

The way she said it sent a little pang of unease through me. "I don't hate you."

"Right." She threw a sad look my way before leaving the bathroom.

I propped my hands on my hips and tipped my head back, drawing in a deep breath. I didn't hate her—I didn't. She was just... young and immature and frustrating as hell. My cock throbbed in my jeans, reminding me once again how long it'd been since I'd had a gorgeous woman throw herself at me.

I adjusted myself, thanking God that I'd had the presence of mind to turn her down. My dick wasn't happy about it, but I liked my job, and I wouldn't jeopardize it, even for her. My only consolation was that Gemma was almost completely inebriated, and with luck, she would forget all about this by the time she woke up tomorrow.

I glanced at my watch. Just after three. Goddamn it. By the time I got home it would be almost four, and I'd have to be up in a couple hours anyway. Resigning myself to staying here for the night, I grimaced as I glanced down at my boots and puke-splattered jeans. I'd definitely experienced worse, but I sure as hell couldn't sleep like that on Gemma's couch.

I peeked out of the bathroom, relieved that she'd crawled into bed. Turning off the light, I cut across the house to the laundry room and toed out of my boots—no saving those suckers—then tossed my shirt and jeans in the washing machine. I'd crash out for a while then dry them in the morning.

Moving through the dark house, I reset the house alarm, used the key fob to lock my truck, then headed back to Gemma's room to check on her. A soft snuffling sound greeted me, and I approached the side of the bed, listening intently to her breathing.

By the time she'd left the bathroom, she'd seemed, if not fully coherent, at least slightly less drunk than when we'd left the bar. She made the soft gurgling sound again, and I rolled my eyes. Just what I needed, for her to choke on her own vomit and die in her sleep.

She let out a grumble as I rolled her to her side, then she snuggled back into her pillow and dropped off again with a little snore. I scrubbed one hand over my face before I reluctantly strode around the bed and climbed in the other side. At least this close, I'd be able to know if something was wrong.

I tucked my arms behind my head and closed my eyes, already dreading the morning to come.

CHAPTER
TWO

JANA

Before I even opened my eyes, I was aware of a bitter taste in my mouth, the cottony feeling like I'd had too much to drink. I cracked one eye open, squinting against the bright sunlight spilling through the window, and warily glanced around. My eyes swept over the familiar walls of my bedroom. Thank God. I was home.

I was also... I peeked under the blanket. Yep. I was bare ass naked. What the hell had happened last night?

I scrunched up my nose and tried to swallow down the taste clinging to my tongue. My eyes felt tired, my body sluggish, and I rolled to my back, stretching my arms wide as I did so. My hand collided with something hard and warm, and I whipped my head toward the right side of the bed.

A huge body occupied the normally empty space next to me, and from a quick glance at the man's face and the dark artwork decorating his skin, I recognized Vince. His torso was bare, his arms tucked beneath the pillow. I waited a moment to see if he was awake, but he didn't stir. I used that to my advantage and unabashedly allowed my gaze to rove over his muscular body.

I knew from our initial introduction that his full name was Vince Incarnato, but most everyone called him Ink. Even so, I'd always thought of him as just Vince. Looking at him, though, I had to admit that the nickname was incredibly apt. Tattoos decorated nearly every inch of skin from his wrists up to his shoulders, then down his back. Twin dimples just above his ass winked up at me, and my fingers itched to pull the sheet down and see if he was just as naked as I was.

Holy shit. Did we have sex last night? God, wouldn't that be just my luck—to finally sleep with him and then have no memory of it?

"What time is it?" I jumped at the sound of Vince's raspy morning voice.

"Um..."

He cracked one eye open to look at me, then pulled his hand from under the pillow and checked his watch. "We've got about another hour. Go back to sleep."

I stared at him. He seriously expected me to go back to sleep when we were both naked in my bed? At least, I was naked, and I needed answers. "Did we have sex last night?"

This time, both eyes popped open, hitting me with a hard stare. "Negative."

"What the hell does that mean? Then why am I naked?"

"Because I wasn't gonna dig around in your shit to try to find something for you to wear."

"What was wrong with the clothes I had on?"

With a huff, he rolled over and swung his legs over the edge of the bed. As he changed positions, I saw that he was wearing a pair of tight-fitting black boxers. Shame.

"Because yours were soaked."

What was soaked? Besides... I ripped my mind out of the gutter and tried to focus. Oh, right. My clothes. I stared at his back, the intricate artwork dancing over his muscles as he stretched. "So we didn't have sex last night?"

He threw a look over his shoulder at me. "No."

He said the word like it was practically three syllables, and it pissed me off. "So what the hell happened?"

"You got drunk, and I brought you home."

"Then why the hell are you in my bed?"

"Oh, I don't know," he said with no small amount of sarcasm. "Maybe so I could make sure you didn't choke on your own puke."

I winced internally, then mentally batted the thought away. "I don't get sick when I drink."

He let out a mirthless laugh. "Really? Because my clothes say otherwise."

Oh, God. Every inch of my body went hot, and I felt heat climbing into my cheeks. "I threw up on you?"

He turned and met my eyes, studying me for several long seconds. "Do you not remember anything?"

I tried desperately to draw back on the events of the last twelve hours or so. There was the show, then we hit up Louie's to celebrate the end of the tour. I had a couple drinks, a couple shots. I remembered riding the bull and Vince telling me it was time to leave. After that... It was like a blank void.

"No..." I drew the word out long and slow, and he let out a little sigh.

He cleared his throat. "Never mind, just forget about it."

"No, no." I tried to scramble from the bed then remembered that I was naked, and I grabbed up the sheet to cover myself. "Tell me."

Now I needed to know. I'd never gotten so drunk before that I didn't remember what I was doing, and the way Vince looked at me worried me immensely. God, why was I always making a fool of myself in front of this man? I hated the way he made me feel sometimes. It wasn't his fault—it was just his personality that made him seem more worldly and mature than I would ever be.

I'd been absolutely infatuated with him from the moment he stepped foot into my living room—and, really, what woman wouldn't be? Vince was huge, standing over six feet tall and built like a brick wall, all muscles and dark tattoos. Icy blue eyes stood out from darkly tanned skin, his strong, square jaw lightly stubbled. His dark hair was slightly longer on top than on the sides, and it stood up slightly where it'd been pressed against the pillow.

Instead of appearing bedraggled and unkempt, the dishevelment made him look dangerous and capable of anything. Coupled with the sex appeal he oozed, I wanted to throw myself into his strong, tattooed arms.

I'd smiled and teased him a bit during our first couple of days together, testing the waters, but he'd taken one look down his nose at me—the one that looked like it'd been broken once or twice, and strangely only added to his handsomeness—and immediately dismissed me as if I were no more interesting than some annoying insect flying by.

I didn't know why his rejection bothered me so much. Maybe because it wasn't a rejection so much as a dismissal. He obviously didn't find me attractive, so I'd built up the walls around my heart, cursing my terrible taste in men once more. I always went for the men I couldn't have, the ones who were emotionally unavailable or had no desire to settle down. Unfortunately, it looked like I would have to cross gorgeous, tattooed bodyguards off my list, too.

Vince scrubbed one hand through his hair, making it stick up even more. "Just saying, maybe you shouldn't have had that last shot of whiskey."

"Apparently." My cheeks burned with humiliation just thinking about it. I couldn't believe I'd thrown up all over him. That was definitely a first for me. It had probably gotten all over me too, which explained why I was naked. He probably just stripped us both and put me to bed.

"Thank you," I said softly. "I'll grab your clothes and put them in the laundry."

"Already taken care of," he replied. "Your clothes are in the sink. They were soaked, and I didn't want to carry them through the house."

I gave a little nod, confused. "Did you wash them in there?"

"Um... no," he said, his shoulders tightening with tension. "You decided to climb in the shower when we got home, so I just tossed your clothes in the sink to drain."

Lord, take me now. This just kept getting worse. He literally had to undress me like a toddler. "Did I... do anything else?"

I swore I saw a hint of red creep over his face before he turned away. "No."

He looked uncomfortable as shit, and I had a terrible feeling I knew what that meant. I'd been drunk and naked, and I'd probably thrown myself at him. I couldn't bear to torture either of us with any more questions, so I clutched the sheet more tightly around me and strode into my closet. Five minutes later, dressed in an armor of leggings and a tank top, I headed to the bathroom.

I almost groaned out loud as I caught my reflection in the mirror. My hair had obviously been soaked when I fell into bed, and now it was matted on one side and sticking up on the other, a rat's nest of crazy, pale gold waves. Jesus. I wouldn't have had sex with me either. I was a hot mess.

Shoving down my humiliation, I pulled my hair up in a messy bun, then quickly washed my face. I needed to get into the studio this morning, but I didn't really care whether I looked like a troll or not.

Vince intercepted me as I came out of the bathroom,

halting me in my tracks. My brain shorted out, and I froze like a deer in the headlights. He was still dressed in only the tight-fitting black boxers he'd worn to bed, and my gaze automatically strayed lower, eagerly drinking in the sculpted muscles and thick bulge in the front. "Uh..."

He cleared his throat, but I could barely hear him over the blood pulsing in my ears. Holy shit. Somehow, I managed to drag my eyes back to his, heat sweeping up my neck and into my cheeks.

He looked as uncomfortable as I felt as he shuffled his feet awkwardly. "Change of plans. Maggie and Harvey are on their way over."

Inwardly, I groaned, and the lust clouding my brain dissipated as reality slammed into me. It wasn't abnormal at all for my assistant, Maggie, to stop by. But Harvey was probably here to do damage control, which meant that last night must have been worse than I thought. I stared at Vince. "Did I make a complete ass of myself at the bar?"

One corner of his mouth tipped up in an almost-smile. "No, you waited till we got to the truck for that."

I closed my eyes. I was going to feel like shit if I puked all over the inside of his truck. I opened my eyes and met Vince's gaze again. "Please tell me I didn't..."

He seemed to know where I was headed with the question, because he shook his head. "You threw up in the parking lot, then passed out for the ride home."

Well, thank God for small favors. "I need caffeine."

Pushing past him, I headed down the hallway into the kitchen. I'd never been a coffee person, and I'd just finished steeping my tea when the doorbell sounded. I took a step toward the hallway, but Vince was already there. "I got it."

My gaze swept over his muscular backside, now clad in his freshly washed clothes. Unfortunately. I smirked. I could only imagine my assistant's reaction had Vince opened the door still half-naked.

A moment later, Harvey and Maggie stepped inside wearing identical expressions of concern. Harvey didn't bother to greet me, just stomped into the living room and took a seat on the couch. I rolled my eyes before meeting Maggie's gaze. "What's up his butt today?"

Maggie bit her lip. "Do you—?"

"Gemma!" Harvey's obnoxious voice cut over whatever Maggie was about to say. "Come sit. We need to talk."

I hated that he refused to use my real name. I'd reminded him time and again to call me Jana, but I seriously doubted he listened or even cared. I bit my lip to keep him from seeing my irritation, then made my way into the living room where I sank into the corner of the loveseat. Maggie gingerly sat next to me, and Vince hovered nearby, a silent but powerful visual. Harvey's eyes darted to him before meeting mine. "We received another note."

This time, I couldn't help the outright eye roll. "So? This guy has been sending me stupid letters for months."

Every actor, athlete, and singer had groupies and obsessive fans. For whatever reason, this guy had latched on to me, sending strange love letters and poems to the studio in the hopes that I would receive them. I'd read the first couple, but they hadn't made a damn bit of sense. The guy apparently had followed my journey over the past two years or so since I'd moved to Texas. He'd spoken of how my music affected him, and how much he'd love to see me perform in person.

I assumed from that tidbit that the guy had heard me on the radio, read about me in the tabloids, and had developed some kind of fascination with me. I really wasn't that interesting, and he appeared to be more infatuated than dangerous. He was just an odd duck, probably some forty-year-old virgin living in his mother's basement who wanted attention. For the past month and a half, I'd been content to just let Harvey deal with it.

"Regardless," my agent continued, "we've decided to increase your security. Beginning now, Mr. Incarnato will be with you 24/7."

Hot tea splashed all over my lap as I jerked up right. Maggie hopped up and ran to the kitchen for a towel, and my eyes jumped to Vince then back to Harvey as I struggled for words. "That's—but—this is ridiculous!"

I didn't need the arrogant, overbearing bodyguard breathing down my neck every second of the day. Especially after last night. I opened my mouth to argue, but Harvey held up a hand. "The label isn't willing to jeopardize your safety."

I sat back, disgruntled. What Harvey meant but didn't say was that Magnolia Way records had too much money invested in me to risk me being hurt. God forbid should they lose their gold ticket.

Harvey turned to Vince. "Mr. Quentin is aware of the situation, and he'll be sending someone over temporarily so you can go get whatever you need."

"Yes, sir," Vince replied. "I've already spoken with him."

I glared at Vince. The asshole had known but hadn't said anything? "I don't understand. Isn't there some other way to—"

"This is nonnegotiable." Harvey pushed his wide girth to the edge of the couch, then stood. "I need to get going. I've got an appointment downtown at ten."

The doorbell rang, and Vince nodded at Harvey. "That's my guy."

Swiftly moving toward the front of the house, he checked the peephole, then held the door for the other man to enter. I glared at him from across the room, but he ignored me completely.

Harvey's words snapped my attention back to him. "The

police are looking into the issue, so it hopefully won't be too long."

He tried for a smile, but it fell flat. Without another word he turned to leave, exiting the house just as the other man from QSG arrived.

Vince closed and locked the door behind Harvey, then led the man toward me. "Ms. Malone, this is Dane."

I lifted my chin in greeting. "Hi."

"Nice to meet you, miss."

Vince turned to Dane. "I'll be back in an hour or so. She's not allowed to go anywhere."

Dane nodded, and I jumped to my feet. "What the hell do you mean, I'm not allowed to go anywhere? All Harvey said was that someone had to be with me all the time."

"Too bad," Vince said, his expression hard. "My game, my rules."

"Fuck your rules, you both suck." I stomped toward the bathroom, my anger growing when I saw the still-wet clothes lying in the sink. I picked them up and hurled them toward the shower where they landed with a wet *thwack,* then slid to the ground.

Seriously. Could this day get any worse?

CHAPTER
THREE

VINCE

Gemma stomped off toward her room, and I ground my teeth together before turning to Dane. She could act like a spoiled brat all she wanted, but it wasn't going to stop either of us from doing our jobs. Dane lifted his eyebrows at me, and I bit back a sigh. "I'll be as quick as I can."

I felt bad for saddling the new guy with her, but I didn't have an option. I just prayed to God that he could follow directions. Gemma was sweet and charming when she wanted to be—ironically, she was nice to pretty much everyone but me—and I was more than a little worried that she would try to talk him into doing something she shouldn't. Together, Dane and I walked toward the door. "She doesn't go out, and no one comes in. Something happens, you call the police, then Con."

He gave me a tight nod. "You got it."

I stepped outside, listening for the tell-tale snick of the lock behind me. As soon as it snapped into place, I cut across the short, winding brick pathway to Gemma's driveway, then climbed into my truck. I backed onto the street, then headed toward home, pulling my phone out as I went. I tapped Con's number, and he answered on the first ring.

"Everything go okay?"

I didn't mince words. "She's pissed. She wants nothing to do with security, let alone having me around every minute of the day."

"Tough shit," Con replied. "Her studio is the one footing the bill, and if they want 24/7 surveillance, that's what they're going to get."

"Fair enough," I responded. "Dane's with her right now, and I'm headed home to get my things. What do we know so far?"

Though Con had texted me earlier to let me know there would be a change in plans, he hadn't been able to go into detail. "Another note was delivered last night," he replied. "This one is the worst of all."

Some obsessive nutcase had been sending love letters to Gemma over the last couple of months, and the tone of the letters vacillated between adoring and possessive. Recently, they'd become increasingly threatening. "How bad?"

"This last one basically said that if she didn't choose him, she wouldn't be with anyone at all."

Shit. "I assume the police are aware?"

"The letter was found in the studio's mail yesterday morning. They called the police right after," Con continued, "and they're tracing the postmark to see if they can nail something down."

I blew out a breath. "Okay. So what kind of timeline are we working with?"

"Plan to be with her full time for two weeks, possibly more."

I rolled my eyes. I could only imagine how badly Gemma and I were going to butt heads over the next fourteen days.

"All right. Last thing—tell your contact at Magnolia Way to tighten their leash on Brandt Meachem."

I explained to Con what had happened last night at the bar. It didn't matter if the drink was intended for the woman he was trying to take home or not. If he'd knowingly drugged Gemma—or any other woman, for that matter—I was going to murder the bastard.

Con sighed. "I'll let them know."

"Keep me posted."

I disconnected and shook my head. It wouldn't be so bad if we could just be nice to each other. Unfortunately, she tended to pull her Queen Bitch act any time I was around, and I snapped right back. And that was only the tip of the iceberg. I couldn't get the sight of her out of my mind. The image was burned into my brain, and I remembered the way her body felt against mine, her curves conforming to my hardened muscles like she was made for me.

The next two weeks would be pure hell, and I had no idea how I was going to survive the temptation of being around her every minute of the day. As it was, I went home each night and jerked off to the thought of those sexy denim cutoffs and fringed cowgirl boots. Her tongue was sharp and deadly, but her body... her body was made for long, sweaty nights between the sheets. The memory of her pressed against me sent heat spiraling through my groin, and I broke out in a sweat.

Shit. I swiped the back of my hand across my forehead, wiping away the perspiration there. It was a lose/lose situation. I needed to get my head in the game, focus on keeping her safe—and keeping my hands off.

I quickly packed my things and was back at Gemma's place less than an hour later. Noticing that Maggie's little black Corolla was still in the driveway, I parked along the street to give her more room, then let myself into Gemma's house using the code. I opened the door and almost bumped into Dane, who stood like a sentry inside the doorway.

I closed the door behind me and lifted my eyebrows in question. "Everything go okay?"

He nodded once. "They're in the kitchen. Good luck."

Rolling my eyes at his sarcastic tone, I locked up behind Dane, then followed the sound of hushed, angry voices. As soon as I stepped foot in the small kitchen, Gemma speared me with her icy blue gaze. "Thought you might have gotten lost."

Despite her syrupy sweet smile, her words dripped with venom. I bristled at her sarcasm but refused to let my ire out. "No such luck. I wouldn't deprive myself of your scintillating company for a second."

Though I continued to glare at Gemma, I could feel Maggie's anxious gaze jump between the two of us.

"Well then..." Maggie fidgeted nervously. "I should probably get going. Oh, before I forget." She pulled a small orange bottle from her purse. "I'm supposed to give you one of these."

She popped off the lid, then shook one tablet into her hand and offered it to Gemma. For the first time, I noticed the half-empty glass of red wine in front of her. Though it wasn't quite noon, I guessed it was five o'clock in Gemma's world.

She snatched the tablet from Maggie's outstretched hand then popped it into her mouth. I could see it hovering on her tongue as she lifted her wine glass and took a healthy sip.

Once she was done, she set her wine glass down with a hard click on the granite countertop.

I watched the entire thing with no small amount of distaste.

Maggie recapped the bottle and moved to put them back into her purse. "Thanks."

"Hey, Mags?" Gemma nodded to the prescription bottle. "Can I have those?"

The redhead looked torn. "I'm really not supposed to leave them…"

"Please?" Gemma affected a pitiful expression. "You know how hard this whole thing has been for me. What if I need them?"

"Well…" Maggie's hand tightened on the bottle before she reluctantly passed it over. "Okay, but don't tell Harvey."

Gemma beamed as she clutched the bottle close to her chest. "You're the best."

I bit down on my tongue to keep my automatic response from flying out of my mouth. Typical spoiled little faux celebrity. Gemma couldn't even make it through one day without medicating herself. There were a lot of people in this world a hell of a lot worse off than she was, but she was too caught up in herself to even realize it. With a little shake of my head, I looked at Maggie. "I'll close up after you."

I showed Maggie to the door, then locked up behind her and strode toward the couch. I dropped my duffel bag on the floor next to the coffee table, resigned to spending the next few nights in this very spot. I was still too antsy to sit and chill, so I made my way back to the kitchen. The sooner Gemma and I hashed things out, the better off we'd both be.

On silent feet, I headed through the doorway and spied Gemma standing at the counter, her back to me. The orange prescription bottle sat open on the counter next to her, as well as various other bottles of supplements, and pills were scattered over the granite surface.

Fury rose up, and I stormed toward her. I snatched up her wrist, and the empty bottle landed with a clatter at our feet. "What the hell do you think you're doing?"

She gasped as she whirled toward me, trying to pull free of my grasp. "Jesus! You scared the hell out of me!"

I scowled down at her. "What are you doing?"

"What?" She looked up at me blankly, like she had no idea what I was talking about—or she was desperately trying to hide something.

"I'm not fucking around, Gemma. What's with the damn pills?"

Her brows drew together, and I finally released her wrist as she gestured to them. "Trying to find a match."

"For what?"

She rolled her eyes. "The pills, you idiot. I'm looking for something similar." She studied me for a second. "What the hell did you think I was doing?"

"You've got pills spread all over the counter, Gemma. Take a guess what went through my head."

She glared at me. "No, I'm not planning to kill myself. But thanks for your concern." She turned back to the pharmacy in front of her but didn't say another word.

Frustration and curiosity welled up. "So, what exactly are you doing?"

"Looking for a match," she repeated, like I was slow. "I need to find a replacement so Maggie won't be suspicious."

"About what? Whether you're taking them?"

"What's with all the questions?"

I shrugged. "Just curious."

She turned to me, and her eyes narrowed. "Why? So you can run and tell Harvey?"

"Jesus, Gemma." I threw one hand in the air. "It's a simple fucking question. Why in Christ's name do you have a dozen different medications spread out like a buffet?"

I picked up the bottle Maggie had handed her before she'd left. "What the hell are these, anyway?"

"I have no idea."

My eyes flared at her response. "You take shit without knowing what it is?"

"No," she drew out the word. "That's why I'm looking for something to substitute."

I glared at the side of her face, which was all I could see of her since she refused to look at me. "But I watched you."

"No." She turned toward me. "You saw what I wanted you to see. Just like Maggie."

When I stared silently at her, she sighed. "You watched me put it in my mouth. I spit it into the wineglass." She gestured at the goblet still sitting by the sink in the island. "That's why I chose the red wine."

I was stunned. And furious. "What the hell, Gemma? Why do you let them do this to you?"

"Not like I have a choice."

"You always have a choice."

She rounded on me. "No, Vince, I don't. The studio owns my life. They choose what I eat, how I look. Hell, I don't even dress myself. I took pills from them once—one time," she spit out. "It made me feel like shit, like I'd lost several hours of my life. I never want to feel that way again."

I pondered that. Sounded kind of like what had happened last night. If that fucker Brandt had drugged her, I was going to knock his teeth down his damn throat. Shoving down my anger, I leaned on the counter next to her and crossed my arms over my chest. "What did they give you?"

She shrugged. "I have no idea. Ever since then, I decided I would never take anything from them again. I have to either pretend to swallow, or..." She shook the pill bottle. "Find a replacement."

My eyes floated over the various vitamins and such that Gemma was examining. I couldn't fucking believe they'd done that to her. No—that wasn't true. I could believe it, but it still pissed me off. She deserved so much better than the treatment she'd been receiving. I hated Harvey and those pretentious assholes even more for subjecting her to this.

"What can I do?"

She slid a curious look my way. "What?"

I gestured to the paraphernalia in front of her. "Tell me how I can help."

"I..." For a moment, she looked completely taken aback. "I guess you can check these to see if they look the same."

She passed me a bottle, and I popped the lid to compare it to the tablets in the prescription bottle. I immediately capped it again. "Where is the 'no' pile?"

She gestured to a drawer between us. "Just toss it in there."

I opened it up, and my eyes widened at the sight of all the bottles stored inside. "Jesus, Gemma."

She lifted one shoulder. "Been doing this for a while."

Clearly. Feeling way more pissed off than I probably should, I threw the bottle on top of the rest then closed it up again. I didn't know how I could help fix this, but I would find a way to do something.

CHAPTER
FOUR

JANA

My phone rang, and I slowed the treadmill to a stop, my chest heaving with exertion as I fought to drag in a breath. My leg muscles wobbled like Jell-O as I stepped off the machine, a result of the hour-long jog I'd just endured as an excuse to stay hidden from Vince.

I couldn't believe I'd spilled my guts to him about the drugs. I never told anyone my business—not even Maggie, and she was my assistant. But her loyalty first and foremost lay with Harvey and the studio. She did her job, whatever she had to do, and I wouldn't jeopardize that for her.

Seeing Vince's anger on my behalf reinforced my decision to not take the medication. Unfortunately, seeing that protective side of him had sent my heart skipping erratically in my chest. I couldn't remember the last time a man had stood up for me like that. Hell, maybe never. Show business was cutthroat, and it was every man—or woman—for themselves.

Vince couldn't care less what anyone thought about him, that much was obvious, and that confidence was a huge turn on. So, I'd done what any woman with a sense of self-preservation would do.

I hid.

For the last three days, I'd been practically under house arrest, and I was doing everything in my power to escape him every waking second. I was terrified that if I spent more time with Vince, I'd end up throwing myself at him again, and I couldn't bear the rejection that was sure to follow.

I shuddered. Hell, no. I swore I would never let him see how attracted I was to him.

I rolled my eyes as I picked up my phone from where it lay on the yoga mat and saw the number on the screen. I bit my lip, already dreading the conversation ahead. There was only one reason to be getting a phone call from the Butler County Jail back home where I'd grown up.

"Hello?"

"Jana, thank God!"

I closed my eyes. "Hey, Mama. What's up?"

I heard some shuffling in the background as Mama moved around. "I need your help, baby girl. These idiots arrested me, and they won't let me out."

I bit my tongue. That was precisely what happened when you'd been charged with possession multiple times. Of course, it never occurred to my mother to follow the rules and not break the law. "Just do what they say, Mama."

"But I didn't do anything!" she cried on the other end. "I swear!"

I didn't believe that for a second. Tears burned the back of my eyes. It was the same old song and dance, the same thing she'd said the last four times. For years, I'd held onto the hope that she would get her life together, but it never happened.

As soon as I turned eighteen and took full control of my finances, I set her up with a monthly allowance. I thought she would have been happy enough to have a steady income, but she always complained that it was never enough. I finally cut her off two years ago when she was busted again for possession. Mama would never change, and I was tired of having my heart broken holding out hope that she would.

My mind floated back to that awful day I'd come home from school at ten years old. The house was eerily quiet, and I hadn't noticed Mama at first, lying prone on the couch. As soon as I saw her eyes, glassy and lifeless from a drug overdose, I called the cops, who showed up within minutes.

It wasn't the first time they'd been at our house, and I was sure it wouldn't be the last. It was, however, Mama's first real stint in jail. When the judge sentenced her to eighteen months, I was sent to live with my grandmother. Rosewood was a tiny town that housed little more than a handful of churches and a family-owned market, but I wasn't going to complain about the lack of things to do; I was just glad to be free of my mother.

Gram took me to church for the first time in my life, and I quickly found my place there in the choir. I eagerly anticipated those Sunday services, and that year-and-a-half was the best of my childhood. When Mama got out of jail, she came to live with us, and for a while, things were better. She kept her nose clean, or at least kept it from Gram, who wouldn't put up with that shit for a second.

During the summer I turned fifteen, everything changed. Gram had been diagnosed the previous winter with cancer, and by spring it had spread into the rest of her organs. She passed peacefully in the middle of the night the first week of June, and I mourned the one person who had truly cared about me.

Two days after Gram's funeral, Mama packed up our tiny, beat up Chevy and drove us back to Hartford, Kentucky. There, we moved in with Burt Henning. He was two years older than my mother, but they'd gone to school together and apparently had reconnected over Facebook.

While I was glad to be back in my hometown with the friends I'd left behind, I hated the situation at home. Burt had a list of priors as long as his arm, and he always looked at me funny, his beady eyes hungry and calculating. One day, about two months after we moved back, Mama sprang a surprise trip on me. "Pack your things," she'd said. "We're going to Nashville to visit a friend."

That friend, it turned out, was Earl Wieden, talent agent. Mama had apparently sent clips of me singing in the choir to various recording studios and agents, but Earl was the only one who'd responded. He listened to me sing and immediately presented my mother with a contract. With the scribble of her signature and a quick goodbye, she disappeared, leaving me with Earl while she went back to Burt and their life in Kentucky. That thought drew me back to the present.

"Why doesn't Burt help?"

"I'm not seeing him anymore."

That was news to me. She and Burt had been together for the past eight years. "What happened?"

"Oh, you'll never believe it, Jana honey." I barely held back a snort as she continued. "I was at Kroger a couple months back, and you'll never guess who I bumped into."

I sat on the yoga mat and tried to summon some interest as I stretched my sore muscles. "Who?"

"Your daddy."

I blinked. "What?"

I wasn't honestly even sure she knew who my real father was. All she'd ever told me about him was that they'd had a whirlwind affair before he'd left her pregnant and alone.

"One thing led to another, and..." She paused, and I could practically see her gesturing excitedly. "Well, we've been seeing each other ever since."

"So, call him."

"He—" There was a scuffle in the background, and I heard the agitation in Mama's voice. "Just hold your horses! Why don't you go do something besides harass innocent people? God. Anyway, Jana baby, I need you to send some money real quick-like so I can get outta here."

I sighed. "I'm sorry, Mama. I can't."

On the other end of the phone, she sucked in an outraged breath. "You have to. This isn't my fault! They set me up!"

Sure. Just like the other times. "I won't do this anymore," I replied quietly.

"You ungrateful little bitch! After everything I've done for you—"

Agony ripped through my heart at her harsh words, and tears stung the backs of my eyes, burning across the bridge of my nose. I swallowed down the lump in my throat so she wouldn't hear it. "Goodbye, Mama."

I hit the end button then dropped my phone to the floor as a tear slipped down my cheek. I thought by now I'd have learned; people never changed. They put on a show, said all the right words, but deep down it was always the same. She was never going to change.

Angrily brushing the tears away, I pushed up off the floor and headed across the hall to my room. The TV was on in the living room, and I hoped that Vince would stay there until I was out of sight. He and I had been taking turns using the workout equipment that I'd put in the spare bedroom. So far, we'd managed to stay out of each other's sight. Now, I had to bite the bullet.

I quickly showered and dressed, then made my way out to the living room. Vince's gaze snapped to mine as I paused at the end of the hallway. "I need to get out for a bit."

He gave a little shake of his head. "No can do. Orders are to stay here."

My anger bubbled up and over—anger at Mama, my anger at whomever was sending me these ridiculous notes, my anger at Vince, the overbearing asshole I lusted after but could never have.

"I don't give a damn what your orders are. I'm leaving this house. You can either come or sit your ass on the couch and wait for me to get back."

Cutting at a diagonal across the room, I snatched my keys from the bowl on the hall table and made for the door that connected to the garage. I had just grabbed the handle when his hand appeared over my shoulder and slapped against the cool metal.

"Not a chance."

I whipped around and shoved against him as hard as I could. The big jerk didn't budge an inch, and it just pissed me off further. "I'm not your fucking prisoner! This is my house, my life, and I'm done!"

Annoyance crossed his face. "You're a pain in the ass, you know that?"

Hearing those words stung more than I thought they would. The bridge of my nose burned as I fought the tears stinging the backs of my eyes. I refused to let him see me upset, so I lashed back at him. "And you're an arrogant prick."

Without waiting for a reply, I reached behind me and grabbed the handle, then threw the door open. I stomped down the steps but was spun around as Vince grabbed my elbow, halting my progress.

"Goddamn it, Gemma, stop."

I glared up at him. "Let me go."

His jaw tensed, and fire flashed in his eyes as he stared down at me. "No. Stop being a fucking spoiled little brat for once in your life and learn to listen."

The hand at my elbow tightened a fraction, and I pulled against his hold. He squeezed my arm, just enough to make a point, and I stumbled back as he released me. "God, you're such a dick. Of all the people in the world, why do I have to be stuck with you?"

He scowled at me. "Is that the problem? You want someone else?"

What I wanted was for life to go back to normal. I wanted the police to catch the crazy idiot sending me love notes. I wanted Vince to want me the way I wanted him. I couldn't stand to have him in my house, sleeping on my couch, knowing how much he despised me. Was it too much to ask for some pot-bellied bodyguard I wasn't attracted to in the least?

"Yeah," I snapped. "Maybe it is."

He gave a slow shake of his head, then finally extended his hand toward my car. "Fine. Let's go. You and Con can figure it out."

I glared at him. "You should count yourself lucky you won't have to put up with me anymore."

I spun on a heel, then stormed to my car and slammed the door behind me. Using the app to lock my doors, I wasn't paying attention and jumped when Vince knocked on the driver side window, a dark look on his face.

I cranked the engine and rolled the window down. "What?"

His blue eyes crackled with anger. "Do you even know where the hell you're going?"

I waved my phone at him. "GPS. I'll figure it out."

His jaw tensed and for a second, I thought he might drag me from the car and haul me back into the house. I held my breath until he huffed out a breath. "Fine. I'll be right behind you."

I let out a deep breath, then rolled up the window, watching in the rearview mirror as Vince climbed into his truck parked across the street and started it up. I reversed out of my driveway, hit the button to lower the garage door, then put the car in gear and started down the street. Throwing a glance Vince's way, I saw him on the phone as he pulled a K-turn in the middle of the road and fell in behind me.

The voice from the GPS spoke up, telling me to make a right as the intersection at the end of my subdivision came into view. Beyond the stop sign, cars whizzed past on the busy four-lane road, and I pressed down on the brake. My foot went straight to the floor, and my heart jumped into my throat as I pumped the brake several more times.

Cars became a colorful blur in my peripheral vision as I clenched my fingers around the wheel and sailed past the stop sign and right into traffic.

CHAPTER
FIVE

VINCE

My heart banged against my ribs as I watched Gemma blow through the stop sign at the end of the road. Her tail lights were lit up bright red, but the car never slowed. The squeal of rubber on pavement filled the air as an oncoming car swerved out of Gemma's path, just narrowly avoiding missing her.

"Fuck!"

Gemma's Honda fishtailed wildly, then it jumped up over the median, sending it into a spin. Con's voice came from the other end of the phone, but I couldn't make out the words. I'd called to apprise him of the situation with Gemma but had forgotten all about him the second I watched her car spin out of control. "Gotta go."

Throwing a glance in the rearview mirror, I slammed on my brakes and yanked my truck to the side of the road, then jumped out. I hit the ground running, already checking for traffic as I sprinted across the road to where Gemma's car now sat facing me. The engine had stalled, but, with the exception of minor damage, the car appeared to be intact.

Thank God.

To my right, the driver who'd swerved to miss Gemma had also pulled over. He shoved the door open just as I ran past. "Call 911!"

Through the windshield, I could see white particles still floating in the air from when the airbag had deployed. I yanked the door open and leaned in, already reaching for her. I framed her face in my hands. "Ms. Malone?" Her eyes appeared hazy and unfocused, and I tried again. "Gemma?"

She licked her lips, then blinked, long and slow before meeting my gaze. "I... I'm good."

My eyes swept over the parts of her that I could see. "Do you hurt? Neck, head, anything?"

Face still trapped by my hands, she tried to shake her head. "Just... just a little sore. Whiplash." She drew a deep breath. "My face hurts."

Thank God she'd been wearing a seat belt or it would've been a hell of a lot worse. "You've got a couple little scrapes, but nothing major. Nose doesn't look broken."

"Okay."

She still sounded dazed, so I reached across her torso to release her seat belt. "Come on. Let's get you out of here."

The driver I'd seen appeared at my side as I helped Gemma from the car. "Is she okay?"

Gemma swayed on her feet unsteadily, and I locked an arm around her waist. "Yeah. You good?"

"Fine." He gestured toward the car with his phone. "Police are on their way, I just hung up with them."

"Thanks."

I turned back to Gemma. "You want to sit?"

She nodded, and I gently lowered her to the ground, where I squatted next to her. "What happened?"

"I—I couldn't stop." Her entire body trembled. "The brakes just... I pressed the pedal, but—"

"It's okay," I said, cutting off her incoherent rambling. I settled my hand on her back and rubbed gently. "Just relax. It's gonna be fine."

A moment later I heard the faint sound of sirens approaching, and I pushed to my feet. I watched as the police pulled up to secure the scene. A second unmarked car arrived a few minutes later, and a tall man in slacks and a blazer stepped out. He met my gaze over the hood of Gemma's car and gave me a tight nod. He stopped to speak with one of the patrolmen before heading our direction.

Not moving from where Gemma sat by my feet, I held out a hand to him. "Vince Incarnato."

"Lieutenant Roy Shepler. Anyone hurt?"

I gestured to Gemma. "Just a few scrapes and bruises from what I can tell."

He lifted his chin in affirmation. "We'll have EMS check her out. What happened?"

"Brake failure, I think." I pointed to my truck across the intersection. "I was following her, and I could see the taillights but she never slowed down. She says she pushed the pedal but nothing happened."

The guy standing next to me spoke next. "I was headed south when she came from there." He pointed toward her street. "The car hit the median and spun her."

"Is that your car?" Shepler pointed to the Ford SUV along the side of the road, and the man nodded. "All right. I'll need you to give your statement to one of the men."

He waved over a patrolman, who guided the driver away, then Shepler turned back to us. "Let's get out of the median."

I extended a hand to Gemma, then lifted her to her feet and guided her across the road. She seemed more stable now, but I kept an arm around her just in case. As soon as we reached the sidewalk, the wail of sirens filled the air, and red and blue lights flashed, heralding the ambulance's arrival.

Shepler turned to Gemma. "How are you feeling?"

"My head hurts," she replied, "but I think I'm fine otherwise."

"We'll have the medic take a look at you. Do you want to do that now or wait?"

She gave a little flick of her hand. "I'll be fine."

"Okay, then. I'd like to hear your side of things."

Gemma shot me a quick glance then licked her lips and turned her attention back to Lt. Shepler. "I was just getting ready to leave, to go for a drive. I was in a hurry because we'd argued, and—"

"What were you arguing about?" Shepler looked at me before turning back to Gemma, whose cheeks had gone from unnaturally white to a soft pink.

"Vince didn't want me to leave. I've been getting strange notes from someone, which is why they assigned a bodyguard to stay with me."

Shepler glanced back to me. "I assume the authorities are already aware of this?"

I nodded. "Detective Traeger over at the eighth precinct has copies of everything. You can double check with him."

Satisfied with that answer, at least for now, Shepler turned back to Gemma. "Continue."

She took another shaky breath. "I don't know what happened. Everything seemed fine at first. But as soon as I got near the stop sign, and I pressed down on the brake..." She spread her fingers wide. "It went straight to the floor. I was confused at first, and I tried again, then realized my brakes were gone. The only thing I could think to do was pull the e-brake."

Shepler made a few notations in a small notebook. "I would say you're extremely lucky, considering how busy this cross street can be."

"Believe me, I know." A shudder racked Gemma's body, and I tightened my hold a fraction, silently lending support.

He snapped the small notebook shut. "Okay. I'd like to take a look at the car while the medics check you over."

Gemma nodded, and I guided her toward the ambulance. Ten minutes later, her scrapes cleaned and antibiotic ointment applied, we headed back over to where Shepler stood with two patrolmen. He turned toward us as we approached and gestured down the street. "You live right up here?"

Gemma pointed to the end of the street. "Next to last one from the end on the left."

"Mind if I take a look?"

"Sure?"

She sounded confused when she responded, but I knew exactly what he was looking for. "They're checking to see if there are any oil spots in the garage from where it may have leaked."

I looked at Shepler. "Mind if I drive her back?"

I wanted to get my truck out of the way, and I knew Gemma was already stressed. The walk wasn't far, but I could tell her adrenaline was crashing after the accident.

Thankfully, Shepler nodded. "I'll follow you."

The lieutenant climbed into the cruiser and followed me to Gemma's house. I got her settled on the couch, then showed Shepler to the garage. As soon as I stepped inside, I saw it, and I let out a swift curse. "Son of a bitch."

Shepler knelt by the small trickle of golden fluid pooled on the concrete floor of the garage. Some of it had run down into the drain a few feet away, but it was obvious enough that a good amount of fluid had seeped out of the lines.

The lieutenant hadn't yet said a word, but I knew he suspected the same thing I did. Coupled with the recent notes, it was too much of a coincidence that her brakes had suddenly failed. I made routine checks around the house, and it pissed me off that someone may have slipped under my radar. Until we knew for certain, I didn't want to say anything to Gemma.

I turned my attention to Shepler. "I've been with her here for the past three days, and her car hasn't moved. I also do perimeter checks every hour, though we don't know for sure that whoever's sending the notes knows where she lives."

"They don't come here?"

I shook my head. "So far, they've been sent to her studio each time. She's received around a dozen over the past two months."

"Interesting." He met my gaze. "You think it was intentional?"

"Absolutely." And it fucking pissed me off that I'd missed it somehow.

He nodded slowly. "I glanced underneath, but the lines don't appear to have been cut. We'll need to bring it in, take a look to see if we can determine exactly what happened. Does anyone else have access to her house or garage?"

"Not that I'm aware of. She uses an electronic lock on the front door—I'm sure you saw—because she hates keys. I know this door"—I pointed to a steel and glass door in the corner of the garage that led to the side yard—"is always locked. I check it each time I make rounds."

He pushed to his feet and strode that direction. It was still locked from the inside, and he yanked on a pair of blue nitrile gloves before he flipped the mechanism, then pulled the door open and inspected the handle from the outside. "Some minor scratches here."

"Someone broke in?"

Shepler lifted one shoulder. "If I had to guess, I would say no. They look more superficial than anything, but I can't afford to write anything off at this point. We'll get one of the techs out here to print it, but I would suggest replacing the lock as soon as possible. We'll leave this one in place until you get it swapped out, then I can have someone check the tumbler inside to see if it's been tampered with."

The thought made me see red. I was never this lax, yet someone had apparently managed to get into Gemma's garage without my knowledge. Granted, without a witness, we wouldn't have any idea of when, exactly, it'd occurred. The knowledge didn't stem the anger and self-recrimination swirling in my gut, and I gritted my teeth before speaking. "I appreciate it."

"I'd like to print both of you, if you think she's up for it."

I tipped my head toward the house. "Come on in."

Gemma stood by the couch, watching curiously. "Everything okay?"

"I'm sure it'll be fine," I lied. "Lt. Shepler just needs to get our fingerprints before he leaves."

"Why?" Her brows drew together in confusion, her arms clutching even more tightly around her middle.

I chose my next words carefully, not wanting to give too much away. "In case they find fingerprints on anything, they'll know which ones are yours and mine."

It seemed to satisfy her curiosity, at least a little bit, and I breathed a sigh of relief despite the unease churning in my gut. Things had just gone from bad to worse, and I had a feeling this was just the beginning.

CHAPTER
SIX

JANA

"Someone want to tell me what the hell is going on here?"

I jumped and shrank away from the harsh voice, and a splash of water hit my feet. The sound of the front door closing reached my ears, immediately followed by the heavy footsteps of the two large men headed my way. The water bottle shook in my hands, and I hastily set it on the counter. A pair of dark eyes settled on me as Vince and the second man approached, sending a slither of unease down my spine.

"Ms. Malone, you remember Connor Quentin, my boss."

"Yes. Hi." I shifted awkwardly.

The man tipped his chin at me, then glared at Vince. "Care to explain what happened?"

A muscle ticked in Vince's jaw. "As I was telling you on the phone, we were just getting ready to come into headquarters when her brakes failed. She blew through the stop sign and hit the median."

Con's face darkened. "Your orders were to stay inside. If you can't handle this, I'll find someone else who can."

"It wasn't his fault," I immediately cut in. Both men's eyes jumped to me, and I trembled under the force of Con's intense gaze. I swallowed hard. "I'm the one responsible. Vince tried to stop me, but I wouldn't listen."

Con stared at me. "You put your life in jeopardy, as well as one of my agent's. I won't tolerate that. You either follow the instructions given to you, or I will terminate the contract right now."

I knew if I dismissed Vince, Harvey would just insist on getting someone else. Arguing with this man would be an exercise in futility, but I steeled my backbone and strove to remain calm and rational. "My brakes failed, that's all—"

"They were bled."

I blinked. "What?"

"Your brakes were drained of all fluid. I spoke with Lt. Shepler on the way over here. They found the bleeder valve wide open and a significant amount of brake fluid in the drain in your garage."

Ice sluiced through my veins. The police had been back to look around and take fingerprints, I knew that, but they hadn't said much. I watched warily as Con tossed a manila folder on the countertop between us. My mouth opened, then snapped close again, and I was dimly aware of Vince murmuring a soft curse beside me.

"Do you understand why you're under protection? Have they told you anything?"

I reluctantly met Con's gaze, then shook my head.

His lips flattened into a thin line of displeasure. "Those letters you've been getting?" He spun the folder toward me and flipped open the front flap. "This one included a couple lovely recipes."

"Recipes?" I tentatively touched the first page on top, a copy of a list of ingredients someone had scribbled on a piece of plain white paper. At the top were the words She-girl Stew.

I slid the paper to the side and read the one beneath. Gemma-balaya.

"I don't..." I trailed off, my mind struggling to make sense of what I was reading.

"This sick fuck is planning different ways to devour you—and not the sexy kind."

I rocked back on my heels, stunned.

"Jesus, Con." Vince's voice came from behind me, and a firm hand clasped my shoulder, giving me strength.

I slowly lifted my gaze to the dark brown eyes across from me. "But I thought... Harvey said they were just sappy love letters."

Con snorted. "Well, there's a fine line between love and obsession, and this guy blew past it a long time ago."

The hand on my shoulder eased and slipped away as I crossed my arms over my midsection. "Why the hell didn't Harvey say anything? I never would've tried to leave if I had known about this."

Con studied me for a moment. "It doesn't take much knowledge or experience to open a bleeder valve and let the fluid run out. Have you gone anywhere else over the last couple of days?"

I shook my head. "Not since..." I drew back, trying to remember the last time I had left the house. "I think it was last weekend, maybe a week ago? I went to the grocery store off Alto Palo."

"Did you notice anything strange when you were driving it?"

"Not that I remember."

Con's brooding, dark gaze slid to Vince. "You've been doing perimeter checks?"

"Every hour," he acknowledged. "Nothing out of the ordinary, but I never thought to check under the car since the garage doors are kept locked."

Con seemed to think it over. "There's a good chance that it was done elsewhere and you just didn't realize it. I don't think anyone would be brash or stupid enough to try to bleed the lines with Ink here making cursory checks unexpectedly."

So where did that leave us? "What do I do now?"

"I don't know if this person knows where you live, but I'd rather err on the side of caution until we determine otherwise. I spoke with Shepler, and we're going to increase police presence for a while." He directed his next words to Vince. "They'll have patrolmen doing drive-bys every hour or so, as well, so you'll have some backup close if you need it."

I nodded, still feeling numb and off-balance. I couldn't believe someone was doing this to me. It all seemed so far-fetched, so juvenile. At least, that's the way Harvey had made it sound. He played it off as if this person were merely infatuated with me. Nothing strange had ever turned up in my dressing rooms while I was on tour, and this was the first time anything ever happened near my home. I felt violated, like the one place I should feel safe had been breached.

Con blew out a breath. "I also need to check—do you know where the key to the garage door is?"

I nodded and pointed to a drawer on the far right. "Should be in here." I dug around for a minute, then produced two generic-looking silver keys on a small ring. "I had the locks changed as soon as I moved in, but I never come in that way, so I just tossed the keys in here."

He nodded. "We're going to get someone out here to change the lock again, just in case. I'd suggest changing the code to the front door and only giving it to those absolutely necessary."

"Okay."

He stared at me for a moment. "Is there anyone who would have had access to that door, or to the keys?"

I shook my head. "They've been in that drawer for as long

as I can remember. I never made a copy for anyone, not even a spare, because I never needed one."

"No neighbors to take care of the house?"

"Definitely not." Hell, I didn't think I could even name two of the people who lived on my street. I'd seen them in passing but nothing more.

"Boyfriend?"

I almost laughed at his mention of a boyfriend. I'd become incredibly selective of my partners and had been celibate for the past eight months. The men I'd dated in the music industry were arrogant and self-centered, and they only cared about using relationships to further their careers. The men outside of the industry were worse.

I'd played at a local fair two summers ago and met a guy who, by all appearances, seemed to be polite and well-mannered—a truly good man. We went on two dates before we'd slept together. He'd rolled out of bed the second it was over, with the comment that he could now tell his friends he'd "banged a celebrity." Asshole. Most of the others I'd met were users or alcoholics, and I had no desire to invite that into my life.

I let out a sigh. "No."

Con mulled that over for a second, then pinned that intense, dark gaze on me. "All right. We'll see what we can dig up. We're not going to have a problem here, are we?"

I shook my head. "N-no. I'm... I'll do what he says. I promise."

"Okay, then." He turned to Vince. "I'll text you details on the locksmith here in a few."

I felt frozen in place as Vince led Con to the door, then locked up behind him. My eyes fell to the manila folder on the counter, and a shiver rolled down my spine. I knew he'd left it there intentionally, as a kind of warning. He was right; seeing the evidence made it all so much more real.

"You want me to get rid of that?"

I lifted my eyes to Vince's, and he tipped his head at the documents in front of me. Finally, I nodded. "Please."

To the best of my knowledge, I hadn't done anything to elicit this kind of reaction. Sure, I knew there were fans who took it a little far sometimes. People on social media weren't afraid to make their feelings known, especially those who hated my music. I knew I sometimes got messages from random men hoping to capture my attention, but Maggie always responded with something polite yet off-putting.

I wondered if she had seen the most recent note, or if she was even aware of the turn the content had taken. I didn't know who all I was allowed to talk to, but Maggie was my assistant, my right hand. Maggie was a singer, too, when she was younger, and we'd actually sung back-up to a few artists together before I'd gotten my big break with Magnolia Way. I would never have made it as far as I had without her encouragement, and I hated to keep her out of the loop.

Finally, Vince looked over at me. "You hungry?"

I shook my head. I couldn't bear the thought of eating right now, even though it was creeping close to dinner time.

"Let me know when you get hungry, and we'll figure out the food situation."

I nodded, but my mind wasn't on food. It was back on the accident this morning that replayed through my mind. I kept hearing Con's voice telling me that my brake lines had been drained, that it hadn't been an accident at all.

I turned to Vince. "I'm sorry."

"Don't worry about it." His voice was gruff and curt, and it only made me feel worse.

Con was right when he said I'd put Vince's life in jeopardy. My actions were rash and selfish, thinking only of myself. "I should have listened to you," I continued. "I just... wanted you to know."

He stared at me for a long minute, then nodded. "I appreciate it."

I stared out the window, thinking about everything that had happened this morning. Part of me wanted to disappear, to just hide away until this was all over. "Maybe I should go wait it out at the beach."

Vince snorted. "Not a terrible idea."

At this point, any place was better than here. My home didn't feel like home anymore. I stared out at the late-afternoon sun spilling over the homes across the street, and I imagined what it might be like to be at the beach.

I could go someplace safe, where no one knew my name or recognized my face. A place I didn't have to worry about Vince or Mama or my stalker. Somewhere I could just be... me.

CHAPTER
SEVEN

VINCE

I peered at Gemma, curled up in the corner of the couch, her face pale and drawn. Her teeth were buried in her lower lip, making her look incredibly vulnerable. Part of me wanted to comfort her, but I had a hunch it was the last thing she'd want.

Things had been awkward between us ever since the night I'd brought her home from the bar, and I had a gut feeling that was part of the reason she'd wanted a new agent to watch over her. Things had never been great between us, but I felt bad for her. She'd been through a lot recently, some of which she'd just learned.

I couldn't believe that asshole manager of hers hadn't said anything. I knew all of the notes had gone to the studio, but I thought they'd at least informed Gemma of the contents. From the look on her face when Con showed her the latest addition, she'd been completely blindsided. The blood had drained from her face, and her eyes had gone round as saucers. I thought for a minute that she might pass out, but she'd managed to pull herself together.

Finally, I could no longer stand it. "Hey." I waited until her gaze lifted to mine. "They'll find him, you know."

Her eyes immediately dropped back to her lap, where she picked at a loose thread on her leggings. "I just don't understand. Like..." She peered helplessly at me. "Did I do something to encourage him?"

"I seriously doubt it. And even if you did"—I locked eyes with her—"no one deserves this."

She tried for a little smile but failed miserably, her eyes sad. "I've been racking my brain, trying to think of who it could be, but..." She lifted her hands, fingers splayed wide. "I just don't know who would do something like this."

"It may not be anyone you know," I replied. "There's no specific definition for obsession."

I'd been reading up on it over the past few days, ever since that last note had arrived. It'd been particularly gory and graphic, citing various ways in which he planned to kill her. Whoever was behind this had obviously done a lot of research, because the letter was incredibly detailed. It still made my stomach turn thinking about it.

"You may have met him once, or it could be someone you've known your entire life. Who knows?" I shrugged. "It's up to the police to figure out the who and why of it. It's my job to keep you safe in the meantime."

"I know." She sighed, then leaned one elbow on the arm of the couch and propped her head on her hand. "And I appreciate it—really. I just wish they could hurry up and find the guy."

"Maybe he'll slip up, and they'll catch him."

"Maybe." She didn't sound convinced, though, and for several minutes, we lapsed into silence.

I sneaked peeks at her from time to time, but she just stared off into space, seemingly a thousand miles away. I checked my phone and noticed the time. The next patrol should be coming through soon, and I wanted to do a perimeter check of the property just in case.

I pushed to my feet. "I'll be outside if you need me."

Gemma nodded but didn't respond, and I headed out the front door, locking up behind me. My truck was parked in Gemma's driveway once more, a bright red beacon to let everyone know I was here. I made a sweep of the yard, checking for anything out of place, any evidence that someone had been here recently, but there was nothing. I checked the windows accessible from the outside again, but everything was locked up tight, just as it had been this morning.

The locksmith wasn't able to come out until tomorrow morning, so I'd blocked the side entrance to the garage in the meantime. Gemma had changed the code for the front door, and as of right now, she and I were the only two who had access to it.

I was still livid that someone had bled her brakes. The more I thought about it, the more I believed it had been done here in her garage. If someone had opened the bleeder valve while she'd been out somewhere, fluid would have drained from the lines each time she'd pressed the brake while driving.

She couldn't have made it very far without running out of fluid completely and losing all stopping power. More than likely, she would have remembered a change in pressure last time she'd driven her car, but she remained adamant that everything had been fine. And I believed her. Which sucked even more, because it meant that her accident was my fault.

Just as I rounded the side of the house, the sound of a car cruising slowly up Gemma's street caught my attention. I saw the distinctive light bar of the cruiser approaching, and I headed out to the street to meet him.

The officer slowed to a stop and rolled his window down just as I stepped off the curb. "Are you with Ms. Malone?"

"I am." I held out a hand. "Vince Incarnato with Quentin Security Group."

"Reimer." We shook hands, then he pointed to her house. "Nothing yet?"

"Nope, everything's been quiet." I didn't truly expect anything less. Unless the person lived close by, I had a feeling he wouldn't strike again until he'd heard news of her accident.

Reimer bobbed his head. "I'm on 'til eleven, so I'll keep an eye out."

I stepped back. "I appreciate it."

Reimer eased back into the street, and I turned to head back inside. There, I checked the garage and all of the windows and doors. Her ranch was a little over a thousand square feet, and it didn't take long until I was back in the living room seated across from Gemma. It was going on dinnertime, and I couldn't remember her eating anything today, with the exception of a pre-workout smoothie this morning.

"You hungry?"

She gave her head a little shake. "I'm good."

I eyed her. "You need to eat something."

Her gaze flicked to mine, the blue depths stormy and shadowed. "I don't know if I can," she finally admitted. "I still feel kind of sick to my stomach."

I understood, but she didn't need to pass out on top of everything else. "Something light, then," I said, pushing from the couch. "Got any salad mix?"

I was sure she did, since it seemed to be the only thing she ate half the time. I had chicken breasts stashed away, and I was already pulling them out by the time she walked into the kitchen behind me. We never actually sat down to eat dinner together, instead keeping to ourselves. I had no idea if she was a vegetarian or not, because I'd never seen her eat meat of any kind.

I held up the chicken. "Will you eat this?"

"As long as it's not fried."

"Good enough for me." I pulled a knife from the butcher's block and gestured toward the table situated in the breakfast nook. "Sit."

Her lips turned down at my command, but she seemed too emotionally drained to do anything other than follow my directive.

I worked in silence, searing the chicken then tossing it with the salad. I slid a plate in front of Gemma and handed her a fork before taking the seat across from her. She twirled the fork in her hand, then finally speared a piece of lettuce and lifted it to her lips.

She was never this quiet. She avoided me most of the time, yes, but she was never afraid to talk back or challenge me in some way. Tonight, she was pensive, deep in thought.

I lifted a brow. "You good?"

She shrugged one shoulder. "Just thinking."

Probably about the situation at hand. I opened my mouth to speak, but she beat me to it.

"I was wondering..." She rolled her lips together. "If there might be a way to... deter him."

I speared her with a glance. "If you're thinking of doing something stupid, like using yourself for bait, you can throw that out the window right now."

She rolled her eyes. "That's not what I was thinking."

"Good, because it's not gonna happen."

She ran her tongue over the front of her teeth in agitation, then set her fork down and leaned forward in her seat. "So... this guy's obsessed with me."

"It would appear that way. Why? What are you thinking?"

"What if I was no longer available?"

I lifted a brow. "That may not deter him. That might piss him off even more and make him lash out."

"Maybe, but at least he'd be doing something instead of silently watching," she pointed out. "Like you said, he'll eventually slip up and get caught."

"All right, I'll bite." I leaned back in my chair and crossed my arms over my chest. "So, let's say you spin this story that you have a boyfriend. You'd have to go public with it to make sure he sees the two of you together. Who are you going to use? One of your musician buddies? The person writing these letters threatened to kill anyone in his way. Are you gonna put him in jeopardy?"

She flinched at my words and her face fell, but knowing I'd made my point brought no satisfaction. "Listen," I said more softly. "Just let the police do their job. They'll catch him. It'll just take some time."

Her wide blue eyes clashed with mine, full of desperation. "What if it was more permanent? Like... a serious relationship?"

I dropped my hands to rest in my lap. "Same boat. You're still putting someone else in danger. Or, even if it did scare this guy off, the relationship would have to last long enough that the guy would forget all about you and fixate on something—someone—else."

She licked her lips. "How long?"

"Hell, I don't know. Six months? A year?"

To that, she said nothing. After a long moment, I picked up my fork and resumed eating. I was almost done with my salad before she spoke again.

"Vince? I mean... Ink."

"Yeah?" The nickname seemed strange coming from her. She was one of the few people who called me Vince, and I actually preferred the sound of my real name falling from her pretty lips.

Her gaze was pinned to the glass of water beside her plate, and it slowly rose to mine. "Um..."

I lifted my brows in question, and her cheeks flared bright pink. She looked shy and almost... guilty?

"Do people call you Ink because of your last name or tattoos?"

I stared at her. "Both, probably."

She nodded slowly. "Right."

Something was... off. I dipped my chin at her. "Gemma?" Her head came up, but her gaze skittered away. "What's on your mind?"

"Nothing. Well... I was just thinking... wondering..." She trailed off, then tried again. "I mean, I know things..."

I peered across the table at Gemma, who continued to babble nervously. What the hell was I missing?

"What if...? I, um..." She drew a deep breath. "God. Why is this so hard?"

"Jesus, Gemma." I set my fork down and leaned back, irritation welling up and spilling over. "Just spit it out already."

Huge blue eyes met mine and held for a second. "What about you?"

"Me?" I blinked at her, my mind scrambling to process her question. "What about me?"

Her cheeks blazed fire-engine red. "Would you... marry me?"

The force of the bomb she'd just dropped knocked me back in my seat, and all I could do was stare at her for several long seconds. She watched me intently, blue irises swirling with a mixture of hope and apprehension, but I couldn't formulate words. I had to be hallucinating, because there was no way this woman had just proposed to me. Right? "Marry you?"

She bobbed her head. "Just pretend—just until this is over."

"Gemma..."

"Please, Vince. I—" She leaned in, reaching one hand toward me, and I automatically recoiled. Her face fell, and her eyes followed her hands as they fell listlessly to her lap. "I'm sorry. I just..."

Fuck.

I scrubbed a hand over my face, but I couldn't think of anything to say. Pretend to be married—really?

Abruptly, Gemma pushed back her chair and snatched up her plate. I turned in my seat as she brushed past me and set her plate in the sink. "Gemma, listen—"

She whirled toward me, holding her hands up, palms out. "No. It was my fault. I never should have asked. Just... don't worry about it. It was stupid. Let's pretend this never happened, okay?"

I opened my mouth again to speak, but she was gone. Heaving myself up from the chair, I set my dish in the sink, then went out to do a perimeter check. Outside, I snuck a glance through the bedroom window. Gemma—what I could see of her—sat on her bed, legs curled up like a child as she hugged a pillow close to her chest.

I felt bad for her—really, I did. But was a pretend marriage really the answer to this? The idea had merit, to a point, but Gemma and I had enough drama to work through. I had a feeling this would only make things worse. She was a budding superstar; if I were to play husband to her, I would be dragged into the limelight, a place I had no desire to be. It could jeopardize both my job and my future. So much could go wrong, and we'd still be in the same boat we were in now.

I hadn't meant to react as badly as I did. The woman constantly had me on guard, almost defensive, but I still felt like an asshole for hurting her feelings. I locked up as I headed inside for the night, then made my way down the hall to Gemma's room.

A sliver of light shone from beneath the door, and I placed my hand on the knob. It was locked. I lifted my hand to knock, but common sense kicked in before I rapped on the door. She was already dejected and embarrassed. I didn't want to risk exacerbating the situation.

Instead, I headed to the couch and sat heavily, dropping my head back and closing my eyes. Thank God Gemma was one of those women who appreciated function and comfort over design, and I could actually spread out. I settled in for the night, but the more time passed, the worse I felt.

I couldn't explain why, exactly, but that crestfallen look of hers killed me. I couldn't imagine the guts it took to ask me something like that, especially given our recent past. She'd looked so ashamed, so embarrassed, which was probably why it bothered me so much. Gemma was normally so vibrant and vivacious that her reticence was completely abnormal.

By the time morning finally rolled around, I was exhausted from guilt and lack of sleep. A soft sound drew my attention to the archway between the kitchen and living room, and I sat up, glancing over the back of the couch just in time to catch a glimpse of Gemma. She threw a quick look my way, and our gazes locked for a moment before her cheeks blazed and her eyes dropped away again. She slunk into the kitchen, and I let out a sigh.

If I was hoping things would be better this morning, I was bound to be disappointed. If I knew Gemma, though, she'd ignore me at all costs and pretend that last night never happened. I didn't know if that was a good thing or bad. Things between us were already so tense, it wouldn't take much to break the tenuous balance.

Scrubbing one hand over my face, I pushed to the edge of the couch and shoved my feet into my boots. Grabbing my phone from the end table where it sat charging, I stowed it in my pocket and headed to the front door, then made my way outside. Even though it was barely after seven, I locked up behind me as I started my perimeter check. It was probably overkill, but after everything that had happened recently, I wasn't willing to risk her safety.

After I made sure everything was secure, I sat down on the wide porch step and dug my phone from my back pocket. I tapped Con's number, and my knee bounced nervously as I waited for the call to connect.

"What's up, Ink?"

He sounded a little short of breath, but as an early riser like the rest of us, I guaranteed he'd been up for well over an hour working out.

"Hey. Any update on the brake lines yet?"

"Not yet. The guys from the precinct are checking the valve for prints, but I haven't heard anything yet. One of the guys will be over after the locksmith leaves. He wants the old doorknob from the garage to see if the internal mechanism has been tampered with."

"I'll make sure to bag it and set it aside." I fell silent for a moment, my mind spinning, anxiety making me jumpy. "So with no evidence, what does that mean?"

"You're stuck for now," came his reply. "Harvey and the studio still want her under surveillance until they get this guy."

"Do they have any leads?"

"Not that I'm aware of," Con said. "At least, nothing solid." He seemed to know instinctively that something was on my mind, because he cautiously continued. "Why?"

"Just thinking," I said slowly. "It occurred to me that we might be able to get this guy's attention, get him to slip up."

"What are you thinking?"

The words felt thick and heavy on my tongue. "He's

obsessed with her, right? What if we make it look like she's off the market?" I held my breath and waited for his response.

Nearly a minute later, he let out a soft sound. "This could blow up in our faces if we're not careful."

"I know," I conceded. "But think of it like this: if this dude sees her with someone new, he'll either get the picture and leave her alone, or..." I trailed off, and Con picked up my train of thought.

"He'll do something stupid and get caught."

"That's my hope."

"So has Ms. Malone considered this at all?"

"It was actually her idea," I said. "She brought it up last night, but I wanted to make sure she didn't change her mind before I ran it by you."

"Fair enough. And she's thinking of having someone pose as her boyfriend?"

"Not a boyfriend—husband."

Con chuckled softly. "Even better, I guess. Who's the lucky guy?"

"That would be me."

There were several seconds of silence before a bewildered laugh came from Con's end. "You're shitting me, right?"

I grimaced. "Who better than the guy hired to keep her safe? I'm already staying with her."

"Ink..."

"We can spin some story about how we've been engaged for a while but were waiting for her tour to end."

"It's not the worst idea in the world," Con said, "but, damn... Are you sure about this?"

No, I wasn't sure at all. This could be a mistake of epic proportions. She was a walking temptation, and I was practically throwing myself at her feet.

"I don't like the idea of my guys being in the spotlight," he warned.

Me either. I had no desire to be flaunted around like that. Personal protection agents were supposed to be silent shadows, and I couldn't do my job properly if I got dragged into the spotlight. If the media caught wind of my name, it could create a shit storm for QSG. The only upside to this at the moment was that once the gym on the upper floor of QSG was set up, I would take over the role of primary instructor for the self-defense courses and wouldn't be needed in the field as much.

"I don't want to jeopardize the business, but better me than one of the other guys. We don't have to release my name to the public," I said. "Plus, it'll only be a few months—just until they find the guy, then we can break things off amicably, just like every other twenty-something celebrity."

"Mhmm…"

Well, it wasn't an outright refusal. "Here's what I was thinking. I'll take her on a pretend honeymoon someplace—there are a couple quiet beaches in Florida that would work well. Airline reservations are hard as hell to get hold of, even for a skilled hacker, so we should be safe enough to fly. Once we land, we'll use a hired driver to take us somewhere obscure. It'll be far enough away that the guy won't immediately be able to follow her, even if our location were to be leaked. Hopefully, he'll slip up and try something stupid here again."

"You've been thinking about this," Con said quietly.

"I have. I don't like it, but if it'll keep her safe…"

Con fell silent for a moment. "Did you know that marriage records are public?"

I hadn't known that. Suddenly, this whole thing seemed a little more real. Anyone at any time could check the records to see if we were officially married. If we went through with this whole scheme, we had to go the whole way. It couldn't be pretend. I would have to marry her.

"I'll double check with her and let you know, but for

now…" I hesitated for a long moment, then sighed. "Let's plan for it. Check into reservations somewhere on the beach, and get the studio to sign off on whatever you need."

"Will do."

Without another word Con hung up, and I stood, then stared at the front door. I had two choices. I could call Con back right now and pretend like this had never happened.

Or… I could do the right thing. Maybe not right, exactly, but it was the only alternative I had at the moment. Given my options, I knew I didn't have a choice.

I entered the house, relocked the door behind me, then made my way to the kitchen. Gemma stood with her back to me as she operated the blender, and I waited until the whirring noise stopped before clearing my throat.

She jumped a little bit and threw a wary look my way. Her lips pressed slightly together, and her chin dropped a notch as she regarded me with no small amount of embarrassment. I was sure she would take back our conversation last night given the chance. If I let her, she would continue on just like this, ignoring me and pretending that none of this had ever happened.

I, however, couldn't forget the look on her face when she'd asked me to marry her. Her expression had been hesitant, timid… hopeful. As strange as it seemed, I was the only one who could help her now.

I held her cerulean gaze for a long moment, then dropped the words that I knew would change my life. "Let's go to the beach."

CHAPTER
EIGHT

JANA

Let's go to the beach.

Individually, each word made perfect sense, but my mind couldn't quite comprehend exactly what he was telling me. I tipped my head to one side. "The beach?"

"You said you've never been there. What better spot for a..." His shoulders twitched, and his gaze darted away before sliding back to mine. "Honeymoon?"

My breath caught, and my heart skipped a beat as hope exploded in my chest. "But I thought—"

He slashed one hand through the air. "Forget what I said. I was being an idiot. My boss liked your idea, and he's already talking to Harvey and the studio."

Part of me wanted to throw my arms around him, and I grabbed the counter behind me to keep myself from doing so. He already looked uncomfortable; I didn't want to freak him out. Though, honestly, I was lucky he was still around after everything that had happened already.

"There's something…" He faltered. "It's a little more complicated than just pretending to be married, though."

I cocked my head. "What do we need to do?"

He hesitated for a long moment, as if searching for the right words. "Marriage records are public." He stared at me, his expression bordering on anxious.

"Okay…?" I drew out the word, trying to decipher his statement.

"Anyone can check to see if we're really married."

It hit me like a bolt of lightning, and I felt my mouth fall open. "Oh."

"Yeah." He looked grim. "So… I'll leave this up to you."

I stared up at him. "You're… You'd really… marry me?"

I watched as a slight tic shuddered across his jaw, and he blinked long and slow before responding. "Yeah. We'll do what we have to do."

My skin went hot as shame assailed me. It was one thing to ask a friend to watch your dog or water your plants, but this…? What had begun as a simple deception had quickly become so much more serious.

"I think, um…" I scrunched up my nose to get rid of the burning sensation and blinked rapidly against the moisture that blurred my eyes as I turned away. "I appreciate it. But I can't."

"Why the hell not?" There was a hard edge to his voice that sent a shiver down my spine.

"I just can't."

One hand wrapped around my bicep and whirled me toward him. "Look at me."

Only inches away, I had no choice but to do so. I glared up at him. "What?"

"Tell me why you've changed your mind."

"I just…" I dropped my gaze to his broad chest. Dark ink

peeked out from beneath the neckline of the tight black tee shirt, and I curled my fingers into a fist to keep from tracing the intricate design. I drew a deep breath. "What would your family say?"

He studied me for a long moment. "They won't find out."

So I would be a dirty little secret. "And... how do you feel about this?"

He leaned against the island and crossed his arms over his chest as he watched me. "It's just a few months."

I bit my lip. "Does that bother you?"

He lifted one shoulder, and his gaze skated over my shoulder and out the window. Finally, he exhaled. "I don't know."

"We don't have to do this," I said softly, even as my heart plummeted toward my toes. "There has to be another way without forcing you to—"

"You're not forcing me into anything." He straightened. "And this is the best scenario at the moment. It creates a diversion while getting you out of harm's way."

"What happens when it's over?"

His gray-blue eyes bore into mine. "We'll figure that out when the time comes."

I closed my eyes before meeting his gaze. "Just... promise you won't regret this?"

He stared at me for a long moment, then finally gave his head a slow shake. "Never."

"That's..." I struggled for words, still overwhelmed by his offer. I didn't know what had changed over the past eight hours, but I wasn't going to take it for granted. I would give Vince literally anything he wanted—pay him whatever I had to—to make this go away. "I really appreciate this. And I swear I'll make it up to you. I'll pay you for—"

"No." His hand tightened on my arm, pulling me infinitesimally closer to him. I sucked in a breath as he dipped his head until it was even with mine, a fierce expression in his eyes. "I won't take a damn dime from you."

"But I—"

"No buts." He tipped his chin and held up a finger. "We're also going to draft a prenup." I opened my mouth, but he cut me off with a slice of his hand. "No negotiations on this."

"Vince—"

"No." He shook his head.

I threw my hands up. "You didn't even listen!"

He crossed his arms over his broad chest as he regarded me, one eyebrow cocked toward his hairline. "I didn't have to."

I scowled at him. "If you think you're doing this for me, it's not worth it. I don't even own this house outright." I could tell by his expression that he was wavering, and I continued. "Seriously. The process can take a long time, and it'll cost more to do the paperwork than anything you would get out of it."

A small furrow appeared between his eyes, and worry caused his mouth tipped down at the corners. "I don't like this."

"I'll be fine," I assured him. "You're already doing me a favor. I won't make you jump through any hoops, and I know my word doesn't mean much, but I promise I won't try to claim anything of yours, either. I already owe you so much for protecting me, and..." I trailed off as the memory of the car accident came to mind and a shiver racked my body.

"Gemma." He waited for me to meet his gaze. "This isn't your fault. We're going to do whatever we have to in order to keep you safe."

I nodded slightly. "Thank you."

My heart stuttered in my chest as his huge hands lifted and cupped my shoulders. "I promise I won't let him near you."

"I know." The words came out on a whisper, but I felt them to my soul as my heart raced with a combination of fear and anticipation. Despite our tumultuous beginnings, Vince would never let anyone hurt me.

His hands dropped away. "So, here's what's going to happen…"

Less than two hours later, Con pulled up in front of the house. I watched from the window as he exited the SUV, and a petite brunette climbed from the passenger side. "Who's that?"

"Abby. Con's baby sister," Vince explained.

"She's beautiful."

Vince threw me a strange look as he moved to open the door, and the duo stepped inside seconds later. Abby's eyes immediately landed on me, and a grin lit up her pretty face. "Hey! It's so nice to meet you!"

I blushed under the scrutiny. I met fans all the time, but it never got easier. I always felt like I was playing dress up, trying to fill a pair of shoes much too big. There were so many artists who were much better than me, and I was constantly amazed that people found me even remotely interesting.

Abby continued. "Ink's told us all about you."

I slid a look his way and caught a tiny smirk lifting the corners of his mouth. My gut tightened. I wasn't entirely sure I wanted to know exactly what he'd told them, but I held out a hand. "It's nice to meet you, Abby. I'm Jana."

She waved away my hand and pulled me into a hug instead. I tensed as her arms tightened around me and awkwardly returned the embrace. Over her shoulder, I met Vince's gaze. There was something there that I couldn't quite read. Abby pulled back and tossed a look over her shoulder at the guys before turning back to me. "Are you ready for this?"

Not knowing exactly what this was, I nodded slowly. "I guess so."

"Perfect." She pulled a camera from the large handbag slung over her shoulder. "Go stand by that wall."

I did as she bade and watched her glance around for a moment. My gaze lifted, and every muscle went tense as a pair of dark brown eyes latched onto mine. Though I'd met him a couple of times now, I wasn't sure I'd ever get used to him. Con was... intense.

He stared at me as if seeking something, and I forced myself to bear up under the scrutiny. I wanted to assure him that I would never jeopardize Vince, that this was only temporary. Instead, I remained silent and still.

"Ink, come here."

He moved forward, and I forced my attention back to Abby. She had the same dark eyes as her brother, but hers were softer, framed by impossibly long lashes that I envied.

"Take a knee," she directed. Vince followed her instructions and knelt on the floor in front of me. Despite the entire thing being staged, my heart gave a little flutter in my chest. As a little girl, I'd dreamed of the day a man would propose to me and make me his wife.

But I'd never envisioned anything like this. The sight of this huge, dominant man on his knees in front of me sent my ovaries into overdrive. My legs shook with the urge to throw myself at him, and I locked my knees to keep from tackling him to the floor and having my wicked way with him.

He lifted a tiny black box then threw open the lid, and my eyes widened at the diamond inside.

"Holy... Is that...?" My gaze jumped from Vince over his shoulder to where Abby stood, camera obscuring half of her face as she took the photos.

"Just go with it," she called from behind the lens.

Automatically, I lifted my hands to my mouth affecting the stereotypical surprised look. Mostly, though, I was trying to cover my true reaction. I hadn't expected a ring at all, let alone the good-sized diamond nestled inside the velvet box.

"Good!" Abby called. "Now, Ink, take it out and slip it on her finger."

My hand trembled as I held it out to him, and it took him two tries to get it on properly. I had a feeling he was shaking just as much as I was. From his position, his head reached my sternum, and he tilted his chin up to meet my eyes. Still holding my hand, he gave my fingers a reassuring squeeze.

I heard the faint snap of the shutter on the camera as Abby clicked away, but in that moment, it seemed as if the rest of the world had slipped away, leaving only Vince and me. If I hadn't been aware of how decent a man he was before, I was now. He'd chosen to put a virtual stranger's needs ahead of his own wishes and desires, and I appreciated it immensely.

"That's enough." I jumped a little as Con's voice shattered my reverie, and Vince dropped my hand before slowly rising to his feet.

Abby retrieved a laptop from her giant tote and met my eyes. "Where's your kitchen?"

Relieved to have something other to do other than daydream about Vince, I eagerly moved toward her. "Follow me."

In the kitchen, Abby pulled out a stool and situated herself at the bar.

"Can I get you something to drink?" I asked.

"No, thanks." Abby shot me a smile. "I'm going to see what kind of magic I can work with Photoshop to whip up an engagement photo for you."

The men entered the room at the tail end of the conversation, and I watched as Vince picked up the door handle the locksmith had removed from the garage door, then passed it to Con.

I met Vince's gaze as he turned back to us. "How are we going to get word out?"

He lifted one shoulder. "I guess just start telling everyone and hope it catches fire organically."

I thought on that for a second, then flicked a glance at Con. "When do we leave?"

He opened his mouth to speak, but Abby beat him to it. "I've got you guys on the second flight out tomorrow morning. Your itineraries are in my purse. Connor, will you go grab those?"

Her older brother rolled his eyes but did as she requested and returned less than a minute later, purple file folder in hand. He passed it to Vince, who opened it up and flipped through the documents.

Thoughts flitted through my mind as I debated my options. "So, we have a little less than twenty-four hours to get everything ready. Do we think that'll be enough time to get word out?"

Con's dark eyes pierced mine. "Do you have a better idea?"

"Well..." I spoke tentatively, afraid he would shoot down my plan. "I have a ton of followers on social media. What if I do kind of a blast of posts over the course of the day tomorrow, each one leading up to our engagement announcement?"

"Kind of like clues leading to the big reveal," Abby piped up. "I like it!"

I shot her a quick smile. "Thanks."

"That's one way to do it," Con said with a slow nod. "I'll leave that to you, then."

"Okay." I was already brimming with ideas as Vince began to read the details aloud for all of us to hear.

"We've got a 10:20 flight out, then a driver will meet us at the airport to take us to Anna Maria Island."

My ears perked up at that. "Where is that?"

"Know where Tampa is?"

I nodded at Con's question. "I've never been there, but I know the general vicinity."

"It's about forty miles south, along the Gulf Coast."

Inside, I bubbled with excitement. "Has anyone told Maggie or Harvey yet?"

Con gave a brief shake of his head. "I'd prefer not to reveal this to anyone yet. If they need to get a hold of you, any communication will go through me first."

"Oh. Okay." It made sense, but I felt a little adrift not being able to talk to anyone.

"Vince will have his cell on him at all times, and he'll be the main point of contact," Con said, "but I ask that you don't tell anyone where you are or what you're doing. You can keep your phone for emergencies, but I suggest leaving it off unless you absolutely need it. Or, better yet, leave it here completely."

"So—" My words were cut off as the doorbell rang. Con immediately turned on a heel and headed that direction. My eyes widened as I threw a look at Vince. "Who is that?"

Abby glanced up at me, then over to Vince before dropping her gaze back to the computer in front of her. That didn't exactly bode well.

His chest rose and fell on a deep breath. "Come with me."

I reluctantly fell into step beside Vince as we followed the sound of voices to the living room. Con stood next to an older man dressed in a suit. As soon as we entered, he turned our way and a bright smile wreathed the man's wrinkled face. "Ah. So here's the happy couple."

Oh, God. I knew this was all part of the plan, but it seemed to be happening so fast. My steps faltered, and I threw a look at Vince. He met my gaze and gently squeezed my waist, urging me forward. "Breathe. Everything is fine," he said quietly, for my ears only.

Heart pounding in my chest, I turned my attention back to the minister standing in the middle of the living room. "Nice to meet you, Reverend. I'm Jana." I extended one hand, and he clasped it within his own.

"You can call me Bob."

His eyes were kind, and a flurry of butterflies kicked up in my stomach. I didn't know if Con had told him the whole story, but I suddenly wanted to spill my guts about every terrible thing I'd done in my life to this man of God.

The reverend turned to Vince and shook his hand. "Are you the groom?"

"I am."

I winced internally, waiting for a bolt of lightning or something equally ominous to appear for our deception. A small hand wrapped around the inside of my elbow, and I tossed a look across my shoulder at Abby.

"You ready for this?" she asked just loud enough for me to hear.

I swallowed hard and pressed one hand to my stomach in an effort to calm my riotous nerves. "I don't know."

She studied me with those huge dark eyes for a moment, then smiled as she gave my arm a gentle squeeze. "Everything will work out."

God, I hoped so, because things certainly couldn't get any worse.

CHAPTER
NINE

VINCE

Beside me, Gemma bounced in her seat as she stared out the window of the plane. "There's so much water."

She moved to one side as I leaned toward her and stared out at the vast expanse of dark blue ocean beneath us. "Crazy, huh?"

She turned to look at me, her big blue eyes pleading. "Can we go to the beach while we're here?"

"We'll see." It really wasn't the best idea, so we would have to play it by ear, see how many people were around.

Her face fell, and she turned back to the window. "I've never been to the beach before."

That surprised me. Gemma seemed to be the kind of girl who had everything at her fingertips, and had seen everything. "Really?"

The plane began to descend, and she buckled her seatbelt then shook her head as she settled back in her seat. "I grew up in a tiny little town in Kentucky. I never even left the state until I was sixteen when I went to Nashville."

I really didn't want to have this conversation in public, but she had piqued my curiosity. "But you've been so many places."

She lifted one shoulder and stared longingly out the window. "We're always in a hotel or something. There's never any time to go explore or do things."

In that moment, I made the decision that before we left Florida, she would get to see the beach. Exiting the plane took a long time, and almost thirty minutes later we grabbed our luggage from the carousel and headed toward the front doors.

"There should be a driver waiting for us."

I scanned the people standing by the doorway, but Gemma beat me to it. She lifted her hand and gestured toward the last set of doors. "Right over there."

A man in a suit held a small sign with my last name, Incarnato, written in big, bold letters. Settling a hand on her lower back, I guided Gemma toward the man, pulling our luggage along as we fell into step together. The man smiled at us as we approached. "Are you Mr. and Mrs. Incarnato?"

For a moment, I was completely caught off guard at hearing Gemma's name used in conjunction with mine. The silver band on my finger felt a little too tight, and I clenched my hand into a tight fist.

"We are," she responded with a huge smile, covering my blunder. "Sorry, we're still getting used to the new titles."

The older man's eyes brightened. "Newlyweds?"

"Yep." She beamed up at me. "I keep forgetting we're married, myself."

An itchy feeling started between my shoulder blades, and I shifted restlessly at the talk of marriage. I was worried that someone would call our bluff, and I didn't want to draw more attention to ourselves than necessary. Gemma, thank God, had better acting skills than I did, because her eyes shined with glee as she grinned up at me. Pasting on a smile, I awkwardly looped an arm around her shoulders.

"Are you here on your honeymoon?"

"We are." She stuck out her hand. "I'm Jana, by the way."

I called Gemma by her stage name so often that I'd almost forgotten it wasn't her real name. Now that we were technically married, I supposed I needed to start addressing her by her actual name.

"Donald." Our driver shook her hand. "That's wonderful. Congratulations." He turned to me. "You must both be so excited."

If he only knew. I released Gemma—*Jana*, I reminded myself—and held out a hand for the man to shake. "I'm Vince. Nice to meet you."

He gestured towards our bags. "Do you have everything?"

I nodded. "This is it."

"I'm parked in the upper lot," Donald said. "It'll take me just a few moments to get down here if you'd like to wait."

"We can walk," I immediately offered. Almost as an afterthought, I turned to Jana. "As long as you don't mind?"

"Not at all." Her eyes hadn't stopped moving over the palm trees and tropical plants lining the building outside.

"Would you like me to carry anything?"

I waved off Donald's question. "I've got it."

The older man kept up an easy stream of conversation as he led us to the car then stowed our bags in the back and climbed inside. "Have you been to Anna Maria Island before?"

I shared a quick look with Jana. "No, this is our first time."

From my right, she piped up, "It's actually my first time going to the beach."

"Oh, that's fantastic," Donald said. "There are so many wonderful things to do here. Although..." the older man chuckled. "With it being your honeymoon and all, staying in is always good, too."

Jana grinned. "I hope so."

I rolled my lips together and slid a warning glance her way. She met my gaze with a look of challenge, then turned her attention out the window again, practically pressing her nose to the glass.

As we turned onto the freeway, Jana bombarded Donald with questions that he patiently answered, all the while pointing out local attractions and places of interest. Her head swiveled left and right as she took in every little detail, her lips parted slightly, and I couldn't help but smile at her obvious joy.

"Oh! Look!" Jana placed one hand on my thigh as she leaned into me, pointing out the window as the Sunshine Skyway Bridge came into view.

"Longest cable stayed bridge in the world," Donald boasted from the driver seat.

The heat of Jana's touch burned my skin through the fabric of my jeans, but I couldn't bring myself to move. I lifted my gaze from her hand to the profile of her pretty face as she stared out the window in fascination. I was certain she had no idea what she was doing, and I didn't want to embarrass her. Ripping my gaze away, I turned my attention outside.

The bridge itself was incredible. In the middle of the five-and-a-half-mile long bridge, the cables rose into two triangles pointing toward the sky, giving it the appearance of two giant sailboats. Jana sucked in a breath, and her fingers tightened on my leg as we started across the bridge. It was a strange sensation, suspended more than a hundred feet over the water with seemingly nothing beneath us for miles.

With nothing but ocean surrounding us, Jana sat back against the seat. Her gaze dropped to her hand in my lap and, finally realizing what she'd done, snatched it away, reaching to fiddle with her purse. I missed the feel of her touch as soon as it was gone, and I mentally berated myself for feeling that way.

God, I was such an idiot sometimes. This whole thing was a complete farce, yet here I was, horny as a teenager for a woman who wanted nothing to do with me.

We finished the ride mostly in silence until we finally crossed the bridge that led to the the island. I watched through the window as we passed several plazas, churches, even a sign for a school, then turned down a side street.

A few blocks later, the white sand of the gulf came into view. From the front of the car, the GPS announced that we'd reached our destination, and Donald pulled into the driveway of a tiny beach house at the very end of the street.

I glanced around as I stepped from the car. The street was lined with palm trees, lending a feel of quiet solitude. Though it was only midafternoon, things seemed calm. I wondered how things would progress over the course of the afternoon and into the evening once kids were out of school and parents were home from work.

I tipped Donald as he pulled our luggage from the trunk. "Let me just make sure the key works and everything looks good, if you don't mind."

"Of course. Would you like me to bring the bags in?"

I grabbed my own and pulled out the key Con had given me before we left. "Just hers if you wouldn't mind."

I cleared my throat, but Jana remained transfixed, staring in every direction, taking in every little thing from the gulls squalling and swooping overhead to the tiny little shells pressed into the pavement. "Jana."

She jumped at the sound of her name then rushed forward, a huge smile on her face. "Can you believe this? We're right on the beach."

I held back a smirk as I inserted the key and unlocked the door then held it open for her as we stepped into the living room. I could only imagine how much it was costing the studio to put us up here for the next two weeks. After the shit they put her through, I thought she deserved every overpriced minute of it.

I thanked Donald as he dropped off our bags, then I locked up behind him and watched through the window as he backed out of the narrow driveway and left. I turned to Jana. "Stay here. I want to check the place out."

No one knew we were coming, so I really didn't expect anything, but I also wasn't going to take any chances. When she rushed to join me, I pointed to the sectional that took up most of the living room. "Sit."

Her brows lowered, and her face fell into a mutinous expression. "Why?"

"Because it's my job to keep you safe, and it's your job to listen. Now sit and stay until I've checked everything out."

She sank down on the edge of the cushion and crossed her arms over her chest. "Would you like me to bark while I'm at it?"

I pressed my lips together to keep from smiling. "If it makes you feel better."

Her eyes narrowed further, but I dismissed her ire as I did a quick scan of the main room. The house was built in a rough L-shape, with the living, kitchen, and dining areas combined into one large room. The living room was basic, with the couch curving around the front and left walls of the house. A small kitchen with bright white cabinets was situated in the far left corner, and a small dining table took up the space just to the right.

Beyond the table, a set of patio doors opened into a small, fenced-in backyard, giving a spectacular view of the pool. I checked to ensure the lock was engaged before turning to inspect the rest of the small bungalow. A short hallway broke off the main room, leading to two bedrooms, a linen closet, and a bathroom.

The bedroom at the back of the house had a sliding door that, just like the dining room, stepped out onto the patio. Through the large bay window on the west wall, the ocean was just barely visible over the fence.

I ruefully took in the queen-sized bed. Too bad the owner hadn't thought to put two beds in here. I couldn't let Jana sleep in here by herself with the door unguarded. She would either have to take the smaller bedroom at the opposite end of the hallway, or I'd be crashing on the floor in here for the foreseeable future.

Once everything was cleared, I called for Jana. "Come on back."

In less than three seconds, she stood at my side, her eyes wide as she took in the vista through the large window. Her eyes lit up, turning the same sparkling blue as the ocean outside. "Is this your room, or would you mind if I take it?" She moved toward the window and gingerly laid her fingers on the glass. "Can you imagine waking up and seeing the ocean every morning?"

I felt like an asshole shooting her down as I explained the problem. "I can't leave you in here by yourself."

"Why not?" She glanced at me over her shoulder.

I pointed to the door. "Because someone could come in through there, and I would never know."

She bit her lip and glanced around. I could see the disappointment written plainly on her face, though she tried to cover it well. Her eyes landed on the bed, then jumped back to me. "We could... share?"

Sweet Jesus. There wasn't a snowball's chance in hell of that happening. Not because I disliked the idea, but because I wanted to share a bed with her—way more than I should. I cleared my throat. "I can crash on the floor if I have to."

"But—"

I waved away the rest of her words. "Don't worry about it. I'll figure it out later."

I had no idea how in the hell I was going to stand sleeping in the same room as her without being tempted. I remembered vividly the way her body looked naked and slick from the shower, the way her breasts felt pressed against my chest, the heat of her hand on my dick. There wasn't a single damn thing about her that didn't turn me on, and now I would be sleeping mere feet away from her—my temporary wife—for the next couple of weeks.

Fuck my life.

CHAPTER
TEN

I wondered what was going through Vince's head at the moment, because whatever it was had twisted his face into an expression of... dismay, maybe? I couldn't quite tell. He was probably disappointed at the prospect of having to put up with me for the next couple of weeks.

Vince seemed to get tenser and more on edge each time I'd mentioned our fake marriage. I knew he was worried about doing his job and keeping me safe, but we were hundreds of miles from home. No one had noticed me at the airport or if they had, no one had approached to ask for a picture or an autograph. I'd caught Vince looking behind us from time to time during the car ride here, so I assumed he was checking to make sure we hadn't been tailed.

As for the bedroom situation... That was going to be a nightmare. Which was too bad, because for the next two weeks, it was just the two of us here in this tiny little house, with nowhere to go and nothing to do... except each other.

The thought almost caused me to laugh out loud. Hey, a girl could dream.

I turned to the man in question. "Can we go down to the ocean now?"

"Not yet," he replied. "This place has plates and cups and things, but no groceries to speak of whatsoever. Let's order some food to be delivered, then we can go out later."

"Why don't we just run to the store? That would save us a lot of time," I pointed out. "Besides, it's only right up the road."

I'd seen a little plaza on the way in that contained a grocery store as well as a handful of various other shops dedicated to beachwear and such.

He shook his head. "Not a good idea."

"Seriously?" I propped my hands on my hips and scowled at him. "Am I allowed to do anything?"

He lifted an eyebrow. "Right now, I'm the only thing standing between you and some psychopathic stalker."

I rolled my eyes. "I wasn't suggesting we announce my identity over the loudspeaker."

He crossed his arms over his chest. "You wouldn't have to. Beautiful women attract attention everywhere they go."

He thought I was beautiful? My heart warmed at the compliment, and I forced myself to tune back in to what he was saying.

"Anyone who listens to country music or has picked up a magazine over the past two years knows your face. Plus, you have social media followers everywhere. They all saw your posts, and you never know where you might run into one of them. It's safer for now just to stay in."

I made a little face, and the corners of his mouth twitched. "Let me get a better feel for the place, then we can discuss it."

"Fine," I sighed, turning toward the door. "I'm going to go sit by the pool."

"Hold up."

I threw my arms up as I whirled back to him. "What now?"

His lips pressed together for a moment, and I wondered if he was fighting a smile again. Jerk.

"Let's make a list of the things we need to order, then you can unpack and do your thing."

Without another word, I traipsed back to the living room and pulled a notebook from my purse. I kept it handy in case any good lyrics ever came to me, so I could write them down before I forgot. Taking a seat at the dining room table, I flipped it open to a blank page then jotted down a few basic items. Eggs, milk, cereal, bread.

"Bacon," Vince added from over my shoulder.

I lifted an eyebrow and glanced up at him. "I can't eat that stuff."

"Don't like it? Or does it make you sick?"

"I love it, actually." I shook my head. "But Harvey would kill me if he found out."

"Harvey can go fuck himself. Besides"—he shot me a rare smile—"you're on your fake honeymoon. Live a little."

I dropped my eyes back to the paper in front of me, my cheeks burning at his teasing remark. This was such a strange situation we'd found ourselves in. How in the hell we'd gone from practically enemies to married in the span of less than two weeks, I would never be able to comprehend. I wished I could get a better read on him, because I had no idea what he was thinking half the time.

Sometimes he was such an asshole. Other times, he acted like a doting boyfriend. I'd caught myself in the car when I laid my hand on his leg, and I was surprised he hadn't pulled away. Maybe he hadn't wanted to say anything in front of Donald. Or it could be because, deep down, he was as attracted to me as I was to him.

I couldn't be sure, but I sure as hell wasn't going to ask. He wasn't exactly communicative on a good day, and I wasn't about to make things more awkward by bringing it up. What I did know for sure was that he never would have come to me on his own. Had the situation with my stalker not escalated, he would probably have just gone on living his life without giving me a second thought.

I tapped the point of the pencil against the page several times before scribbling *bacon* on the blue line. We added several more items for dinner plus fresh fruits and vegetables. As I wrote, he pulled out his phone and began to text rapidly.

I couldn't help but wonder who he was talking to. A girlfriend? Jealousy burned through my veins like fire. I had no claim on him whatsoever, but I hated the thought of Vince with another woman. It would explain why he'd never made a move on me, though.

I couldn't help the words that spilled from my mouth before I could stop them. "Are you letting her know you're here?"

Icy blue eyes lifted to mine. "Who?"

I nodded toward the phone in his hands. "Your girlfriend."

He pinned me with a hard stare. "Do I seem like the type of guy who would marry you if I had a girlfriend?"

He had me there. "No, I—I'm sorry. It's just..." I bit my lip. "It sounds strange, but I keep forgetting we're... married."

"I get it, believe me." His rigid posture relaxed. "It's kinda weird, right?"

"Little bit." We shared a smile, and I dipped my head, happiness unfurling in my chest.

No girlfriend. *Check.*

"I can call that in if you're done with it." He finished typing, then gestured with his chin toward my list.

"It's okay." I shook my head. "I'll take care of it."

"If you're sure."

I'd brought my phone along, mostly to take pictures since Con had asked that I not speak to anyone while I was here, but it was still in my bag. I retrieved it and handed it to Vince. "Here, I'll trade you."

He cocked a brow. "What do you want me to do with it?"

"Just hang onto it. I won't need it, right?" I wanted him to trust me. Mostly, I wanted him to know that I trusted him to keep me safe.

With a slow dip of his chin, he tucked my phone into his back pocket, then held out his phone for me to take, and I slipped it from his hand, my fingers brushing his in the process. Intent on ignoring the fluttering in my belly at the sensation of his warm skin against mine, I focused on the task at hand. I quickly scrolled through the closest grocery stores according to Google, then held the phone to my ear as I waited for the call to connect.

"Hi," I said when a man on the other end answered. "I'd like some groceries to be delivered to..."

I threw a look at Vince, and he rattled off the address. I relayed it to the man, then rose from the chair, notebook in hand as I began to recite the items one by one. I felt Vince's eyes on me as I moved toward the bedroom.

I sat on the edge of the bed, and my gaze fell to my left hand where it rested in my lap. The diamond sparkled in the sunshine pouring in through the window, and it shot little rainbows against the bedroom wall as I turned my hand left and right, examining it. The ring felt odd, yet my pulse kicked up each time I looked at it.

I couldn't stop myself as I spun it around my finger and made a final request. "Um... One more thing if you have it..."

The delivery man confirmed my order, and I hung up, clutching Vince's phone to my chest. Through the sliding doors, I stared out over the back yard, practically salivating at the thought of getting out into the afternoon sun and relaxing for a bit.

The past few days had been stressful, and I was grateful that the studio had agreed to send me away. They could just as easily have sent me to a hotel, but somehow Con had managed to convince them that it was safer here. I definitely owed him for that.

Motion from the corner of my eye caught my attention, and I watched as Vince opened the doors in the dining area and stepped onto the patio. God, the man was gorgeous. He moved with the powerful, innate grace of a man who'd been trained to fight and defend. His eyes never stopped roving over his surroundings, searching for danger even in the most unlikely of places.

I wondered what he was truly like, deep beneath the layer of cool indifference he wore like a cloak. I'd seen glimpses of that man over the past few days, and it'd only served to pique my curiosity. I wanted to see him relaxed, wanted to see him smile—truly smile—and enjoy himself. I decided it was my new mission. By the time we left here, I was going to figure out who the real Vince Incarnato was.

Flipping the lock, I slid open the glass door that led to the patio and crossed the brick patio to where Vince stood. "This is beautiful."

"It is." He glanced down at me. "Did you get everything taken care of?"

"Yep."

He studied me for a long moment, and my heart banged against my ribcage. Finally, he turned his gaze back out over the pool. "Make sure you let me pay for it when it comes. I'll forward the expense report to Con, and he'll take care of it from there."

"Okay. Thanks." I nodded before heading toward the pool. I stepped close, then dipped my toes in, loving the way the sun had heated it to the temperature of bathwater. I glanced back at Vince. "Since we can't go to the beach yet, can I at least hop in the pool for a bit?"

He dipped his chin in a curt nod. "Let's go change, and I'll come out here with you. I should be able to hear the delivery guy well enough when he arrives. Did he give you a timeframe?"

He held the door for me as we entered the house, and I threw a look at him over my shoulder. "He said it would be about an hour."

I paused in the living room, one hand on my suitcase. I should do the right thing and take the back bedroom. But doing so would put more distance between us than I wanted —and I desperately wanted to use this time to find if the attraction was mutual, or if I was the only one who felt something.

Slowly, I lifted my gaze to Vince's. He watched me with those intriguing blue eyes that didn't miss a thing, and butterfly wings battered my insides under his scrutiny. The way he watched me sometimes... His actions didn't quite line up with his words.

Heat flared over my skin, and my fingers twitched at the memory of his muscular thigh beneath my palm. I had a golden opportunity to explore whatever this was between us, and I wasn't going to pass it up.

I tipped my head, peering up at him through my lashes. "Are you sleeping with me tonight?"

CHAPTER
ELEVEN

VINCE

Are you sleeping with me tonight?

The words echoed in the silence between us, and I swallowed the answer that immediately sprang to the tip of my tongue. She looked innocent, almost subservient, and it raised my suspicions tenfold. Surely she didn't mean it the way she sounded. Right?

Of course she didn't. After I'd explained everything to her earlier, I was certain she was just trying to follow the rules we'd set in place to keep her safe. I was glad that, for once, she seemed to be taking it seriously. Those slumbrous bedroom eyes, though, were nearly my undoing.

She was a potent combination of naïveté and sensuality, and I swore if I spent a hundred years with the woman, I could never figure her out. She'd acted like a self-absorbed princess most of the time I'd known her, but there were rare, unguarded moments when I thought I saw the real Jana.

From beneath those long lashes, she eyed me expectantly, and my gut twisted. I didn't have the heart to kick her out of the bedroom overlooking the beach. We could figure out the sleeping arrangements later. "Take the one you like. I'll use the one in the back."

With a tiny smile, she rolled her suitcase down the hall and shut the door behind her. I retreated to the second bedroom, changing as quickly as I could, keeping one ear tuned to the opposite side of the house as I did so. Leaving my clothes on the floor, I tugged on a pair of swim trunks then headed down the hall. Noticing Jana's door was still closed, I stopped in front of the linen closet and pulled out two pool towels, then moved into the living room to wait for her.

The soft pad of footsteps had me lifting my head, and I damn near swallowed my tongue. I was not at all prepared for Jana in a tiny red bikini. I'd seen her naked, but somehow this was even more erotic. The triangular top showed off her tits to perfection, and the skimpy bottoms were slung low over her hips and decorated with a gold chain. I wanted to grab that chain and yank her close, peel that tiny excuse for a swimsuit off her.

My dick hardened, and my balls grew heavy at the thought of stripping the fabric down her silky-smooth legs, running my hands over the lean muscles and soft curves. I could practically feel her round ass and full tits filling my palms. I wanted to put my mouth on her, taste her, fucking devour her—

No. *No*, my brain repeated emphatically. Hands—and mouth—off.

My fingers twitched, and I gritted my teeth against the urge to reach out and touch her. Damn it, didn't she have something more appropriate? Like a one-piece suit? With sleeves?

I knew they made those fuckers—I'd seen one in the most recent issue of Sports Illustrated. I'd thought at the time that it defeated the purpose of wearing a swimsuit at all, but now I was beginning to see the merit of covering every inch of skin.

I clutched the towels in front of me, praying to God that she wouldn't see the hard-on pressing eagerly through my shorts. My body's reaction to her pissed me off, and I squared my shoulders. "Ready?"

"Yep."

Her smile lit up her entire face, and I forced myself not to smile back. "Good. Let's go."

"Okay..." Her brows drew slightly together as she regarded me like I was giving orders to march off to battle instead of twenty feet outside to the patio.

I opened the door and held it for her as she moved past me and, against my will, my eyes dropped to her bottom. Pert and round, gently swaying from side to side as she walked, her ass looked like a cherry ripe for the picking.

Goddamn it. These next few days were going to be a hell of a lot harder than I'd anticipated—in more ways than one.

I settled into a chaise lounge beside the pool, and Jana wasted no time slipping into the water. Sinking beneath the crystal blue surface, she pushed off the wall and glided gracefully to the opposite end. The pool wasn't terribly deep. About three-and-a-half feet at the shallow end, the deep end would barely cover the top of her head.

When she reached the far edge of the pool, she turned and swam back toward me. I glanced from side to side under the pretense of taking in our surroundings, surreptitiously watching Jana from the corners of my eyes. I was grateful for my sunglasses as she threw a look my way, like she could feel my stare on her.

Glancing around, I took in the backyard. It was fenced in and well-maintained, surrounded by lush palm trees that blocked the view from the neighboring homes. A smallish rectangular pool took up most of the space, and a tiny grill sat off to one side. The fence was high enough so that someone walking by couldn't see over, which was a blessing. A gate at the far end of the patio opened directly onto the beach, and a small grassy area ran the length of the fence to the left of the pool.

A few minutes later, Jana exited the pool, and I tensed as she settled in the lounge chair right next to mine. Droplets of water glistened on her skin, and I watched as one slid over her stomach and down her side. My mouth went dry, and I swallowed hard. Jesus.

Forcing my gaze and my thoughts away from Jana, I focused on every little sight and sound around me. Things were still quiet, and it felt like we were secluded in our own little world. Hopefully the next two weeks would pass without incident. All I had to do was keep her corralled near the house. Of course, with Jana that was easier said than done.

A half hour later, I heard the soft rumble of an engine approach, and I glanced toward the direction of the street. "I'll bet that's our guy."

"Perfect." Jana hopped up. "We'll get the groceries put away, then we can head down to the beach."

"Not so fast," I said, catching her arm as she walked by. "I need you to stay out of sight." For a moment, she looked hurt, and I felt the need to explain. "We need to keep your identity a secret, especially now that we're here."

She stared at me for a moment then nodded. "Right."

I opened the door for her, and Jana headed to her bedroom while I cut across the living room toward the front door. I was two steps away when the knock came, and I peered through the peephole at the young man under the portico. I opened the door just enough that my body filled the space. "Groceries?"

The young man nodded. "Jana Incarnato?" It was the second time today that her name had been used in conjunction with mine, and it still sounded strange. I nodded. "That's us."

I followed the young man as he strode to the trunk of his car, and I helped him carry in two cases of water as well as various grocery bags full of stuff. Once I'd double-checked everything, he ran my credit card and finalized the transaction. I had taken one step toward the door when the kid's voice stopped me.

"Oh, I almost forgot." He held a drugstore bag in my direction, and I reached for it just as Jana came barreling down the hall.

Clad in a wide brimmed hat and giant sunglasses, she snatched the bag from the kid's fingers with a brilliant smile. "I'll take that. Thank you so much."

I watched in disbelief as she turned abruptly and fled back toward her room. Shaking off the strangeness of the situation, I turned back to the kid. He remained frozen in place, his eyes glued to Jana's backside as she moved away from us. Something settled over me when I saw him watching her, and I tensed, every muscle in my body going completely rigid. I cleared my throat hard, and the kid jumped, his gaze snapping back to mine.

"I, uh... Thank you, sir."

He bolted for the front door, and I locked up behind him with a slight shake of my head. I seriously doubted he had recognized her in her crazy beach get-up, and more than likely it was just seeing Jana in a swimsuit that had scrambled the kid's brain.

Truth to tell, I didn't blame him one bit, because she did the same thing to me.

CHAPTER
TWELVE

JANA

The sand squished beneath my feet, giving way and sucking me in, like the mud near the riverbank I'd played on as a kid. It was the whitest sand I'd ever seen—the only sand I'd ever seen in person—and I marveled at the way it stretched from one end of the beach to the other.

The breeze picked up, and I placed one hand on my hat to keep it from blowing away. The sun was hot on my skin, reminding me that it'd been too long since I'd taken any time to do something for myself. With Vince's rigid security measures, I wasn't sure how often we'd be able to go out, and I was determined to make the most of the moment.

I increased my pace, eager to get down to the ocean. The sight had literally taken my breath away. It was so vast, so wide, that it seemed never-ending. Parts of it were navy, other areas green, and some closest to the shore were aquamarine. Tiny shells pricked at my feet as I made my way across the sand, but I brushed off the pain and continued, not wanting anything to strip the joy from this moment.

Vince hovered just a few feet away, and I practically ran into the surf. I sucked in a breath as the cool water lapped over my feet and ankles, making me dance backwards out of the way.

"Oh! It's cooler than I thought it would be."

Vince gazed out at the ocean. "By the end of summer, it'll be much warmer."

I nodded. It was the same as the creek that ran behind the trailer park where I'd grown up. The runoff from the mountains filled the rivers and streams during the spring and early summer, but by the end of the season it warmed to almost bathwater temperature. I turned it back to him. "Can we walk a little bit?"

Though he didn't move, I knew he was taking in every single detail of our surroundings. Finally, he gave me a curt nod. "That should be fine."

We'd locked up the house before we came down here, so I knew our things were safe enough inside. Even down here at the beach, only a few dozen people were visible lounging or playing on the bright white sand.

"Which direction?"

He glanced up and down the beach. "Doesn't matter. The island is only about seven miles long, and we're just north of the midpoint."

I pursed my lips and shielded my eyes, glancing in each direction. Finally, I pointed north. "Let's go this way today. Maybe tomorrow we'll check out the southern strip."

Silently, Vince fell into step beside me and we walked on, lost in thought for several minutes. A half mile or so up the beach, a cute little bistro sat along the shoreline. Shell pink with white trim, it had a deck off the back for patrons to view the sunset while they ate. "There's food close by if we want to go out."

Vince shook his head. "We're supposed to be lying low."

I suppressed a huff. I didn't know why I'd hoped things would be different here. I bit down on my tongue to keep a sharp retort from escaping. The idea of a fake honeymoon had definitely sounded better in theory, because the reality was looking pretty crappy so far. I drew in a deep breath. My anger at Vince was misguided. I knew he was just following orders, but that didn't mean I had to like it. "So, basically nothing has changed? Different house, same guard, same rules?"

Vince side-eyed me from behind his mirrored sunglasses. "Basically."

"Awesome. Can't wait."

Vince's lips quirked at my sarcasm. "At least the view is better here."

"Are you saying my house is shit?"

My question seemed to catch him off guard. "No. Just... different."

"Hmm..." I glanced out at the ocean, watching the birds overhead, but I could feel his gaze on me.

"It does surprise me a little, not gonna lie."

It was the first thing he'd offered voluntarily, and I turned to meet his gaze. "Why's that?"

"I thought you'd choose something more... extravagant."

Because he thought I was spoiled and self-centered. I probably should have expected something like that, but his words cut into my heart like a dagger slipping between my ribs.

My shoulders twitched as I fortified the walls around myself. "The belief that all singers make a ton of money right off the bat with a record deal is a misconception. I got started as a backup singer to some of the more popular artists. It's only been about a year and a half since I've really ventured out on my own. There's a lot of money tied up in recording, and though I tour, only the headliners make a decent profit.

"When I moved to Dallas, I wanted to put down some roots, but I didn't want to buy anything ostentatious. I'd rather save my money now and live modestly than try to keep up with the Joneses and be broke in ten years."

He was silent for a long moment, then—"Smart."

Though I refused to look at him, I heard a faint thread of admiration in his voice. Not wanting to acknowledge it, I changed the subject. "I'm getting kind of hungry. What about you?"

"I could eat."

I rolled my eyes. Such a guy thing to say. He could always eat. In fact, I was pretty sure Vince would never stop eating given the choice. I had no idea how he stayed in shape with as much as he consumed over the course of a day. Though we'd avoided each other as much as possible while he'd been staying with me, I couldn't miss the dent he'd made in my pantry. Not that I minded. I was a terrible shopper. I always seemed to go when I was hungry and grabbed all kinds of things that I regretted later. Vince had helped polish off most of my open bags of snacks so they didn't go to waste.

I slowed to a stop and gestured with my head back toward the house. "Let's head back and start dinner, then."

I studied him surreptitiously as we turned around to head home. Well, our home for the next couple of weeks, anyway. Temporary house, temporary marriage. I almost laughed out loud, though I was far from feeling the humor of the situation. My heart still felt bruised at the way Vince had so easily stereotyped me as a high-maintenance blonde bimbo who was only concerned about appearances. Would he ever see me for who I really was? I seriously doubted it.

Inwardly, I heaved a sigh. He seemed to be acting stranger than normal, and I hoped that wasn't a sign of things to come. I liked knowing exactly where I stood with someone, and now

I felt like I was floundering, grasping for purchase. I knew all of this was a fabrication to keep me safe. I just couldn't stop my heart from wishing it could be more.

CHAPTER
THIRTEEN

VINCE

As I stacked the last of the dishes in the sink, I glanced over the bar into the living room where Jana was curled up at one end of the plush sectional, a pair of fuzzy pink socks adorning her feet.

The sight made me want to smile. She wore little else in the way of clothing, only a camisole and a pair of tiny shorts, but she always had a pair of those fuzzy socks on. *What's with that?*

I didn't realize I'd spoken out loud until Jana's head swiveled my way. "What's with what?"

Embarrassed to have been caught watching her, I dropped my eyes back to the sink and fiddled with the utensils for a moment. "Your socks."

I dried my hands on a dish towel as I glanced over at her again. She lifted one shoulder. "My feet are always cold."

I cracked a grin. "Have you tried wearing clothes?"

She rolled her eyes. "I didn't say the rest of me was cold, just my feet."

"Gotcha." I sank onto the couch a few cushions away and spread my arms out over the back. "What're you watching?"

"I don't honestly know." She gently tossed the remote my way. "I don't get a chance to watch much TV, so if there's something you want to turn on, go ahead."

"This is fine." I turned my attention to the reality show on TV. From what I'd gathered, a dozen or so strangers were all on an island, apparently looking for love. Twenty minutes later, I was reluctant to admit that it had sucked me in.

"What a tool." I gestured to the guy on the screen. "Do women actually go for that shit?"

Jana shrugged. "I guess so. In my experience, all the good ones seem to be taken."

I snorted. The only men she'd been with recently were money-hungry, douchebag pretty boys, so it didn't surprise me that she hadn't found anyone worthwhile. Keeping the comment to myself, I turned my attention back to the TV until the show ended.

Jana slapped a hand over her mouth to cover a yawn, and I glanced over at her. "Are you ready for bed?"

Her face scrunched up in apology. "Sorry. It's been kind of a long day. You can stay up if you want."

I'd been dreading this moment all day long, but I couldn't put it off any longer. I picked up the remote and turned off the TV. "That's okay, we can head to bed. I need to do a quick once over of the house, then figure out where I'm going to sleep."

Part of me stupidly, irrationally, hoped she would voice her offer to let me sleep in bed with her again. Before I could say anything I would regret, I continued. "Why don't you use the bathroom first, and I'll shower up when you're done."

Without waiting for an answer, I headed to the sliding door by the patio and checked to make sure it was locked.

Though I didn't look at her, I heard Jana's soft footsteps pad down the short hallway and into the bathroom.

Heaving a sigh, I checked each window and door thoroughly, wasting as much time as possible before I had to meet her in the bedroom. Once I was sure that everything was locked up tight, I grabbed a change of clothes from my suitcase and slipped into the bathroom to get ready.

I took a quick shower, not wanting to leave her unattended too long, then hopped out and yanked on my clothes. I steeled myself as I flicked off the light and headed toward the bedroom. Jana was waiting on the edge of the bed when I entered.

She'd worn the tiny tank top and shorts all evening, but somehow, the sight of her wearing them here in the bedroom was a thousand times more erotic. I wanted to slide the spaghetti-thin strap down her shoulder, explore every inch of tanned, toned skin. Forcing my gaze and thoughts away from her, I scanned the bedroom again.

The floor was tiled, probably for low maintenance reasons, but there was at least a rug under the bed. The rug made a three-foot border around the bed, and the thin layer of woven fabric was better than nothing. Pulling a blanket from the closet, I folded it in half for extra padding and laid it on the floor at the foot of the bed, placing myself between both the sliding door and the door to the hallway.

I gestured with my chin toward the bed. "Can I steal a pillow?"

Silently, Jana reached behind her to snag a pillow, then threw it my way.

"Thanks." I dropped it to the floor then found an outlet close by to charge my phone. Jana still sat on the edge of the bed, and I finally lifted my eyes to hers. "Do you need anything else before we hit the hay?"

She shook her head slowly. "Nope. I'm good."

I spun on a heel and took two quick steps toward the door, then flipped off the overhead light. The rustle of sheets met my ears as Jana slipped under them, and I bit my tongue, willing myself not to look. I settled onto my makeshift pallet and tucked my hands beneath my head, staring at the ceiling. The blankets made it more comfortable, and it definitely wasn't the worst place I'd ever slept.

"Night." Jana's soft voice floated on the still air down to me.

"Night." I closed my eyes and tried to shut off my brain to settle in to sleep, but all I could see was her. I remembered the look of wonder on her face the moment we stepped onto the beach and she'd seen the ocean for the first time. I heard her tinkling laugh as the cool water lapped over her toes, the huge smile lighting her face more radiant than the sun.

And that tiny red bikini... God, she was so gorgeous. I'd had to constantly fight my hard-on around her, because the sight of her sleek body was like a drug to my system. I shifted uncomfortably and bit back an oath as heat raced to my groin.

Fuck, I couldn't think of her like that. She was slowly burrowing under my skin with those sweet smiles that made me want to show her everything, spend every minute of the next thirteen days exploring the island from top to bottom.

I wanted to say to hell with the rules—but I couldn't. We were here for her safety, and it needed to stay that way. In order to pull this whole thing off, I needed to spend more time watching our surroundings and less time checking out Jana's tight ass and perfect tits, barely concealed in that stretchy fabric.

Damn.

A soft creak of the mattress drew my attention back to her as she shifted in bed. I drew in a deep breath and let it out slowly, finally managing to wrangle my wayward thoughts under control. I closed my eyes and willed myself to go to sleep. But I was trained to be attuned to my surroundings, and my ears perked up at every little sound—and there were a lot of those.

For the next several hours, I lay on the floor in a state of torture as Jana tossed and turned in the bed just a few feet away. I couldn't help but wonder if she was as uncomfortable and on edge as I was. Finally, in the still-early morning when I could drag it out no longer, I hauled myself to my feet.

With a grimace, I stretched my sore muscles then glanced over at the bed. Jana slumbered away, her face relaxed, long blonde strands spread out behind her on the pillowcase. She seemed so small, so vulnerable, and a strange sense of possessiveness washed over me.

I gave a slight jerk of my head, shaking off the strange emotion. Though I'd spent years in the military watching over others, this was the first time I'd ever been in a situation like the one with Jana. Protecting a civilian—especially a woman —was different. They were softer, more delicate... and infinitely more tempting. I shut down that train of thought, chalking up the surge of protectiveness to the basic primitive need to keep her from harm.

I quietly exited the bedroom and closed the door behind me, then headed into the kitchen. I'd never been a coffee person, and apparently Jana wasn't either. Neither of us had added it to the grocery list, and I couldn't remember ever seeing her drink it. I smiled. As different as we were, at least that was one thing we had in common.

The sun was just breaking over the horizon as I stepped into the back yard. I shot a glance toward the sliding doors where Jana hopefully still snoozed away in bed and drew in a lungful of the salty ocean air. After being with her almost every minute of the past twenty-four hours, I needed some time to myself to get my head on straight.

Jana was a walking wet dream, and it felt like my insides

were literally twisted up in knots over the woman. My pulse kicked up and blood pumped furiously through my veins at the thought of her in that sexy swimsuit. I dropped my head back on a soft groan.

The only way I could think to solve the problem was to exhaust my body so completely that I couldn't even get turned on by her. I had serious doubts it would work, but I had to try something. Because touching her was not an option. If I ever laid a hand on her, I knew it would be over.

Staying as quiet as humanly possible, I warmed up then moved into some of my Krav Maga workout. I preferred to work with a partner to sharpen my skills and reaction time, but the movement felt good, and time slipped away as the sun rose higher in the sky. I was breathing heavily by the time Jana stepped onto the patio in a sports bra and another pair of tiny shorts.

Despite my fatigue, I felt my dick twitch at the sight of those lean legs. So much for hoping my body would be too tired to react to her. I clenched my teeth as she practically skipped over to me, her perfect white smile lighting her face.

"What are you doing?"

Trying to kill myself so I'll stop getting so worked up over you. I cleared my throat. "Working out."

"Well, yeah." She rolled her eyes. "I know that. But I mean"—she wiggled her fingers in my direction—"what kind of moves are those? Is that some type of karate?"

"Krav Maga," I corrected.

"Krav Maga." She tested the words on her tongue, then bounced on her toes, her eyes shining with interest. "Can you teach me?"

I froze. "What?"

"You know." She made the hand gesture again. "The self-defense stuff."

"Um..." I couldn't deny that it would actually be a good

idea for her to learn, but self-defense was up-close-and-personal. My hands would be all over her, every inch, and I broke into a sweat just thinking about it. "I don't think that's a good idea."

"Why not?"

My mind spun to come up with an excuse. "Beginners normally start on the mats. The grass can get slick, and I don't want you to get hurt."

It sounded feeble to my ears, and they burned as she stared incredulously at me, like she wasn't buying the bullshit I was selling. Neither was I.

She pursed her lips. "Well, it's not like some stranger is going to wait until I'm in some soft, padded area to attack me."

And there it was, the logic I so desperately despised. I grunted. "You don't need to learn."

"What if I need to protect myself?"

"You won't," I snapped. "I'm here to take care of that."

"You won't be around forever," she pointed out.

Damn. Score one for the blonde. And why the hell did hearing those words hurt so bad? A dull ache thudded through my chest, infuriating me further. "I'm here now."

"So?" She threw her hands in the air. "What about when you're gone?"

"Goddamn it, Jana, just leave it alone."

"I don't understand—"

"Enough!" I barked out. "I'm not fucking teaching you, and that's final."

"What the hell is wrong with you?" Tears shimmered in her eyes as she glared up at me. "You're such a dick."

She spun on a heel and stormed into the house, and the sliding door slammed in her wake. She was right. I was a complete asshole. All she'd done was ask that I teach her some moves to defend herself, which wasn't an unreasonable request at all. But the thought of running my hands all over her body knowing I would never be able to have her... It was too much.

I was pissed at myself for overreacting and hurting her feelings again, but I didn't know how to fix it. I'd either push her away or cross the line and do something I couldn't take back. Because I knew I didn't have the self-control to have her in my arms without wanting to kiss her and so much more.

Now I'd ruined the tenuous balance between us because I couldn't set my attraction for her aside to do the right thing.

It was going to be a long two weeks.

CHAPTER
FOURTEEN

JANA

I threw down my pencil and heaved a sigh as I rolled to my back. My brain was fried, and I couldn't come up with anything good to save my life. I'd tried off and on to work on some new lyrics, but any motivation and inspiration had been zapped.

For the past three days, I had alternated between lying by the pool and watching whatever happened to be on TV, which most often, seemed to be one reality show or another. While I had enjoyed relaxing for the most part, I had pretty much reached my limit being stagnant, and I was ready to throw myself into the ocean. God, how did people live like this? I was not made to be sedentary.

My body vibrated with irritation, and I stared vacantly at the ceiling, debating what to do. Things between Vince and me had grown even more tense than before. Every night, he slipped into the role of protector, sleeping at the foot of the bed. Each morning, he was gone long before I awoke, apparently to work out in the small rectangle of grass next to the pool.

I still harbored a fair amount of resentment toward him for refusing to show me any self-defense moves. To my way of thinking, it made sense to know how to protect myself, and I couldn't figure out why he wouldn't want to teach me. Unless, of course, he just despised me so much that he didn't want to spend one more minute with me than absolutely necessary. I supposed that, given his attitude for the past couple of days, it was a distinct possibility.

Considering the house was so tiny we literally almost tripped over each other, we technically ate dinner together each night. Even so, I would bet we hadn't exchanged more than a hundred words since our fight on the patio three mornings ago.

I couldn't figure him out. One minute he was my white knight in shining armor, ready to leap to my defense; the next, he was an overbearing, arrogant asshole who seemed to think that, because I was a woman, I was incapable of caring for myself.

That pissed me off more than anything. I'd been on my own for most of the twenty-two years I'd been on this earth, and I would still be on my own long after he was gone. He was a chauvinist if I'd ever seen one. I should probably consider myself lucky that he let me use the bathroom by myself, because I certainly wasn't allowed to do anything else.

Although I'd broken down and practically begged, he had staunchly refused to entertain any notion of going back to the beach. As far as I could tell, the island was perpetually calm and quiet, exactly what we had seen when we arrived. No one had approached us while we were out that first day, and I didn't think anyone had been able to recognize me under the hat and sunglasses.

Unfortunately, Vince seemed to be taking his bodyguard

duties more seriously than ever. There was no doubt in my mind that if I tried to escape to the beach on my own, he would drag me back and tie me to a chair for the remainder of our time here.

I hated that I was stuck here with him. We were literally a thousand miles from home, away from whoever was stalking me, yet he refused to bend at all. I'd been too mad to even revisit the subject since yesterday, and even if I did bring it up, I was certain he would shoot me down again.

A thought suddenly occurred to me, and I wasn't quite sure why I hadn't realized it before. I had some leverage here. If I made enough noise, complained enough, Harvey would be forced to step in. I didn't really want to throw a temper tantrum after the conversation I'd had with Con at my house last week, but I was getting desperate. Gritting my teeth, I steeled myself as I pushed up from the bed and stalked into the living room.

Vince sat sprawled on the couch, arms stretched over the back, feet propped up on the coffee table in front of him. He glanced my way as I entered the room. I paused several feet away and stared at him for a moment, waiting for him to speak. Not surprisingly, he didn't. Instead, one dark eyebrow rose in silent question, stirring my ire.

"I'd like to go down to the beach."

He was silent for a long moment. Then he shook his head. "No can do."

"Why the hell not?" I motioned toward the windows. "It's almost dark anyway. Even if we did run into somebody, there's, like, zero percent chance they would recognize me."

"Doesn't matter. We're staying here."

"Fine. Then I want my phone." I stepped forward and held my hand out expectantly.

His gaze dropped to my hand, then rose slowly again to meet my eyes. "What for?"

"This is ridiculous." I made an aggravated gesture with my hand. "I want to call Harvey."

"Why?" Vince scoffed. "So you can call and throw a temper tantrum like the spoiled, self-righteous little girl you are?"

"Says the overblown, chauvinistic tyrant."

He lifted one shoulder as if he couldn't care less that I'd just insulted him. "Tough shit. This tyrant's keeping you safe, which you would understand if you utilized that one remaining brain cell reserved for common sense."

I sucked in an outraged breath. I knew I wasn't the smartest person in the world, but neither was I stupid. The heat of humiliation raced through my veins, and I fought to shut down my emotions as I lashed out at him.

"Keeping me safe?" I let out a mirthless laugh as I crossed my arms over my chest and stared down at him. "How's that working out for you? Because I'm pretty sure I could've been killed due to your negligence."

His face darkened. "Are you this much of a bitch to everyone, or am I the unlucky bastard who gets saddled with your bad attitude?"

"Pretty sure it's just you," I snapped. "I seem to get along just fine with everyone else."

"You sure have them fooled, because you're a pain in the ass when you don't get your way." He gave a short laugh. "Since you seem so determined to throw yourself in harm's way, maybe we should've left you at home where your stalker could find you. I'm sure he wouldn't have made it out of your subdivision before turning around and taking your bratty ass back."

God, he was such an asshole. I glared at him. "Believe it or not, most people actually like me."

"That's a lie if I ever heard one," he snapped. "Your personality is as fake as those tits."

Cold washed over me, and I could practically feel the blood drain from my face. He may as well have reached out and slapped me. Of all the things he could've said to me, that was the worst. I directed my gaze over his shoulder as silence fell like a lead curtain around us. Tears burned the back of my throat, and I bit my tongue to keep them from rising higher and spilling from my eyes.

I dug my fingernails into the palm of my hand, using the bite of physical pain to distract myself from his hurtful words. I couldn't bring myself to look at him. Instead, I pulled my shoulders back and lifted my chin. I'd be damned if I would give him the satisfaction of knowing his words had impacted me, that they'd cut deeper than a knife.

Swallowing down the emotion that had risen in my throat, I fell back a step, then turned to leave. I almost hoped that Vince would stop me, but he didn't. All the fight left me as my heart cracked wide open.

In the span of only a few seconds, Vince had solidified exactly where we stood. He didn't care about me at all. Though I'd continued to hope that maybe he was just holding back, I knew in that moment I was wrong. It hurt more than I wanted to admit, and I was furious with myself for allowing a man to dictate my happiness and self-worth.

Bypassing the bathroom completely, I headed straight for the bedroom and quietly closed the door behind me. As soon as the darkness enveloped me, the tears came, falling hard and fast. I fought to control my breathing as my lungs heaved and my chest constricted.

This whole thing had been a huge mistake. I had no idea how we were going to keep this farce going when he obviously hated me so much. I climbed into bed and hugged my pillow close, pouring every ounce of despair into the cotton fabric.

The remaining slivers of my heart shattered with each sob that racked my body. He made me feel horrible, insignificant.

Worst of all, he'd just validated every negative thought I'd ever had about myself. I was beginning to wonder if maybe I really was as awful as he said I was.

Vince was about as brutally honest as a person could get, and if nothing else, I could always count on him to speak the truth... And the truth hurt like hell.

CHAPTER
FIFTEEN

VINCE

A sick sense of dread curdled in my gut as I watched her stiffen and turn slowly toward the bedroom. I dropped my feet to the floor, ready to stand and stop her—beg her forgiveness. The second I leaned forward, though, I caught myself.

Fuck.

I couldn't go after her—not like this. I felt like shit for hurting her feelings, but what the hell was I going to do? The reminder of every word I'd said tasted like acid on my tongue, and I longed to pull her to me, tell her I hadn't meant any of it.

I wanted to... but I couldn't.

Aside from that, a huge part of me was still pissed at myself for what had happened back home. Her words hit me hard, because I blamed myself for not noticing someone had tampered with her brake lines. It was no consolation that we couldn't pin down an exact time, but I hadn't forgiven myself, and apparently, neither had she. The hell of it was... she was right. She deserved someone better, .

For the past few days, ever since that morning out on the patio, I'd done my best to ignore her. I'd pushed her away, unable to stand being in her company for more than a few minutes—and not because I disliked her. Each time she was near, I felt the overwhelming urge to pull her close and lose myself in a kiss that I knew would change my life irrevocably forever.

Seeing her half-naked in those skimpy swimsuits tested the limits of my self-control, and it was all I could do not to strip the tiny scrap of fabric from her body and pull her under me. Over me. Fucking anywhere—as long as I could have her.

I'd shot down every opportunity to leave the house, telling her that we needed to keep her out of the public's eye. But that was only half of the story. The truth was, I was terrified. Going out, even for a walk on the beach, would force me to interact with her, and if we ran into someone who was interested in talking, we'd have to act like we were married.

The last thing I wanted was a replay of the scene in the airport when she'd slipped her hand into mine. Her skin had been so soft, so perfect, I couldn't help but wonder how the rest of her felt. It called to mind the night in the shower when she'd been pressed against me from chest to thighs, and I nearly broke into a sweat at the thought.

I craved her like I'd never wanted anything else in my life. Though she'd thrown herself at me that night, she'd been drunk—possibly drugged—and out of her mind. I refused to make a fool of myself by laying a move on her and being turned down. It wasn't the possibility of rejection that stopped me, but everything else. Her safety, as well as my job, was at stake here, and I couldn't risk it.

I sank back against the couch and scrubbed my hands over my face. Fuck. I'd made a huge mess of things, and I had no idea how to fix it. Hell, maybe things were beyond repair.

Guilt pressed in on me, rendering me motionless. I didn't

know how long I sat there staring blindly at the TV before I finally turned it off and stood. I had to at least apologize.

I did a quick once-over of the small bungalow, then used the bathroom and headed to bed. The room was completely dark when I entered, though that was no surprise. She probably needed the privacy of the dark after everything that had happened. What I'd said was horrible and completely uncalled for, that was a given.

But I couldn't figure out her reaction. The Jana I'd come to know over the past couple of weeks had a backbone of steel, a sharp retort at the ready. But not today. Instead of fighting back like normal, she'd turned and fled. That alone told me how badly I'd hurt her, and the knowledge made me feel sick to my stomach.

I couldn't shake off the way she'd looked at me the moment those words left my throat. Her eyes were like an open book—I'd read everything in the blue depths from "you're an idiot" to "you're right, but I don't want to admit it."

This time, though, there was nothing. Absolutely nothing. They'd been completely devoid of emotion as if I'd reached into her chest and ripped out her heart. I literally watched the walls go back up over her expressive eyes, the vibrant sparkle leaching away as she shut down and pushed me away.

What made everything worse, though, was the amount of trust she'd placed in me. She was so certain that I would protect her, keep her safe, and the thought was both bolstering and daunting. It was hard to fathom having that kind of faith in someone.

Silently, I closed the door behind me, then crept toward the bed. Not wanting to scare her, I dropped to one knee next to the mattress. A silvery shaft of moonlight spilled through the sliding doors and over the bed, illuminating her pretty face. What I saw there made my heart clench. A trail of dried tears was visible over the curve of her cheek, and I hated myself for putting them there.

I stretched one hand toward her then halted, frozen in midair. Helplessly, I let it drop to my side. I'd done this to her. God, I was such an asshole. Heaving a sigh, I pushed to my feet. Making my way to the foot of the bed, I collapsed onto the pile of blankets and lay back, staring at the ceiling.

Guilt and unease swirled in my stomach. I had to find a way to make it up to her. By holding back and keeping her prisoner in the house, I was only hurting us both. There was no reason we shouldn't be able to coexist in harmony. Besides, it was my fault that things had been so awkward.

After tossing and turning for hours, I finally fell asleep only to wake again just after dawn. Jana slept soundly as I crept from the room, for which I was grateful. I knew I needed to apologize, but I wasn't ready to eat crow just yet. I needed to come up with a game plan. I grabbed a bottle of water from the fridge, then headed out to the patio for my daily morning workout.

For the next hour and a half, I kept an eye on the sliding door, watching for the slightest movement inside the house that would indicate Jana was up and about. Finally, around nine o'clock, a tiny shadow passed in front of the door as she made her way to the kitchen. I hopped up from the stretch I was doing and hustled toward the house. I wanted to catch her where she had no escape, no choice but to listen to me.

My gaze zeroed in on her as soon as I stepped inside, and there was no mistaking the tense set of her shoulders. She kept her eyes cast downward, ignoring me completely as she grabbed a water bottle, then made to leave the room. I set one hand on the counter, effectively blocking her escape. Every muscle in her body went completely rigid, and though she refused to look at me, I heard her swallow hard.

"Jana." Her eyes lifted to my chest, and she stared straight ahead. I'd take it; it was better than nothing. "I need to apologize."

I hadn't meant to put it so bluntly, but the second the words were out, her gaze snapped to mine. The pretty blue irises, normally so full of life and warmth, were cold and hard. "You need to or want to?"

Damn. The girl wasn't pulling any punches this morning, was she? "Both," I admitted. "You were absolutely right. I've been an ass about this whole thing."

Her eyes narrowed suspiciously, but she didn't say a word. I forced myself to continue. "This, all of this, is new to me. Being a bodyguard, having a—"

The word wife sprang to my lips, and I clamped my mouth shut to keep it from flying out. I started over. "It's not a good excuse, but it's the only one I've got. I've been trying to keep you safe, trying to follow the rules, but it's only made things worse. There's no reason you shouldn't learn to defend yourself."

"There's not?"

"No," I said firmly. Jana was gorgeous and talented, no question about it. But what I admired most was her strength and resilience. I was sure it had taken balls of steel—or whatever the female equivalent was—to ask me for help to pull this off.

She was independent and headstrong, and I knew she would never relinquish her freedom, even in the face of danger. She wanted to ensnare her stalker, wanted to learn to protect herself. And I respected the hell out of that. "I'll show you what you need to know. Tell me what you want to do, and I'll do my best to make it happen."

For several long seconds, she eyed me like she couldn't believe a word she'd heard. "Why are you doing this?"

"Because I'm tired of fighting." I dropped both hands to

my sides. "I just want to get through the next week and a half without hating each other."

Two little lines appeared in the space over her nose. "I don't hate you," she said softly.

It felt as if a weight had been lifted off my shoulders. "I still can't guarantee that we'll be able to go out much, but I don't want to spend the next ten days cooped up in the house."

A delicate shudder shook her body. "Me, either. I'm starting to go crazy."

I cracked a small smile. "What would you like to do?"

"Honestly?" Her eyes darted out the window toward the ocean. "I'd like to go back to the beach. I would love to see it first thing when the sun comes up, go for an early morning run when it's peaceful and quiet."

"Tomorrow," I promised. "We'll go down to the beach in the morning when there are fewer people out."

Blue eyes filled with caution blinked up at me. "Really?"

"I promise," I replied. "Let's just try to enjoy the time we have left here, okay?"

Her lips slowly lifted, curling into the prettiest smile I'd ever seen. "Okay."

I knew it was going to cost me every shred of sanity and control I harbored within me, but seeing her smile like that was totally worth every bit of it.

CHAPTER
SIXTEEN

JANA

Something tugged on my foot, and I kicked it away, snuggling back into my pillow and yanking the covers up to my chin.

"Come on, sleeping beauty. Up and at 'em."

I cracked my eyes open, but the room was still dim in the early morning light. The shaking of my foot resumed.

"Come on, trouble. Time to get your lazy butt up."

With a growl, I bolted upright to face Vince. "What the hell do you want?" I snarled.

A grin slowly spread over his face as he folded his arms across his broad chest. "You said you wanted to go for a run at sunrise. Here's your chance."

I glanced at the clock. "We still have another hour."

"Not if you want to see the best part," he said, dropping his arms to his sides. "I'll meet you in the kitchen in five."

"Ten," I countered with a yawn as I flopped back to the warm sheets.

"Jana..."

I screeched as his fingers tickled across the bottom of my

foot, and I yanked it away. I glared at him, but he just smiled. "Five minutes, trouble, and not a second longer."

With that, he sauntered out of the room. I couldn't muster the ability to form a retort, and my mind was still blurry, moving too slowly to find the nearest object to throw at him. I swore the man got off on torturing me. Knowing I wouldn't be able to go back to sleep, I reluctantly crawled from the bed. I made my way to the bathroom first, where I relieved myself, then splashed some water on my face to help wake me up.

Vince lounged against the wall of the narrow hallway as I exited the bathroom, bringing me up short. He threw a glance at his watch before meeting my gaze again. "Two minutes."

A low chuckle met my ears as I flipped him off, then headed back to the bedroom. My body was still half asleep, but I somehow managed to wrangle myself into a sports bra and a pair of yoga shorts.

"Jana..." Vince's voice floated from the living room as I tugged on a pair of socks.

"I'm coming!" I shoved my feet into sneakers, then stomped out to the dining room where Vince waited not so patiently by the patio door.

"Took you long enough."

"Have I told you recently how much I despise you?" I asked as I stepped outside. The cool morning air assaulted me, and I shivered.

"You're such a gem when you first wake up. Is that where your stage name came from?"

I didn't spare him a glance, but I could hear the smile in his voice. We cut across the back yard, then exited onto the soft sand of the beach.

"Let's walk for a minute," he suggested as he closed the gate behind us then fell into step next to me.

I smothered another yawn as we reached the water's edge,

and I did a few quick stretches as I looked up and down the nearly empty beach.

"Where to?" he asked.

"Back to bed."

Vince rolled his eyes and gave a quick tug to my ponytail. "The pier it is." Without another word, he turned and lurched into a long, loping stride.

"Hey!" I called to his back as I took off after him. "Asshole."

I caught up to him within just a few seconds, and we fell into an easy rhythm as he shortened his stride to match mine. A cool breeze blew in over the ocean, and goosebumps raced down my arms and over my stomach. "Damn, it's cold out right now."

Vince nodded toward the horizon, which was just beginning to lighten with the first orange rays of sunrise. "It'll warm up quick as soon as the sun comes out. By then, you'll be thankful for the breeze."

The sand beneath my feet was packed tightly by the tide that had come in early this morning, but it still offered a resistance I wasn't used to, and after a few minutes, my leg muscles began to burn. I was grateful when we finally rounded the end of the island and reached the pier. "Can we take a break?" I panted.

Vince smirked at me. "Are you tired already?"

My eyes swept over him. He looked as fresh as if he'd just stepped out of the shower, no sign of exertion or perspiration anywhere. "Shut up," I grumbled. "Let's walk the pier, then we can head back."

By the time we reached the end of the pier, the sun had lifted fully over the horizon, its reflection dancing in the rippling waves below. I stared out at the water, looking so dark and deep. On the surface, it looked so calm, but so many dangers lurked beneath. "I don't think I could ever get tired of this view."

"Me, either." Vince's voice came from behind me, and I turned. His gaze was fixed on me, and I faltered for a moment. Was he talking about the ocean, or... me? My heart leaped at the thought of him referring to me as beautiful, but reality came crashing down again just as quickly.

Heat crept up my cheeks, and I redirected my gaze back over the midnight blue water, terrified that I was reading too much into things. I was just a job to him, nothing more. Even saying that we were becoming friends would be a stretch. We were roommates for a limited time, two people making the best of a bad situation.

A dull ache took up residence in the region of my heart, and I forced it down as I turned back to Vince. "Ready to head back?"

He lifted his chin at me. "Whenever you are."

We were silent as we headed down the pier, then stepped into the soft sand. Conversation halted as we fell into a jog on the way back to the house. About a hundred yards from the gate, Vince turned to me, a challenging glint in his eyes. "Race you."

Not one to be outdone, I shoved him away then sprinted forward as fast as I could. Within seconds, he was by my side and already starting to take the lead. I growled, pumping my arms faster, willing my feet to dig into the stand and propel me forward. Vince reached the gate first, his fingers brushing the hard plastic a second before mine.

"I win." He turned to me with a smug smile as he held the gate open and waited for me to precede him inside.

"Only because your arms are longer," I shot back. My legs felt like jelly, and I wobbled around the pool before collapsing into a chaise lounge facedown. "I feel like I'm dying. Just leave me here."

A throaty chuckle filtered over my shoulder. "I'll get breakfast going. Come on in whenever you're done being lazy."

I jumped as he swatted the back of my thigh, and a tiny smile curled my mouth. He could be such a jerk sometimes, but I was incredibly thankful that he was trying so hard to be nice. After our rough beginning, it meant a lot. Once I'd caught my breath, I hauled myself up from the lounge chair, then made my way inside on still-shaky legs to take a quick shower. By the time I got out, the smell of toast and bacon tickled my nose, drawing me toward the kitchen.

A country station played from somewhere—probably Vince's phone since I hadn't seen a radio—and the smooth baritone voice drew me like a moth to light. Who was that? The song was a popular one, but I was certain I'd never heard the man before. It was odd, because I knew, at least by voice, most of the singers in the industry.

I stopped dead in my tracks at the end of the hallway, and my eyes scanned the room. Vince stood at the counter with his back to me, concentrating on whatever he was chopping on the cutting board in front of him. The sound of the knife hitting wood mingled with his sexy voice as he crooned along to the lyrics.

I felt blindsided, completely taken aback. He was good. No, he was better than good—he was incredible.

"You said you couldn't sing," I accused from my place just outside the kitchen.

Muscles that he hadn't bothered to cover up with a shirt tensed for a moment, then relaxed. "Never said I couldn't sing," he corrected. "I said I don't."

"Why the hell not?" I snapped as I stepped up beside him.

"Because I don't want to," came his reply.

I slapped a hand on the counter next to the cutting board. "That's not an answer. You're really good."

He lifted one shoulder as if it didn't make a difference in the world. "Don't like to sing in front of people."

I thought about that for a second, and about the stage fright I battled for years. "Someone could help you with that. There's—"

"No." His response was swift and abrupt. "Not singing."

God, the man was exasperating. "I don't understand. Why won't you at least try?"

Even from off to the side, I could see him roll his eyes. "Yeah, I'm sure the guys would have a field day with that shit."

And suddenly the lightbulb came on. He didn't have stage fright—he was afraid of what his friends would say. I was affronted on his behalf. No way would anyone ever make fun of him, especially not someone he called a friend.

The song he'd been singing ended, rolling into a new one —a duet. An idea sprang to life. "Sing with me."

He threw a bewildered look at me. "Didn't we just discuss this?"

"Yeah." I hopped up on the counter next to where he was working. "But it's just me."

"Yeah. And you're a professional." He rolled his eyes.

Instead of replying, I started singing along with the female part. Vince turned to face me, and our eyes locked. The words flowed from my tongue, and I felt like I was singing to him. A warm sensation swept over me, catching me off guard. *Desire.* After our argument I'd pushed my true feelings for him down deep, but now they came flaring to life once more.

Vince gave a little shake of his head but didn't look away. "How do you expect me to compete with you?"

"Just sing," I replied before picking up the lyrics again as it launched into the chorus.

Looking torn and more self-conscious than I'd ever seen him, Vince picked up the male part. Quiet at first, he grew bolder, his voice blending harmoniously with mine as we finished out the song together. I drew out the last note and grinned at Vince. He smiled back, a lightness entering his eyes, and I hopped down.

"There. That wasn't so bad, was it?" I gently hip-checked him, and he chuckled.

"No, trouble. Not so bad."

"Good." I pointed to the pan. "Now finish making me breakfast so you can show me some moves."

One dark eyebrow ratcheted toward his hairline. "Bossy little thing, aren't you?"

I grinned. "That shouldn't be news to you."

He shook his head. "No, it's not. Get out of my kitchen and go sit."

Turning toward the small dining table, I jumped and let out a shriek when the slotted spatula he'd been holding connected with my butt. I threw my hands over both cheeks to cover them as I whipped toward him. "Hey!"

He used the spatula to point at me. "You deserved that for making me sing."

I couldn't help but smile. "Still don't regret it. Now"—I made a chopping motion with my hand—"chop-chop."

I jumped out of the way with a laugh as Vince swatted at me with the spatula again. "Woman, I swear..." He trailed off, and I grinned at the exasperation tingeing his voice. I could definitely get used to this playful side of him.

Two hours later, sweat poured down my temples as we stood in the small grassy area of the backyard discussing self-defense maneuvers. "If you're ever out in public and fear for your life, yell 'fire' instead of 'help.' People are more likely to come running."

I lifted a brow at him. "Um... why?"

"People instinctively hesitate to put their own lives in jeopardy. They hear the word help and fear the worst—that they'll be shot or kidnapped along with the person in trouble. Fire, by comparison, doesn't hold the same threat."

"Well, that's messed up."

"Sad, but true." Vince shrugged, then moved into position once more. "Ready?"

I took a deep breath and swallowed. "Go."

Facing me, he wrapped both hands around my neck in a choke hold. I took a huge step backward, bending at the waist and ducking my head, putting pressure on his thumbs and breaking his hold. I quickly slipped under his arm and spun away from him, out of reach of his grasping hands. Once I was free, I jogged a few steps away, then turned to look at him, breathing heavily.

"Nice job. That's enough for today. We'll come back to it tomorrow." He shot me a grin. "You're doing well."

"Thanks." I offered him a little smile and shook out my limbs. "I had no idea how hard this would be. You make it look so easy."

"It takes a lot of time and practice to master some of the more advanced moves." He held the door for me as we stepped into the welcome air conditioning of the house. "I'll be teaching a variety of different classes for QSG if you want to keep learning or hone your skills."

My steps faltered as I strode toward the kitchen to grab a bottle of water. Could I still see Vince after all of this was over? Maybe the better question was, how could I not?

I nodded slowly. "I might have to do that."

Because seeing him, even in a strictly professional capacity, was better than not seeing him at all.

CHAPTER
SEVENTEEN

VINCE

Jana stood in the open doorway of the fridge, peering inside as if hoping that something different would magically appear.

I smiled at the look of abject dismay on her face. "What's for dinner, trouble?"

She threw a look over her shoulder. "Chicken or... chicken."

I didn't know if she'd intentionally used the line from one of my favorite movies or not, but it made me smile nonetheless. It was something I'd found myself doing more and more often in Jana's presence. Over the past couple of days, we'd settled into a rhythm of sorts. Our argument the other night seemed to clear the air and, ever since then, things had been better than ever.

I still regretted what I'd said, especially now that I was getting to know her better. There were so many facets to Jana I didn't think I'd ever discover all of them. I was finding new things each day that I liked about her, more things that we had in common. It was dangerous territory, and one I'd promised myself—repeatedly—that I wouldn't venture into.

It was getting harder and harder not to admit my attraction to her. We spent hours together each day, almost like a real couple. Except... not. Nothing about this was normal. We were carrying on a temporary marriage to keep her safe—which was my number one priority. Fact was, she was my principle—the person I'd been charged to watch over and keep from harm. I couldn't do that if I was constantly distracted by my feelings for her.

Even if she was interested in a fling, I wasn't sure I was. My cousins and siblings had all settled down already, and most had kids of their own. Thirty had already come and gone two years ago, and for some reason, I figured I'd have a family of my own already.

Though I'd enjoyed my youth, I felt time pressing in on me. I was only getting older. Rationally, I knew that a lot of men—and women, these days—were waiting longer and longer to settle down. But each day that slipped past made me acutely aware that I was still all alone and would stay that way until I did something about it.

I'd enjoyed women's company before, though mostly in the bedroom. It'd been a long time since I'd really talked with one. Jana and I had done nothing but talk for the past two days. Somehow she'd managed to get me to sing—which I'd never done in front of another person with the exception of my mother.

My brothers had made fun of me growing up and though I knew it was good-natured sibling rivalry, I'd never attempted to sing in public. It was strange how comfortable I was with Jana. Without even realizing it, she'd managed to get me to open up.

She'd reciprocated, telling me stories about her life in the music industry. But any time I broached the topic of her life before she moved to Dallas, she shut down. I wanted to reassure her the way she'd reassured me, coax her into opening up and confiding in me.

All that aside, it didn't matter what I wanted. There was no way she would ever want me the way I wanted her. She was basically a celebrity, even if it was only in the world of country music. She had thousands of fans who adored her, evidenced by the man who'd become obsessed with her. There were hundreds of men she worked with who would be a better match to her than I ever would.

I shook my head. Jesus. When the hell had I gone soft? I was practically trying to find a way to fit myself into her life, and she barely even knew I existed as a man. She saw me as her bodyguard—nothing more. Or, if she did, she'd never let on.

Ever since I could remember, she'd been standoffish around me. I could only assume that meant she wasn't attracted to me. No, she was making an effort to get along until the police caught her stalker. Then she could go home, back to her glamorous life where we would part ways. Forever.

I wasn't sure why I hated the thought of that so much. Probably because I'd never been one to let things unfold by themselves. Anytime I wanted something, I went after it. Her, though... I couldn't do that. She was astronomically out of my league, not to mention any decisions I made with her could potentially affect my job. I hated to walk away without knowing if there was anything between us, but it was better this way.

Jana shut the door then slouched against the counter, staring woefully out the window. "I'm so tired of the same thing. There are only so many ways you can cook chicken before it all begins to taste the same."

"What do you want?" I asked.

Her gaze slid back to me, and I swore I could see a flicker of something in the bright blue depths. It never ceased to amaze me how blue her eyes were. Mine were blue, too, but I'd always thought of them as plain. Kind of gray, icy, cool. But hers... I'd never seen a more vivid blue before. Cerulean like the sky on the brightest day, they drew me in, tugged at my heart.

Finally, she gave a little sigh. "Honestly, I would kill for a steak."

I lifted one shoulder. "So call it in."

She lifted an eyebrow. "You'll grill up a steak for me?"

"Sure. Why not?" Did she think I couldn't or wouldn't?

The corners of her mouth tipped down in a frown. "I appreciate it, but Harvey would kill me."

"That asshole's not here," I reminded her. "Besides, I don't know why you're so caught up in what he thinks."

"Um... Because he pays my bills?"

She looked at me like I was dumb, and I rolled my eyes. "That shouldn't extend to determining your diet. If you were unhealthy, I could understand, but you're perfect just the way you are."

Her gaze dropped to her toes, but not before I watched a soft pink sweep up her neck and into her cheeks. I fucking loved when she blushed. It made me want to pull her close, kiss her pretty, full mouth, rosy cheeks, then lower, over her neck and chest until I'd finally exposed those gorgeous breasts of hers.

Damn. I wished I knew what she was thinking. Was she merely flirting, or was there more to her reaction? It wasn't the first time something I'd said had elicited that type of reaction, and I lived for those rare moments when I caught her open and unguarded.

Part of me wanted to ask, but I'd be lying if I said I wasn't worried about the answer. People fawned over her all the time.

She got compliments from everyone, and I was certain my words sounded no different. But those looks... I wanted those to be for me and me alone. I wanted to be the only person to bring a blush to her cheeks.

Still, I said nothing. If she didn't feel the same, I didn't want to look like an asshole. It wouldn't be the first time I'd made a fool of myself, but this was an entirely different scenario. She was already under stress, and I didn't want to add to that. I liked the way things had become between us, and I wouldn't jeopardize it for the world. I didn't want to go back to the stilted, awkward conversations of weeks past.

Her words tore me from my introspection. "I'll let you pick tonight. Whatever you want is fine with me."

That was a lie if I'd ever heard one.

Without another word, she turned and wandered into the living room. I watched, eyes narrowed, as she sank into the corner of the couch. The blush from earlier had disappeared, replaced by what I thought was disappointment. She stared out the glass doors that led to the patio, and I studied her features. She wasn't pouting, but she did look sad, and I'd have to be an idiot not to realize why.

Jana was like a bundle of energy, always vibrating with barely-restrained motion. I knew how hard it was for her to be still, especially in a beautiful place like this. For the past week I'd kept her locked down according to orders.

What I'd told her the other night was true—I would put her safety first, whether she liked it or not. But tomorrow would make a week that we'd been here, and when I'd spoken with Con earlier, he told me there was no indication of anyone learning our whereabouts.

Although I didn't use them much, I did have a couple different social media accounts, so I hopped on to check out the progress online. Jana had told us she'd planned to do a blast of posts that culminated in our engagement photo and subsequent elopement.

When Con had dropped us at the Dallas-Fort Worth airport, he'd taken a picture of us—from the back so my face wouldn't be plastered all over the internet—walking into the airport on our way to our honeymoon destination.

I flipped through various photos now. Pictures of high heeled silver shoes, a sparkly necklace and earrings, and a close up of white satin, which I guessed was supposed to be her dress. By the time I reached that photo, even I could have guessed what she was hinting at. It was the next photo, though, that suspended the breath in my chest.

Abby had somehow managed to manipulate the picture she'd taken in Jana's living room and turn it into a masterpiece. In the doctored photo, Jana stood next to an ornate, brightly lit Christmas tree. I knelt in front of her, my face cleverly cropped from view. Her left hand was encased in mine, displaying the sparkling diamond as I slid it into place.

My attention was drawn to Jana's expression. Her hand partially covered her mouth, but her eyes... Her eyes were liquid and soft, full of wonder. They seemed to sparkle with pure joy, so much so that it sent a chill through me.

Had she actually looked like that, or was this some special effect Abby had added? I tried to draw back on the moment, but I couldn't remember, damn it. I'd been a little off-kilter myself, just moments away from marrying a woman I'd only met two weeks earlier.

I ripped my attention away from Jana's face and scrolled down. People were speculating on our marriage, and the comments ranged from glowing congratulations to downright crass and degrading. People could be such assholes sometimes.

Jana had been a trooper so far, with the exception of our little hiccup a few nights ago. A gilded cage was still a cage, and I knew it was wearing on her. With each day that passed, she smiled less and less and seemed more on edge. Since everything appeared to be safe and quiet, I figured she was due for a night out. I strode toward the couch, stopping only a few feet away.

"Do you want to get out of the house?"

Her gaze slid away from the window to meet mine, and she blinked once, long and slow. I could practically see the wheels turning, wondering if it was a trick question.

The corner of my mouth kicked up in a smirk when she didn't answer. "You would be a terrible poker player, you know."

She rolled her eyes. "I mean, I'm not going to argue if you want to get out of the house. What do you have in mind? A walk down to the pier?"

I shook my head. "Let's go to dinner."

She stared at me for a long moment. "But..."

I flicked one hand in the air, effectively stopping her. "We'll wait until dusk, after the dinner rush is over."

"Really?" She regarded me suspiciously as she sat up straight. "Are you sure?"

I nodded. "I think it'll be good for both of us."

In a blur of motion, she was already on her feet and halfway across the room. "I'll go get ready!"

I chuckled as she bolted to the bathroom, slamming the door in her wake.

I knew she would be a while, so I settled on the couch and flipped on the TV for some background noise, then pulled out my phone and scrolled through my emails.

When the water in the bathroom cut off, I made my way to the bedroom and grabbed a change of clothes. Jana entered moments later, wearing nothing but a towel wrapped around her torso. The knowledge that she was completely bare underneath—at least, that's how I imagined her—hit me like a punch to the gut. My mouth went dry, and I quickly averted my gaze as she swept into the room, headed straight for the closet.

"I'm hopping in the shower."

"Okay." Without sparing me a glance she sifted through the outfits hanging in a neat row, and I escaped to the bathroom, closing the door behind me.

Holy shit. I swore, every time I thought I had my feelings for her under control, my traitorous body had to go and prove me wrong. My dick ached, and I fisted it as I flipped on the water and stepped under the warm spray.

Visions of Jana filled my mind as I leaned one hand on the tile wall of the shower and stroked myself from root to tip. Warm water sluiced over me, easing the way for my hand as it moved up and down my shaft.

I pictured myself loosening the knot of her towel, letting it drop to the floor and taking in every inch of her gorgeous body. She smelled so damn sweet all the time, and I couldn't help but wonder how she would taste. I wanted to kiss her from head to toe, sink so deep inside her I couldn't tell where she ended and I began.

My muscles tensed as heat raced through me, and my balls grew heavy and full. I gritted my teeth as I pumped twice more then came on a silent groan. Feeling slightly more relieved than I had a few minutes before, I finished showering then dressed for dinner. Jana was still getting ready, so I headed back to the sofa. For the next forty-five minutes I zoned out to whatever show was on TV until I heard the soft creak of the bedroom door opening.

Jana swept down the hallway toward me, and the hard-on I thought I'd extinguished in the shower flared up again at the sight of her. Goddamn, she looked good enough to eat. Her long locks shined like gold, and her beautifully tanned skin glowed bronze against the bright yellow sundress that hit at mid-thigh, clinging to her breasts and hips. A giant pair of sunglasses once more covered half of her face, but they did absolutely nothing to hide her beautiful features.

I discreetly adjusted myself as I stood, forcing my gaze away from her as I busied myself turning off the TV and grabbing my phone and keys. "You ready?"

"Hell yes. Let's get out of here."

I chuckled at her enthusiasm. "I've never met anyone as impatient as you."

"Not impatient, exactly." She shrugged one shoulder as she made her way toward the front door, then waited for me to go first. "But when you have people breathing down your neck all the time, telling you what to do…"

I slid a glance her way. Her tone sounded defeated, and something akin to sadness had dimmed her pretty blue eyes. "I know what you mean."

I locked the door behind us, then we cut across the driveway and out to the road. I hiked a thumb toward the north end of the island. "I was thinking maybe we could check out that restaurant up this way. Maybe we'll catch the tail end of the sunset if we eat out on the deck."

She tipped her face up to me and grinned. "That sounds perfect."

That smile of hers hit me like a sucker punch, stealing my breath and threatening to cut me down at the knees. It lit up her whole face, brightening everything around us. Even beneath those sunglasses, her eyes were so wide and so blue that I could drown in them. Like this, she made me feel like I was ten feet tall, the center of her whole world.

My gaze traveled the length of her, from the top of her head to the tips of her pink-painted toes. She was absolute perfection, everything I never knew I wanted. Everything about her drove me absolutely crazy. Thoughts of Jana consumed every free moment, and she had me so tangled up in knots that I swore I was going to lose my mind before this was over.

I sighed as we set off down the sidewalk. Looked like my hand was going to get a hell of a workout over the next few days.

CHAPTER
EIGHTEEN

JANA

I couldn't help the little bubble of happiness surrounding me as we headed toward the restaurant. It was the first time Vince and I had truly been out of the house, and I was so excited I wanted to throw my arms wide and dance for joy. Over the past few days I'd learned to never take anything for granted, especially not being able to go out any time I chose.

A host greeted us as we climbed up the wide wooden steps. "Two tonight?"

"Yes, please."

He tipped his head and grabbed two rolls of silverware. "Inside or out?"

I looked up at Vince. As if reading my mind, he nodded to the deck out back. "Outside."

The host made a notation on his seating chart, then led us to a small table on the deck overlooking the ocean. "Gabi will be right with you."

Vince grabbed a laminated menu from the condiment stand in the middle of the table, and I glanced toward the horizon, turned burnt orange from the setting sun. "This is beautiful."

As soon as the words left my throat, a pretty, young waitress—Gabi, according to her name tag—appeared by our table. "Can I get you something to drink?"

"Iced tea for me, please."

She nodded at my request then turned to Vince. A tiny kernel of jealousy lodged in my throat as her eyes drifted over his wide shoulders and biceps that strained the sleeves of his dark polo. Completely unaware of her perusal, he ordered a Coke, then turned his attention back to the menu as the waitress reluctantly dragged her gaze away from Vince and drifted inside.

"What are you having?"

His eyes lifted to mine, and I forced a smile. "I haven't looked yet."

I'd been too busy watching the waitress check him out to even look at the menu. Unaware of the detour my thoughts had taken, Vince continued. "Get a steak if you want one."

"Maybe." I picked up a menu and began to scan the items, then let out a soft sigh as I gestured to the ocean lapping at the shore just a few hundred yards away. "As good as it sounds, I'm probably better off ordering seafood."

"Probably." Vince grinned. "I'll take you to a steakhouse next time you're craving a steak."

Next time? My cheeks burned as I dropped my gaze back to the menu in my hands. The waitress came back to deliver our drinks, then took our orders. I decided on the shrimp and scallops while Vince ordered an entire platter of seafood, plus several sides.

I glanced at him, amazed, as the waitress returned to the kitchen. "I don't know where you put all that food."

He leaned back in his chair and patted his flat—and very ripped—stomach. "I burn a lot of calories."

I let out a very unladylike snort. "Must be nice to eat whatever you want and burn it all right back off."

"Whatever," he scoffed. "You need to stop listening to all those assholes. I've watched you pick at your food like you're afraid to eat it because they've drilled it into your head that you're somehow not good enough. That's bullshit. There's not a damn thing wrong with you. Don't let those idiots make you feel bad, because you're absolutely—"

He cut off suddenly, his gaze darting away as he gave his head a little shake. "You're fine the way you are."

He looked like he wanted to say more, but he picked up his phone and began to fiddle with the screen. I watched him for a moment, not missing the tense set to his shoulders, the slight tic in his jaw. A warm glow flared to life around my heart, and I felt the heat climb over my chest and up my neck, and into my cheeks.

He thought I was perfect—he'd said as much earlier. I tried so hard to be confident, but I always seemed to fall short of the mark. People were always comparing me to someone else, and everyone had an opinion on how I should be. I'd heard it all—I was too fat, too thin, too pretty, too plain, too honest, too fake.

I'd be lying if I said Vince's words didn't affect me. Thank God I still wore my sunglasses so I could conceal my expression. Despite years of trying to harden myself, I still wore my heart on my sleeve, and my eyes were like an open book for anyone to read. It wasn't the first time he'd seemed to look straight into my soul and known exactly how I felt.

For the next few minutes, we lapsed into silence. Vince avoided me completely as he immersed himself in something on his phone, and I stared out at the beach, lost in thought. I swore I'd seen something in his eyes earlier, heard something in his voice. I'd shelved all thoughts of exploring any possible attraction between us over the past few days, but now I wondered... Was it possible he felt the same way about me?

The waitress delivered our meals, tearing me from my introspection. She hovered by the table for a moment, her eyes fixed on Vince, and I bristled. The jealousy I'd felt earlier flared once more, sending heat racing over my skin. "Can I get some ketchup, please?"

Her head whipped in my direction, and she quickly nodded. "Of course."

She headed back toward the kitchen, and I glanced across the table at Vince. He'd set his phone down and was currently digging into his food, completely unaware of my internal struggle.

I offered a tight smile to the waitress as she returned with my ketchup, but it was a futile effort because her gaze was locked on Vince. Anger simmered in my stomach, sending prickles of heat over my skin. It was irrational to feel possessive of him, but I couldn't help it.

I picked up my fork and speared a scallop, then lifted it to my lips. My heart raced in my chest, making it almost impossible to swallow. Twirling my fork between my fingers, I bit my lower lip and surreptitiously studied the man across from me. We'd become friends, sort of, over the past few days, and I hated to ruin that... but part of me needed to know if there was more simmering beneath the surface.

I slipped off my sandal and crossed my legs, shifting slightly closer to him as I did so. I moved my foot experimentally, and I watched him stiffen as my toes brushed the inside of his calf. Both of us froze, waiting for the other to move. My chest lifted and fell rapidly, and I fought to control my breathing as excitement and pleasure curled through me. For several long minutes, we remained that way, both of us refusing to give an inch, either to pull away or to push for more.

"How is everything?"

The appearance of the waitress again made me drop my foot to the floor, and I watched Vince turn toward her.

"Good, thanks." He offered a polite smile, apparently blissfully unaware of Gabi's obvious interest.

Her gaze roved over the dark ink covering his arms. "I've always wanted a tattoo," she gushed. "How many do you have?"

"A few dozen, maybe?" Vince looked thoughtful. "I lost count a while back. I've been adding to the collection for several years."

My eyes widened as she traced one design curling around his forearm. "I love this. How long did it take to do?"

"Ah..." He shifted slightly in his chair. "A couple hours."

"Wow." She smiled hugely. "Well, I'll let you finish. Just let me know if you need anything," she said as she stepped away, letting her gaze linger on Vince just a little too long.

Unable to comprehend what I'd just seen, I stared at her back as she retreated inside the restaurant. My gaze bounced back to Vince, but he was focused on his food once more, and I swiveled my head toward the doors the waitress had disappeared through. It was almost as if she didn't care that I was sitting right here. I tossed my napkin on the table and slipped back into my sandals. "I'll be back. I have to use the bathroom."

I headed indoors, my eyes searching for the bathroom sign, and I cut across the dining room to the back corner. After I used the bathroom, I stood at the sink washing my hands, studying my reflection in the mirror. What was wrong with me? I knew I shouldn't let the situation bother me so much, but I couldn't reconcile the confusing mixture of feelings welling up inside.

Vince hadn't given any indication of being attracted to the waitress, despite the fact that he was, in reality, an attractive single guy. Irritation flared at the memory of the waitress's blatant ogling of the man who was—to the eyes of the public, at least—my husband.

I knew she hadn't missed the ring on his finger, because I'd watched her gaze drop to his left hand before greedily drinking him in again. I understood where she was coming from. The sight of those tattoos peeking out from under the shirt, along with all those hard muscles, made me stupid. I could no longer deny the attraction I felt to him, but he hadn't given any indication of wanting me, either.

I knew I would be complicating matters, but I needed to know once and for all exactly where we stood. If nothing else, I was at least going to show the waitress that it wasn't okay to ogle a man right in front of his wife—or temporary wife, as the case might be.

Tossing the paper towel in the trash, I straightened my shoulders and pulled open the door. My heart beat erratically, but I fought to keep my expression neutral as I stepped onto the deck and strode toward our table. I bypassed my seat and rounded the table, headed straight for Vince.

His eyes widened a fraction, and almost as if he knew my intentions, he shoved his chair away from the table. Curving one arm around his neck, I slid onto his lap, heart pounding so hard I swore he could feel it slamming against my ribs where my chest brushed his.

"What do you think you're doing?" His voice was pitched low, and his warm breath hit my cheek as he spoke. "You're drawing attention to us."

I turned my head slightly and met his silvery blue gaze. "If either of us is drawing attention from someone, it's you."

One corner of his mouth kicked up in a smirk. "The waitress?"

I rolled my eyes. "Like you had to ask. I can't believe she practically hit on you right in front of me."

"Jealous?" His tone had a mocking quality to it, and I bristled.

"No," I snapped. "It's the principle of the thing."

He leaned in closer, his lips brushing my ear as he spoke. "Keep your voice down. People are looking."

His words only served to piss me off even more, and I angled myself slightly away, my brows drawing down in anger. "Let them look. As far as she knows, we're married, and it irks me that she keeps checking you out."

His hand landed on my knee, then slid further up my thigh until it rested beneath the hem of my sundress. I sucked in a breath as his fingers drew little circles over my flesh, goosebumps exploding in their wake. "Keep it up, and I'll bend you over this table and spank your ass right in front of everybody."

My heart skipped a beat, and my anger dissipated into thin air at his low spoken words. Did he really just say that to me? Refusing to let him see how much the idea turned me on, I met his gaze with what I hoped was a teasing smile. "Promise?"

His fingers found the curve of my ass and pinched lightly. I jumped, and my hand flew to cover his where it rested along my hip. I opened my mouth to speak, but the pretty waitress materialized beside our table before I had the chance.

"Can I get you any dessert?"

"No, thanks," Vince replied smoothly, a glint in his eyes. "I think my wife has something waiting for me at home."

I was caught somewhere between shock and laughter, and I watched in bemusement as the waitress's cheeks flared bright red. With a curt nod, she slid the checkbook onto the table. "Have a nice night."

"Oh, we will." Vince's voice was filled with promise—though I knew that couldn't bode well for me. I shifted on his lap, away from pinching fingers, and pressed my lips together to contain a smile as she flew back to the kitchen.

As soon as she was gone, I turned back to him. "Wow. I wish I'd thought of that."

He smiled, a pair of dimples carving small crescents into his cheeks. "Happy now?"

A sudden realization caught me off guard. I *was* happy. Most of the men I'd dated, especially in the music industry, had thrived on the attention they received from people. It was nice to see a man stand up for me, even if he was only pretending. "Thank you."

His chin dipped in a nod, but I felt the need to explain. "No, really. I appreciate it. Anyone else I've dated would've flirted right back, maybe even gotten her number to call her later."

Blue eyes stared into mine. "Then you haven't been with the right men."

Heat flared around my heart, sliding through my chest, then slithering lower until it pooled in my core. I held his gaze, unable to tear myself away as I slowly shook my head. "No, I haven't."

CHAPTER
NINETEEN

VINCE

I held out my hand. "Come walk with me?"

"At night?" She darted a quick look toward the beach before slipping her palm into mine. "Are we allowed to do that?"

I managed to bite back a smile. "Nothing that says we can't," I replied. "Wait till you see the moonlight on the water. You're gonna love it."

I helped her off my lap then stood, reveling in the feel of her slender fingers in mine. It was a terrible idea, but one I hadn't been able to talk myself out of. She was just a job, and our time together would be over just as soon as the police found her stalker. According to Con's last message, they were investigating a few new leads, one of which sounded promising.

I wasn't sure how much time Jana and I actually had left, so I wanted to make sure she enjoyed every minute. I tried to focus on her and not the disappointment that had settled like lead in my gut. I knew this was all for show, but I couldn't help how right it felt to have her by my side.

I slipped several bills into the folio on the table and tucked her sunglasses into the neckline of my shirt. Tightening my fingers around hers, I tugged her toward the wide steps that led down to the beach. At the bottom, I pulled her to a stop and motioned for her to remove her shoes. I held her hand while she bent over to remove first one sandal, then the other. No matter how stupid it was, I couldn't force myself to let go of her.

A smile curved my mouth at the sight of her stepping out of her sandals. Little brat had been playing footsie with me under the table. At first, I thought it was an accident, so I'd pretended I hadn't even noticed. But then she hadn't moved. I'd been tempted to reach under the table and pull her foot into my lap, show her exactly what she was doing to me.

She straightened and I took the shoes from her, letting them dangle from my fingertips as I propelled her onto the sand, still slightly warm from the sun. I watched her expression light up as she took in the moonlight rippling over the ocean. "It's so beautiful."

I couldn't tear my eyes away from her. "It is," I agreed, not referring to the ocean at all. She darted a look at me, and I swore I could see her cheeks flare pink at my implication. I squeezed her hand. "Want to walk down to the water?"

"Sure."

Hand in hand, we picked our way across the sand down to the edge of the surf. She jumped back as the cool water lapped over her toes. I reluctantly released her as she began to look for stray shells buried in the sand.

"It's better to look for them after high tide," I said. "The ocean brings all the shells in at high tide, then leaves them when it goes back out."

"Can we come back when—" Her question was cut short

as she let out a little squeak of surprise. "Oh, my God! What was that?"

The weight of her petite body slammed into me, her arms and legs winding around me like a vine. Already scanning for whatever had frightened her, I scooped her into my arms, lifting her easily against my chest. Still holding her tightly, I turned, checking every direction, searching the darkness. Seeing nothing, I dipped my head to look her in the eye. "What's wrong?"

One arm curled around my neck, she pointed at the ground, her words shaky. "I don't know. Something ran over my foot."

I glanced down in time to see a handful of white creatures burrow back into the sand, and relief poured through me. "Probably just a ghost crab."

Her eyes widened as she turned back to me. "What the hell is that?"

I fought the urge to smile but lost the battle. "They're tiny white crabs that primarily come out at night."

"Those things are seriously creepy." A delicate shudder moved through her, and her legs tightened around my waist.

She was too close, and I was too turned on. Trying to break the tension, I bent over, dipping her backwards toward the sand. She threw a panicked look downward, clutching at my shirt, her fingers curling into the fabric. "What are you doing?"

"You just took ten years off my life, woman. I should let the crabs have you." I swung her low enough that the strands of her long hair brushed the ground.

She seemed to know that I wouldn't drop her, and her fear bled away, turning to laughter. "Stop! Vince, please!" she called out between giggles.

Taking pity on her, I lifted her back into my arms where she met my eyes with a lethal glare. "That wasn't very nice."

"I couldn't help teasing you just a little bit," I replied, the corner of my mouth kicking up. "I mean, seriously. Who's afraid of a little crab?"

She playfully slapped my chest, and silence fell as I stared into her eyes. Heat raced through my body, and with her pelvis flat against mine, I was certain she could feel the evidence of my lust there. Her gaze dropped to my lips, and my pulse shifted into overdrive. I curled my fingers into her flesh and started to lean in before common sense took over.

Shit. No matter how badly I wanted to kiss her, I couldn't let it go that far. Easing my hold on her bottom, I slowly lowered her to her feet. She leaned heavily on me, her eyes darting around to make sure the crabs were gone.

"Come on," I said softly. "Let's head home."

I placed a hand on her lower back to try to dispel the awkwardness of the moment. I knew it was my fault, but it was something I had to do. She was a client, and a fairly high profile one at that. We were technically married, but that piece of paper didn't mean a damn thing to her other than her safety.

There was no way I could ever let it go far enough for anything to happen. As real as it all seemed, I had to remember one thing—this was just pretend.

CHAPTER
TWENTY

JANA

"So, are you scared of anything else, or just crabs?"

I shot Vince a mock glare as we cut across the sand on the way back to the rental house. "I wasn't scared of the crab, it just... startled me."

He laughed, a low sound in the back of his throat. "You sure about that?"

"Yes." I lifted my chin defiantly, fighting the smile tugging at the corners of my mouth.

"Mhmm." He gently bumped me with his shoulder. "Scaredy cat."

I rolled my eyes. "Whatever."

"All right, all right," he conceded. "So, you're not afraid of the crab, even though you tried to climb me like a tree."

I snorted but couldn't help the smile that spread over my face. "You're such a jerk."

Beside me, Vince laughed. "Seriously, I've never seen anyone move so fast in my life."

Now that my initial surprise had worn off, I could laugh at

my reaction. "Fine, I may have overreacted"—I held up my thumb and forefinger an inch apart—"just a tiny bit. But, in my defense, I wasn't expecting them."

"I know, right? Who would suspect there would be crabs at the beach?" he asked drily, and I lightly backhanded his arm.

"It's nighttime. I assumed they all... I don't know." Exasperation tinged my tone. "Don't they dig themselves into the sand or something?"

Vince grinned. "Yeah, to hide from you."

I rolled my eyes. "Ha, ha. You're so funny."

"Coulda been worse." He shrugged. "Florida has some of the most deadly snakes in the world."

I snapped my head around to look at him. "That's a joke, right?"

"Nope." He kept walking, as if it didn't bother him in the least. "Coral snakes, water moccasins, rattlers. It's always a good idea to watch trees and bushes where they hang out. They like to get up off the hot ground."

I knew that, of course. We had snakes in Texas, but somehow this little bit of news detracted from the beauty of my temporary paradise. "Well, that sucks."

He slid a look my way. "I take it you're not a fan of snakes?"

A shudder of revulsion worked its way down my spine. "No. *Hell no*. No snakes, no spiders. Nothing creepy."

"Creepy?" His mouth tilted into a smirk.

"Yeah. Creepy. Eight legs are way too many legs for any living thing to have. But at least they have legs," I said, on a roll now. "It's not natural for something to not have legs at all. That's just... disgusting."

"It's actually good to have snakes around," Vince commented. "They eat all the little rodents."

"Not for this girl." I pointed at myself. "You know what else can take care of rodents? An exterminator."

"Point taken." Vince laughed. "I'll add that to my list—Keep Jana safe from creepy animals."

We had reached the house, and ever the gentleman, Vince held the gate open for me. I felt a little tickle on the back of my neck as I stepped inside the patio area, and I swiped at it. The palm fronds surrounding the fence danced on the light breeze as I felt the phantom sensation again.

From behind me, Vince spoke, low and serious. "Jana... Don't move..."

His voice was low, filled with wariness, and I immediately froze. "What's wrong?" I whispered.

The crawly sensation skittered across my shoulder blades again, and a high-pitched squeal left my mouth. Oh, my God. Something was on me.

Panic took over, and I waved my arms wildly, trying to brush off whatever was on me. "Get it off, get it off, GET IT OFF!"

I twisted and contorted my body in an effort to get the thing off. All the while, Vince never even tried to help. I shot a glare his way in time to see him stumble against the wall, bent at the waist. Confusion welled up as the sound falling from his lips registered. The jerk was laughing. My gaze dropped lower to the palm leaf clutched in his hand. Shock rooted me to the ground, then anger took over.

"You asshole!" I launched myself at him, but he caught me easily. Dropping the palm leaf, he fended off my clumsy slaps to his chest, still choking with mirth.

"Truce, truce!" he called between laughs.

"You're such a dick!" He winced a little as I punched him in the chest one more time. "I can't believe you did that to me!"

I turned to storm off, but he caught me around the waist and pulled me back. "C'mere, trouble. It was just a joke."

I yanked backward, trying to pry myself from his grasp. "I told you how much I don't like them!"

"I know, I know." Vince loosened his hold but didn't release me. "I'm sorry. I was just teasing."

In hindsight, I should have known. The tickle of the palm leaf didn't feel anything like a spider. But my mind had been so preoccupied by thoughts of creepy, crawly things that I'd fallen for his trick.

"I hate you." Even as the words left my mouth, I melted against him, a strange combination of emotions swirling inside me as I sank into the warmth and security of his broad chest.

A pair of huge hands swept slowly up my spine, then back down. "No, you don't."

"Fine. I don't hate you." This time, he let me go as I leaned away from him. "But I'm still mad at you. Jerk."

"You know I would never let anything hurt you for real." He turned and steered us toward the house. "But I kinda owed you for that little stunt you pulled at the restaurant. Brat."

My heart banged against my ribs as he draped one arm over my shoulders and dropped a kiss on the top of my head. I was so taken aback by the gesture that I almost missed a step. As if realizing what he'd done, Vince let his hand drop, his fingertips skimming my arm as it fell to his side. Disappointment hit me first, followed immediately by a warm glow around my heart.

Something had changed between us tonight. I wasn't sure what would happen next, but I knew instinctively that Vince would fight it. He'd deemed himself my protector and was reluctant to cross any lines. But I had no such qualms. I just had to figure out how to break down his resistance and make him see that I wanted this too.

CHAPTER
TWENTY-ONE

VINCE

One arm wrapped under her breasts, her head was tucked beneath my chin, her body flush against mine. Even all hot and sweaty, she felt so damn good.

Every single thing about her turned me on—the way her hair smelled, the way the curves of her tiny body fit my muscular frame. For better or worse, things between us had shifted dramatically. And I wouldn't change it for the world.

I still couldn't believe I'd kissed her last night. It wasn't a real kiss, but it'd been automatic, as if I'd done it a hundred times. That look on her face had done me in—the one that spoke of a mixture of shock and fear. I'd wanted to lift her into my arms and promise to keep her safe forever. Unfortunately, we'd already been here for a week. All she'd have left of me once we got home were the evasion tactics I was currently teaching her.

With her chin tucked into the crook of my right elbow, I tightened my hold around her neck. "Now, show me how you're gonna get free."

Her hands came up and wrapped around my forearm, trying to drag it away from her throat. She let out a frustrated little growl when I dragged her backward a few steps, demonstrating how easily I could overpower her. I loosened my hold and set her away from me, then met her gaze.

"Your goal isn't to fight me—it's to escape," I explained. "Since you're small, it's going to be difficult for you to fend off an attack. Six seconds is all it takes to choke someone out. You need to remain in control and use your entire body to get free. Let's try it again."

I pulled her back into a reverse chokehold. "I'm holding you with my right arm, so you'll need to escape to your left. Small step forward with your left foot, then slide your right foot between our bodies and rotate your shoulders."

I tapped her right thigh, and she followed my instructions, slowly spinning until she was facing me. "Keep your body low as you move, then once your shoulders are free of my arms, push off as hard as you can and run like hell."

I turned her and pulled her against me, then dragged her backward a couple of steps. Her feet tangled with mine as she fought for purchase. She dug in her heels and rotated her hips toward me. "Come on, Jana. Break it, break my hold!"

She threw all of her weight into the spin, loosening my grip, but I grabbed for her again as she tried to evade my hold. Her adrenaline was running high, and I saw the move coming before one slender leg kicked forward, right toward the soft spot between my legs. I shifted slightly to the side, but her foot connected with my groin, and I let out a grunt of pain as I dropped to one knee.

Damn, I'd forgotten how bad that hurt.

"Shit!" Jana threw herself forward and grabbed my shoulders. "Are you okay?"

I forced out a laugh. "I will be in a sec."

"I'm so sorry." She pulled me into a hug, and on my knees the way I was, my cheek pressed against her stomach. We were both sticky and sweaty, but I didn't give a single fuck. I wrapped my arms around the back of her legs and held on tight.

Damn, she felt so good. Too good.

She let out a little squeak as I shifted my weight, rolling us until she was pinned beneath me, my weight settled firmly between her hips. "Don't ever apologize. You did exactly what I told you to do. You go back to check on someone and they do this." I gestured with my chin to my precarious position between her legs. "This is exactly what a sexual predator wants."

Big blue eyes stared up at me, one hundred percent focused now on my words. I wrapped my hands around her throat. "Show me what you do."

Her right hand came up and wrapped around my forearm, and her left hand cut across my chest until the flat of her palm lay against the base of my neck. Her feet crawled up my body until her right leg was braced over my shoulder and the left swung in front of my face, forcing me to lean back.

Grabbing my wrist with both hands, she rolled to the side so my arm was trapped between her legs. Arcing her back, she pressed her hips upward, putting enough pressure on my elbow to snap the joint.

"Easy!" I yelled.

She immediately released me, rolling to her feet and jogging away. "That was pretty good, huh?"

She threw a cheeky grin my way, and I couldn't help but laugh as I climbed to my feet. "Yeah, it was."

She was proving to be a damn quick learner. She wasn't proficient by any means, but I was proud as hell that she was taking the instruction seriously. That cocky little smile gracing her lips made me want to pick her up and toss her tiny ass over my shoulder, dominate her in every way known to mankind.

I dipped my chin. "You know I owe you for that."

She squealed and tried to dart away as I lunged toward her. I caught her wrist and tugged her toward me, but she slipped from my grasp, dancing backwards. Not taking my eyes from her, a predatory smile lifted my lips. "Where you goin', trouble?"

She licked her lips and glanced past me—to the pool at my back. A gleam entered her eyes, but she tried to play it cool. She shrugged. "I'm hungry, aren't you?" She took a step closer. "What are you feeling for lunch? I was thinking—"

All of a sudden she rushed me, arms outstretched, reaching for my chest. I grinned as I fended her off. Grabbing her around her narrow waist, I whirled her so we were reversed and she was inches away from the edge of the pool. She held fast to my forearms, balanced only on the balls of her feet. I watched her face as she hung there, suspended over the edge of the pool. If I let go, she'd fall in, and she knew it.

She let out a little shriek as I released her waist and grabbed her wrists instead, lowering her another foot closer to the water. "Payback's a bitch, trouble."

"If I'm going in, you're coming with me." She grinned hugely and levered all of her weight backward, trying to pull me in with her.

I had to outweigh her skinny ass by at least eighty pounds; she had absolutely zero chance of budging me, but it didn't stop her from trying. Digging her heels in, she used every ounce of muscle she possessed to try to pull me with her.

Her face twisted in consternation, and I let out a laugh. She was so damn adorable I couldn't handle it sometimes. Relaxing my muscles, I leaned forward, and we toppled toward the water together. I surfaced and stood to find Jana hastily swiping long strands of blonde hair from her face.

"You asshole!" She sputtered with laughter and swiped her arm across the surface of the water, sending a wave splashing over me.

"Now you've done it." I growled and dove toward her. She was hampered by the water as she tried to move out of arm's reach, and I easily pulled her under. She popped back up, pressing down on my shoulders, and I allowed her to dunk me before wrapping my arms around her waist and lifting her off her feet.

She threw her head back on a laugh as she clutched at my shoulders. "Okay, okay, truce!"

"That's what I thought." I grinned.

Face to face, we stared at each other, and all of a sudden it sank in just how close we were. Jana's chest rose on a breath, brushing against mine. The sports bra she wore was thin, and I could feel the outline of her tight little nipples through the fabric. My dick leaped to attention between us, and I was momentarily amazed by my body's reaction. Even after taking that shot just minutes earlier, my cock was eager as ever at the prospect of being near Jana.

Every trace of mirth vanished from Jana's face, and she wrapped her legs around my waist. There was no way she couldn't feel my arousal for her. I adjusted my grip, sliding my hands under her bottom. Goddamn, I loved her ass. I loved to look at it, but that was nothing compared to actually touching her, reveling in the feel of the soft globes filling my palms.

I was flirting with fire, but for the life of me, I couldn't remember why it was a bad idea. Jana evoked feelings in me, both emotional and physical, that I'd never experienced. I'd tried to rationalize it by telling myself it was only because I hadn't been with a woman in months.

But I knew better. It was Jana that was different. I couldn't think when she was around, and I couldn't keep my eyes off her. She was a walking wet dream, a perpetual distraction. I couldn't focus on anything but her.

Her lips were only inches from my own. Tiny droplets of water clung to her skin, and I wanted to run my tongue over her, lick up every single one. I dropped my gaze to her mouth, full and sensual. Her lips rolled inward then parted slightly on a soft sigh as her fingers sank into the hair at the base of my neck. She was begging for it—and I was going to give it to her.

I dipped my head just as a high-pitched ring pierced the air. Both of us froze. The ring came a second time from my cell phone, and Jana lifted her gaze to mine. I wanted to ignore it, to recapture the spark I'd felt a moment ago zinging between us.

A third ring pealed incessantly.

Damn it. "I should get that."

I simultaneously cursed and blessed whoever the hell had just ruined the moment as Jana unwound her legs from my waist. Cool water replaced the feel of her hot body against mine, and I wanted to pull her back to me. My fingers twitched against the curve of her ass as she slowly slid down my body until she was on her feet.

Shaking my lust-addled head, I made sure she was steady, then braced my hands on the side of the pool and launched myself up and over. I threw a quick glance over my shoulder to where Jana had paused on the steps of the pool.

She was bent over at the waist, hair draped over one shoulder as she wrung water from the long strands. It glimmered in the sunlight, and I wanted to run my fingers through it, gather it up and pull her close, take that kiss she was so willing to offer just a few seconds ago.

Turning, I adjusted the massive hard-on tenting my shorts and almost groaned at the contact. I'd jerked off at least once a day for the past week, but it hadn't satiated my desire for her at all. Each encounter left me feeling unsatisfied and empty.

My gaze dropped to her ass, barely constrained by a tiny scrap of teal fabric. My cock jumped to attention once more, and I let out a little growl as I snatched up the phone. Fuck. It was going to be a long ass week.

CHAPTER
TWENTY-TWO

JANA

My heart slammed against my ribcage, and I dragged in an unsteady breath as I pressed one hand over my chest and leaned against the door. While Vince took the phone call, I used the opportunity to slip inside and put some distance between us. I needed a second to myself to process everything that had happened—and everything that hadn't.

I swore he was about to kiss me before his phone rang, breaking the moment. I couldn't figure him out. One minute he was the big, bad bodyguard, keeping me locked away in the ivory tower. The next, he was laughing and smiling, joking like we'd known each other forever.

Despite the innocent flirting over the past few days, I felt a real spark with him. He made me feel giddy, like I was walking on air, but I had no idea if he felt the same way. Our past was so riddled with drama that I didn't know how to reconcile his recent behavior. The hard ridge I'd felt through the thin material of his shorts told me it was more than just friendly banter, but I had no idea if he would ever let himself feel more for me.

Not for the first time, I wished I had someone to talk to other than Vince. Since he was currently the subject of my speculation, he was the last person I could turn to. A rash desperation took hold, and I scrabbled through my bag, looking for my cell phone.

Vince had given it back a few days ago, once things between us had smoothed over a bit. I'd thrown it back in my purse, and now I snatched it up. While I waited for it to turn on, I stripped out of my soaked sports bra and shorts, then slipped into dry clothes.

As soon as my phone powered up, my screen was bombarded with hundreds of notifications that had come in through email and text message over the last week. Ignoring all of them, I pulled up my phone log and quickly tapped Maggie's number, then waited impatiently for it to connect.

Maggie didn't even bother with a hello. "Jana, please tell me that's you!"

"Of course it's me." I laughed. "Who else would it be?"

"Thank God! I was starting to worry about you."

I smiled at her overprotective reaction. She could be super paranoid sometimes, but I loved her to death. "I thought Harvey told you I was headed out of town."

"Yeah," she huffed. "But you never know. The whole thing just sounded sketchy with your elopement and everything. You never even told me you were seeing anyone."

I could hear the accusation in her voice, but Con's strict instructions came back to me, and I smoothly ignored her unspoken question. "I know, I'm sorry. Everything happened so fast, and we wanted it to be a surprise..."

Ha. Wasn't that the understatement of the year? Getting married had sure surprised the hell out of me.

"Right..." Maggie sounded worried. "Well, as long as you're okay."

"I'm good," I reassured her. "I was kind of just calling to check in, see how everything's going."

"People are losing their minds over here," she replied. "Your social media has been going crazy, with everyone wanting all the details."

"Thanks for taking care of that," I said. "I know everything happened kind of suddenly."

"It's fine," she said. "I'm just glad to hear from you and know you're okay."

"I'm great."

She must have heard the hesitation in my voice, because her tone turned contemplative. "Are you enjoying yourself?"

I shrugged one shoulder as I sank onto the corner of the bed. "It's been kind of boring, honestly. We've only gone out once since we've been here."

Maggie let out a crack of laughter. "Have you been stuck in bed the whole time?"

My cheeks burned at the implication, and my gaze slid to the pillows just a few feet away. I'd be lying if I said I hadn't imagined what it would be like between Vince and me, especially after the past few days. He'd shown me a side of himself I hadn't known existed, and for the first time since I met him, I really believed there might be a possibility of something more.

I must have waited too long to answer, because Maggie laughed again. "I'll take that as a yes."

I rolled my eyes, mentally slapping away the image of him in bed next to me, all sweaty and sexy. "Just been hanging around," I said, trying to keep the details to a minimum. "Swimming, walking on the beach. It's been fun."

"You never take a vacation," Maggie cut in. "You should enjoy it while it lasts."

"I know." I threw myself back onto the bed with a sigh. "But Vince says it's not safe yet."

"Vince is with you?" Maggie asked.

"Well, yeah." I rolled my eyes. "Who else?"

"But I thought you were on your honeymoon?"

Her question caused me to bolt upright. Shit. My mind raced to come up with an acceptable excuse but failed.

"Wait a second," she said. "Are we talking about the same person? As in Vince Incarnato—your bodyguard?"

"Um..." I licked my lips, debating whether I could lie my way out of this. She was going to find out eventually anyway, so I gave in. "Yeah. We're... together."

"You married him?"

Incredulity saturated Maggie's tone, and I bristled. "Why do you say it like that?"

"Oh, I don't know," she snapped. "Maybe because you guys have been at each other's throats since he came to work for you. Damn." She huffed a mirthless little laugh. "He moved fast."

There was no concealing the derision in her tone this time. "It's not like that," I bit out. "He's a good guy."

Ten whole seconds of silence ensued, then a sigh filtered through the speaker. "Do you love him?"

The question hit me like a ton of bricks to the chest. "Enough to marry him," I said softly, realizing how true the words were.

"Are you sure he's not taking advantage of the situation?"

I had to laugh. If either of us was taking advantage of anyone, it was me. "Definitely not," I said.

Maggie persisted. "Seriously, though. How long have you known this guy? How can you be sure?"

"Because he's nice to me. Because he treats me like a human being instead of tabloid fodder."

"But—" She made an agitated sound on the other end of

the phone. "Seriously. How do you know Vince isn't the one sending you these crazy letters, or involved somehow?"

I let out a laugh. "He had nothing to do with those letters."

"But how do you know for sure?" she insisted. "He could kill you and take everything you own, and—"

"He demanded a prenup," I cut in. A stunned silence met my statement, and I continued. "Plus, I haven't changed my will. I would never do anything rash like that without making absolutely sure it was for the best."

She was silent for a long moment. "Jana..."

"Just... Trust me." I didn't bother to tell her we hadn't followed through with the prenup, but the idea of Vince being my stalker was laughable. The man's morals were more stringent than a nun's. "Vince is... the best."

On the other end, I heard Maggie let out a beleaguered breath. "Listen. I don't know exactly what's going on, but just don't get your hopes up, okay?"

Part of me longed to confide in her and spill the truth, but I couldn't. I promised Con that I wouldn't speak a word to anyone, and I wouldn't. All I could do was brace myself for Maggie's *I told you so* six months from now when Vince and I had a very public break up. "I appreciate it," I said softly. "Thanks for everything."

We said goodbye, then I ended the call and turned off the phone before slipping it back into my bag. I stood for several moments, arms wrapped around my waist, replaying Maggie's words. I knew there was something special between Vince and me—I just knew it.

But was he more open and flirty because he cared about me, or because I was convenient? The question plagued me as I curled up on the bed and hugged the pillow close, my heart aching.

CHAPTER
TWENTY-THREE

VINCE

I swiped my phone off the chaise lounge and answered it mid-ring, unable to read the screen in the blinding sunlight. "Incarnato."

"Busy?"

I immediately recognized Con's voice, and I swore under my breath. "Nope. Caught me in the middle of working out. Whatcha got for me?"

"Just touching base," Con replied. "I'm guessing no one has made her yet. No mention of any spottings on social media."

That was good to hear and all, but it didn't help my current situation. I glanced down at the hard-on pressing against the front of my shorts. All the blood in my body had flooded south, and it was taking my brain awhile to catch up and come up with a suitable response.

"Ink?"

"Nope." Throwing myself into the chair, I forced my attention back to Con. "We've been out a couple times, but no one has recognized her, or, if they have, they haven't said anything."

"Keep it that way." There was a long pause on his end, then— "Everything good?"

"Yeah, why?" Even I could hear the defensiveness in my voice, and I fought to dial it back.

I could practically hear the wheels turning before he spoke, his tone both wary and curious. "This isn't a typical situation. Just making sure you haven't had any trouble."

"No trouble here," I said smoothly. Not the nefarious kind, anyway. Jana, though... Great tits, perfect ass, the five-foot-five blonde bombshell in my care was the worst kind of trouble there was. She was the kind of woman a man would happily hand over his balls to have.

Son of a bitch. I banged my head against the headrest of the chair. I couldn't believe I'd let things get so out of hand, even if she was encouraging me. Another three seconds in the pool with her and I'd have kissed her. A minute more and we both probably would have been naked.

Con hummed a little sound. "Police have a lead that they're investigating. Phelps told me they've applied for the warrant and plan to bring him in for questioning today or tomorrow if everything goes well."

I let a measured breath out through my nose. I had mixed feelings about the news he'd just imparted. On the one hand, I was glad that the threats against Jana would stop. If the police had enough evidence to press for a warrant, they must be pretty certain the guy was responsible. On the other hand, it meant my time with Jana was almost up. "Is it solid?" I asked.

"From what I understand," Con said slowly, "they're pretty certain they've got the right guy. Up until just a couple days ago, he worked as a janitor in Magnolia Way's studio."

A tingly sensation rushed over my skin. That meant he'd been in close contact with Jana, possibly for months. "Any news on the lock from Jana's house? Fingerprints, anything tying him to the car?"

"The techs analyzed the lock and determined that the damage was only superficial. I would guess he used a key, but we'll find out more once they question him. The guy also has a prior record for assaulting his ex-girlfriend."

I rolled my eyes. No surprise there. Men like that usually started small, with assault or harassment, then escalated into something more sinister. It was looking more and more like he was the one responsible. If he'd worked practically beside her, it would have been easy for him to follow her home.

Con continued, "He was caught stealing and was relieved of his position. When they searched his locker, they found a pair of sunglasses belonging to Ms. Malone. Prints have been pulled from several of the letters she received, so they'll cross check those as soon as they have him in custody. So far, it's looking pretty open and shut."

"Right. Well, that's... great." I tried to hide the disappointment in my voice, but I knew I had failed when a long pause came from the other end of the line.

"How are things with you?" Con asked warily.

"We've had our bumps," I replied honestly. "She threw a fit a few days ago when I wouldn't give her phone back so she could call you and bitch about me."

A low chuckle filtered through the speaker. "If it helps at all, I think you can ease up on her a bit. Seems like these guys have a handle on the situation here. I'll touch base tomorrow or the next day to let you know how everything panned out."

"I appreciate it."

"Hey, Ink?"

"Yeah?"

"The studio agreed to pay double for the assignment, so at least you'll get something out of this when it's all said and done."

The thought made me see red. "I'm not with her for the fucking money," I snapped.

I knew those assholes from the studio didn't give a shit about her, especially not her slime bag agent, Harvey. For all I cared, they could take that cash and shove it up their ass. I'd be damned, though, if I gave them the satisfaction. Whatever extra pay I got I would split with Jana. After everything she'd been through, she deserved it.

Con hesitated. "Not many men in your position would say the same."

I didn't have a response for that. He'd already read way more into the situation than I was comfortable with. "I've gotta go," I said. "That girl's attracted to trouble, so I better make sure she stays out of it."

"You do that," came Con's response. "Just remember..."

He trailed off, and I bristled. "What?"

"This ends when you come back."

It was like a kick to the gut. But he was exactly right. This —all of it—was just an illusion, a fantasy that would end the moment we went home. It still pissed me off. "And?"

He sighed. "Just don't do anything you'll regret."

"Call me when you know something." With that, I hung up and tossed my phone on the chaise lounge. Closing my eyes, I scrubbed my hands over my face.

What the hell was I doing? Things between Jana and me were getting out of control. Christ, had Con's phone call not interrupted us, I probably would've taken her right there in the shallow end of the pool. How the hell could I have been so stupid?

I'd almost crossed the line with her, with a client, something I swore I'd never do. It didn't matter what I felt for her or that she seemed to want it, too. My first—and only— priority was to keep her safe. And I couldn't do that if I was constantly distracted by her.

I let out a sigh, then turned my gaze toward the sliding doors that led into the bedroom. Beneath the reflection from the sun, I could just barely make out Jana's form moving around the bed. A primal urge came over me, tempting me to pick her up, throw her on the bed, then fuck her until we were both senseless. Clearly, I was already halfway there since I was contemplating having sex with her in the first place.

I prayed to God that the police would get this shit figured out and fast, because I was going to lose my mind if I had to spend any more time with this woman without getting my hands on her—all over her—exactly the way we both wanted.

CHAPTER
TWENTY-FOUR

JANA

I turned to glance at Vince. "How about we walk down to the pier?"

We'd seen it during the day, but now, at night, part of it was lit up, looking like a runway leading out to the middle of the sea.

He glanced in that direction, then shrugged. "Fine with me."

Silence fell as we started out across the sand. The sound of voices and laughter drifted toward us from the shore, but the beach itself was nearly deserted. Ever since he'd taken that phone call yesterday, things between us seemed more tense than usual. Whatever moment had passed between us in the pool had immediately dissipated, and he'd withdrawn completely, back to the cold, aloof man he'd been before.

I hated it. I wanted the real Vince back—the one I'd joked with and played cards with. I wanted the man who teased and laughed and smiled. The one who looked at me like he actually cared about me—not the singer that everyone else saw, but me, Jana.

After a few minutes, I couldn't stand it anymore and finally broke the silence. "Where are you from?"

"Originally?" I glanced up at Vince, his face illuminated in the moonlight, and nodded. "Pennsylvania, just north of Pittsburgh."

"Is your family still there?"

"Almost all of them." He smiled a little then. "I have four brothers, plus dozens of aunts and uncles and cousins back home. They all live just a few miles from one another."

His words caused me to miss a step as I whipped toward him. "Seriously? There's five of you?"

He smiled down at me. "Yep."

"Wow. What was it like growing up?"

"Loud. Hectic. Things got broken a lot."

I grinned at him. "I imagine your mom was ready to tear her hair out half the time."

"Probably. She was tough, but fair. She's a good woman."

"I'm sure," I said softly as we fell into step again. I couldn't imagine what it would be like to have a huge, close-knit family like that. Ever since I could remember, it had been just Mama and me. According to Mama, Daddy was a silver-tongued devil who'd charmed his way into her bed then left as soon as he found out she was pregnant with me. I couldn't believe she would even consider getting back with him—assuming the man was actually my father.

I could feel his gaze on me. "What about you?"

"Just my mom."

"Are you guys close?"

I shook my head. "Not exactly."

"That sucks." There was no sarcasm in his tone, no sympathy, just a matter-of-fact statement.

"You have no idea." I sighed. "We had a... falling out a

couple years back. I just couldn't stand watching her slowly destroy herself."

"Drugs?"

"Everything," I admitted. Growing up, there had never been money for food or new clothes, but somehow Mama always managed to budget just enough for smokes and booze and the occasional high. The older I got, the worse her addiction became. "Men, alcohol, drugs. You name it, she's done it. It actually got so bad that I had to go live with my grandmother when I was ten."

"What happened?" Vince's voice was soft, giving me the courage to continue.

"She overdosed, almost killed herself." Vince swore softly, and I nodded absently. "I remember walking home from school and coming into the house. It seemed so quiet, which was unusual. When Mama was home, the TV was always blaring one of her soap operas. That day though... There was nothing. I saw her lying on the couch, and at first I thought she was asleep."

"They saved her?"

I nodded. "I called the police right away, and they gave her Narcan. It was the craziest thing I've ever seen. One second, she was lying there like a corpse then the next, she took this huge, deep breath, and opened her eyes. It was literally like she woke up from the dead."

Vince was quiet for several long seconds. "I'm sorry you had to go through that."

So was I. I cleared my throat. "Anyway, I went to live with my grandmother for a few years. Mama went to jail that time, and we lost our trailer. When she got out, she came to live with us. Over the years, we kind of lost contact. She only reached out when she needed something, usually money, and finally I got tired of it. I cut her off completely a couple years ago when I moved down here."

It was actually one of the main reasons I'd chosen to come down here. My contract with my first agent, Earl, had been up, and I wanted to get as far away from my roots as fast as I could. I packed up and never looked back.

"Is that the last time you talked to her?"

I dropped my gaze to the sand beneath my feet and bit my lip. I still hadn't told him the truth of what had propelled me out of the house the morning I'd wrecked the car. "Actually, no," I admitted. "That morning we found out someone tampered with the brakes on my car..." I glanced up at him. "She called me from jail just before that."

"So that's why you needed to get out of the house," he stated.

I gave a little nod. "Yeah."

We had just reached the pier, and I was desperate to change the topic. "Have you ever been out on the ocean at night?"

I gestured towards the ocean, and he shook his head. "No, but I've done some deep-sea fishing excursions before."

We fell into step together as we started down the long pier, walking out over the ocean. "That sounds like fun."

"Do you like to fish?"

"Not at all." I shook my head. "I tried it once, but I just can't get into it."

"Can't sit still that long?" he teased.

"There is that," I said with a smile. "But really, I just hate the feel of those tiny, slippery, scaly bodies."

Vince laughed. "I should've known. If it's slimy or creepy, you want nothing to do with it."

A grin spread over my face. "Pretty much. I'm not super girly, but that's one thing I just can't do."

"It's not for everybody," he said easily.

Silence descended once more, and we made our way to the end of the pier. There were no lamps overhead now that we were out this far, only the moon and stars twinkling overhead, their reflection glowing on the dark water below. The waves gently lapped against the piles supporting the pier, and the slight breeze carried any sound away. Like this, it was as if Vince and I were out in the middle of nowhere, in our own little world. The wind picked up, and I pulled my sweater more tightly around myself. The skirt of my dress swirled around my knees, plastering the fabric to my body.

I leaned my elbows against the railing and stared out at the endless body of water in front of me. Next to me, Vince did the same. After several long moments, I broke the silence. "Sometimes I never want to go back."

Vince slid a look my way. "The beach life seems way more fun because it's different. But you'd miss your life back home."

"Maybe." But I knew better. I loved singing, but I hated the industry, having to always put on a happy face and pretend everything was perfect, even when I felt like I was dying inside. Here, with Vince, there was no pressure. "Here, I feel... free. I feel happy."

"Nothing good can ever last."

His words were soft, and I sighed. "I know. But I'm not ready for it to end yet."

He nodded slowly. "I know."

We stood there for nearly a minute, just looking up at the stars. I couldn't remember the last time I'd just stopped and stared up at them. They were so bright, so clear, and it reminded me of how very small I was. It was humbling, reminding me to be thankful for everything good in my life. Mostly, I was grateful for the man next to me who'd made this experience so incredible. "Thank you for doing this."

He tipped his head to one side. "Walking with you?"

"No, just... This. Everything."

I couldn't look at him, but I could feel the weight of his gaze as he turned toward me. "What do you mean?"

The breeze whipped a strand of hair across my face, and I brushed it away before tilting my head up to him. "We haven't always gotten along, so I just wanted to tell you how much I appreciate you going along with all of this."

He studied me for a second. "You know I wouldn't have done it if I didn't want to."

A wry smile tipped the corners of my lips. I doubted anyone could make Vince do something he didn't want to do. But being coerced into getting married was probably a stretch, even for him. "I know you don't really like me, but—"

He straightened suddenly, turning toward me. "I don't know why you keep saying that."

I mimicked his actions, tipping my head slightly to one side. "What?"

Vivid blue eyes stared down at me, turned icy gray in the moonlight. "That I don't like you. Why do you keep saying that?"

Heat climbed into my cheeks, and I shrugged. "Because it's true."

"It's not true. I've never said that."

"You didn't have to," I countered. "This whole thing was my idea, and I dragged you into it."

"I wouldn't have done it if I didn't want to," he reiterated.

I rolled my eyes. "Right, because—"

My words were immediately cut off, replaced by a gasp of surprise as his heavy palm curled around the back of my neck. My hands flew up, bracing against his firm chest as he tugged me close. Those crystalline eyes bored into mine before dropping to my lips.

I was helpless against him as his mouth covered mine, his lips firm yet soft, tender yet demanding, as he kissed me. My eyes fluttered closed, and I curled my fingers into the fabric of his T-shirt. I felt off-balance, as if I might float away at any second, and I swayed slightly against him. His lips moved on mine, increasing the pressure and urging me to open for him.

The hand on the back of my neck slid upward, tangling in the strands of my hair and tipping my head to one side. His tongue swept over mine, and he tasted faintly of spearmint, like the gum he was always chewing. He tasted so good, felt so right, both of us perfectly in sync.

Things had been tumultuous between us since the beginning, and I couldn't believe this was actually happening. He'd closed down after our almost-kiss yesterday, and it suddenly felt as if this was all too good to be true.

Abruptly, I yanked back and stared up at him. "Is that a pity kiss?"

One dark eyebrow hiked up. "Didn't we already establish this?"

I don't do anything I don't want to do. I blinked up at him and ran my tongue over my lower lip. "Okay."

His hand tightened in my hair, and one muscular forearm looped around my waist, pulling me back to him. "In case you're wondering," he said, his lips only millimeters from mine, "I've been wanting to do that for a long time."

CHAPTER
TWENTY-FIVE

VINCE

I sat by the pool, staring up at the stars, thinking about that kiss on the pier. Despite telling myself it was wrong, I couldn't keep my hands off her. Not touching her, not kissing her, was like trying not to breathe. I couldn't do it. She was passionate and vibrant, more than I ever dreamed of.

And that kiss... I couldn't get it off my mind. I'd kissed a lot of women in my life, possibly upward of a hundred. There was an indefinable chemistry in a kiss that felt more intimate than sex. I'd found over the course of my adult life that a kiss determined the path of a relationship.

Some of the women I'd dated had never made it past the kissing phase. Other women, some I hadn't been particularly attracted to physically, their kiss just did it for me. But none of them even held a candle to the way I'd felt with Jana. It was like she'd poured part of herself into me, imprinted herself on my heart, tattooed her touch on my skin.

I flexed the fingers of my left hand. I could still feel the heat of her flesh where she'd tucked her small fingers into mine on the walk back. The simple silver ring glinted in the moonlight, and I rubbed my thumb over the smooth metal. I felt our time together ticking away, but I wasn't ready to let her go, damn it.

Soon enough, she would go back to the real world, back to her friends and the life of fame she adored. I wasn't stupid; I knew I didn't fit into that kind of life. I wasn't the kind of man she needed. The reality was like a bitch slap to the face. Somewhere along the line, I'd really come to care for her.

As soon as we got back to the house, we'd gone our separate ways; Jana went inside while I had retreated out here to think. Behind me, I heard the soft scrape of the sliding door open then close again. My ears perked up, and I held my breath as heat flared in my chest. It was as if my thoughts had conjured her, lured her to me. Did she want me as badly as I wanted her? God, I hoped so.

Silent as a cat, Jana approached. She didn't say a word as she nudged my legs farther apart and settled between my thighs on the chaise lounge. Her bottom pushed back against my dick, and she snuggled in close to me. The sweater she'd worn earlier was gone, and she shivered slightly at the coolness of the evening.

"Cold?" My voice was low and raspy, full of relief that she'd searched me out.

Grasping my wrists, she lifted my arms and wrapped them around her. "Not anymore."

Tightening my hold, I pulled her even closer, wishing we were skin to skin. We remained that way for several minutes, enjoying the quiet night and the feel of each other.

I tore my gaze away from the stars dotting the sky to the beautiful woman in front of me. She still wore the red halter dress she'd had on earlier, and I glanced down into the valley of her breasts, put on display by the low cut of the dress. I wanted to trail my fingers down between the plump mounds, cup them, play with the perfect pink peaks I'd salivated over since seeing her in the shower.

My chin grazed the sleek slope of her shoulder, and I dipped my head, brushing my lips over her skin. Jana tipped her head slightly to the side, giving me carte blanche. Her smell invaded my nostrils, wrapping around me and pulling me under, drawing me further under whatever spell she'd managed to weave over me.

I dropped kisses up the base of her neck and bit down lightly, holding her as a shiver racked her body. I pulled her more tightly to me and brushed my nose over the shell of her ear before taking the lobe between my teeth and giving a gentle tug.

A soft sound escaped her throat, and I reluctantly released her flesh. Jana leaned slightly to one side and turned to me. I met her gaze, darkened in the moonlight. Her blue eyes were liquid fire as she stared up at me, and I couldn't resist the temptation. Dipping my head, I brushed my mouth over hers. Her lips parted, and I deepened the kiss, possessing her mouth, taking what was mine.

I sank my hand into her hair and turned her head, angling her to fit me better. My right hand still rested on her stomach, and I could feel her muscles contract as she arched into me. I skimmed upward and pulled the tie of her dress free, allowing the triangular cups to fall open and expose her pretty tits to my view.

I pulled back to examine her. "God, you're gorgeous."

She gasped as I plucked a pink tip between my fingertips. "Vince!"

Tightening my hold on her hair, I pulled her back to me and claimed her mouth again. My tongue swept over hers as I played with her breasts, circling one nipple, tweaking the other. Jana writhed against me, and my cock hardened in my jeans.

Jana's knees fell open, and the skirt of her dress slipped down to her hips. Coasting downward, I slid my hand between her legs—and froze.

Grabbing her hair, I pulled away and broke the kiss. "You're not wearing panties." It was a statement, but I couldn't fucking believe it. "Were you bare under your dress all night?"

She shook her head and licked her lips before giving me a cheeky smile. "Just since we got home."

"You were gonna let someone else see you?" She jumped and let out a little squeal as I slapped her pussy. She tried to slam her knees together, but I pried them apart, exposing her to me as I draped them over my thighs so she was spread wide open.

I knew I had no right to claim her, to touch her, but I couldn't help myself. It was as if she was made for me. I wanted her, needed her like my next breath of air. I slipped my fingers between her slick folds, loving the way she thrust against my hand. "You're all mine. No one else sees this part of you but me."

"Only you," she whispered.

Right answer. She was all mine, every single inch of her. I sank two fingers deep inside her and kissed her hard. My hand left her hair and wandered down to her breast, using my fingertip to trace a circle around the tight peak. I slipped lower, feeling the heavy weight of her as I cupped her in my hand. I'd lied to her before; I loved her tits. She was so incredibly responsive, so open and transparent in her feelings.

A little moan welled up as I brushed my thumb over her clit, thrusting deep with my fingers. I nipped her lower lip, and she jumped, hips arching into me as I circled the tiny bundle of nerves at her entrance.

"Oh, God... Vince!"

Her leg muscles trembled, and I could feel how close she

was. Sinking my fingers deep, I pressed my thumb down on her clit and pinched her nipple. The slight bite of pain pushed her over the edge, and her entire body went rigid as she shattered on a long, quiet cry. I fucked her with my fingers as she rode out the orgasm until her body went limp and she melted into me with a little hum of pleasure.

I rearranged her in my arms, and she clutched at my neck as I stood and carried her toward the door. Somehow I managed to maneuver us inside and lock up before I carried her through the darkened bungalow to the bedroom. I halted next to the bed, still holding her, dreading letting her go. "Tell me to stop."

Her face lifted to mine, open and vulnerable in the moonlight. She shook her head, her words a whisper. "Not now. Not when I finally got you to see me."

"I've always seen you." I propped a knee on the bed and lay her back. "God, have I seen you."

The vibrant red dress was bunched up at the waist, exposing nearly all of her to my view. Her arms were bent, hands lying on the comforter above her head. The position put her tits on full display, and I couldn't resist the urge to touch her. Settling on my knees between her spread thighs, I kneaded the generous mounds and teased the tight pink tips with the pads of my thumbs. She arched into my touch, and her eyes closed, her teeth sinking into her lower lip.

I bent and took one pert tip between my lips, curling my tongue around the pretty pink nipple. With a little mewl, her hands sank into my hair, and her hips bucked upward. My dick ached to be inside her, and I pulled away. "Fuck, woman. You're going to be the death of me."

I slid off the bed and grasped the fabric of her dress. Her hips lifted to aid me, and I yanked it down her thighs, then dropped it to the floor before reaching for her again, desperate to feel her. "I swear I can't wait one more second."

"Me, either." She struggled to sit up, then her hands were on me, pulling at my shirt. I ducked my head, allowing her to pull it over and toss it to the floor.

I pulled my wallet from my back pocket and extracted a single condom. "I've only got one, so we'd better make it last."

She shook her head and yanked open the drawer of the nightstand. "I've got us covered."

My eyes darted uncomprehendingly to the brand-new, unopened box of condoms. I knew they weren't in there the first day when I'd searched everything. All of a sudden, I remembered her strange interaction with the delivery boy who'd brought our groceries. My gaze slid back to hers. "You ordered those."

I didn't know if it was an accusation or a compliment, but she nodded, her tongue swiping over her lower lip.

I crawled over her, forcing her to her back. "You planned this?"

She jumped a little as I lightly smacked the undercurve of her ass. "Hey, a girl can hope."

Her words were breathless, but they rang with total honesty. I dipped my head and kissed her hard. She clutched desperately at my head, and our mouths and tongues tangled until we were both panting for breath, hearts racing.

I broke the kiss and met her pretty blue gaze. "I hope you're ready for what you've started... because you're mine now."

CHAPTER
TWENTY-SIX

JANA

His words sent a shiver down my spine. God, yes, was I ready. I sucked in a breath as his hands coasted down my inner thighs and his fingers swept through my slick folds. My back bowed, thrusting closer, offering myself to him. Heat licked over my skin, and I swore I was going to burst into flame if he made me wait one more second.

Fingers swirling around the little bundle of nerves, he leaned forward and captured my mouth with his. This kiss was hard, borderline brutal as he nipped at my lips, then down my jaw. His teeth sank into my neck, and goosebumps raced over my skin as I arched at the sensation and let out a soft cry.

"You like that?"

"Yes," I managed to pant out. Yes to anything—yes to everything. I reached for him, looping my arms around his shoulders and pulling him down to me. "Don't stop," I begged.

His chuckle stirred the air near my ear. "Oh, honey, I'm just gettin' started."

It wasn't fair that I was completely naked and he was still mostly clothed. I reached between us and fumbled with the opening of his jeans. My arms weren't quite long enough, and I let out a frustrated growl when the button refused to come free.

Vince brushed my hands away and took over, popping the fastener from its hole and shoving the material down his legs. My eyes widened when I realized he'd gone commando, too. I lifted a brow. "And you gave me shit for not wearing underwear."

His grin was blindingly white and feral-looking in the semi-darkness. "I told you, trouble." He slid his thumb through my folds again as he spoke. "This is for my eyes only."

"I—" My words were stolen on a gasp as he sank two fingers deep inside me.

He worked his shaft with his free hand, running it slowly up and down as he watched me, his fingers still moving in and out to the slow, methodical rhythm he was using on himself. It was erotic to watch, and liquid fire pooled in my core at the sight.

"Vince, please..." I sank my teeth into my lower lip and grabbed the comforter as he circled my clit before pulling his fingers free. Snatching up the condom, he tore the wrapper and rolled it over the swollen head of his erection.

The mattress dipped beneath his weight as he climbed up between my legs, and I was already grabbing for him as he braced his hands on either side of my shoulders. A soft chuckle left his throat as he closed the distance between us. "You are the least patient person I know."

"Can't be patient with you," I complained. I didn't care that I was baring myself to him. I was too eager for everything he offered to worry about guarding my heart against him. "I need you."

"I know, baby." He lowered himself until his chest

brushed mine, the dark hair there tickling my skin and making my nipples stand up eagerly. "I know exactly how you feel."

Maneuvering one hand between us, he lined the head of his shaft up with my entrance. His lips found mine just as he thrust hard, sinking into me with one hard stroke. He filled every inch of me, stretching my sensitive walls. I bit back a cry as pleasure like I'd never known washed over me.

He retreated, and my body clenched around him, trying to hold him close as he pulled out to the tip then slammed back in. I clutched at his shoulders, curling into him as sparks of electricity shot through my body. His tongue swept over mine, and he kissed me breathless until I thought I was going to pass out from ecstasy and lack of oxygen.

I ripped my mouth away from his and dragged in air as he continued to piston in and out, his cock hitting my G-spot with every deep stroke. Winding my legs around his waist, I locked my feet together at the base of his spine and moved with him, matching him thrust for thrust. Molten fire flowed through my veins as he moved, pushing me closer and closer to the edge.

Suddenly he changed tempo, throwing me off balance. A tiny whimper escaped, and he smirked down at me. "I'll take care of you, pretty girl. You close?"

"God, yes." I dug my nails into his shoulders. "I'm going to kill you if you don't start moving."

With a chuckle, Vince lifted my left leg and kissed my ankle bone, then draped it over his shoulder so I was completely open to him. "Do those threats work for everyone else?"

"Usually." I licked my lips as he moved in and out with torturously slow, shallow thrusts. "Vince, I swear to God..."

My next words disappeared on a gasp as he slammed into me. My body jolted under the force of it, and he pulled out, only to ram into me again. I threw one hand over my mouth and bit the fleshy part of my palm to keep the scream welling up my throat from escaping.

Vince grabbed my hand and pinned it to the bed over my head. "Haven't you figured it out yet?" He dragged his cock out, then shoved back in forcefully, splintering my attention.

I arched, my head digging into the mattress as tiny tremors shuddered through my body. "Wh-what?"

He leaned forward, pushing himself deeper into me, and every muscle in my body shook under the strain. I was so close, literally trembling with the need to come. I squeezed my thighs, trying to pull him even closer, but Vince resisted, pulling out until he was barely inside me. His cock teased my entrance, and he dipped his head, capturing my nipple between his teeth. I let out a soft shriek as he lightly bit down, then rolled his tongue over it to soothe the sting.

I glared up at him as he released me with a confident smile. "I'm in charge here, gorgeous."

"If you don't—"

He released my hands and kissed me deeply, passionately, cutting off my threat and fueling the desire between us. My muscles contracted around him as he moved in and out, his pace growing increasingly frantic. My nerve endings tingled, and heat pooled in my core, the flare of pleasure growing and spreading outward until it erupted.

Blood rushed in my ears and I thought I might have screamed, but the orgasm ripping through my body dulled everything around me. My stomach muscles tightened until they ached, and I gritted my teeth, letting out a high-pitched mewl as my body rode the line between pleasure and pain.

Vince continued to pound into me, and his lips unerringly found mine for another kiss. I could taste his distinct flavor as he devoured every inch of my mouth, his tongue sliding against mine.

Gently slipping my ankle off his shoulder, he guided it

behind his back. I followed suit and I locked my legs around his waist, swallowing the guttural growl that welled up his throat as he thrust deeper, harder. With one last stroke he let go and came on a soft roar, and I instinctively tightened my muscles around him, never wanting to let him go.

Braced on his elbows, he held himself up to keep from smashing me into the mattress, but I didn't want a single inch separating us. I clutched his shoulders tighter, pulling him down to me.

He huffed out a soft chuckle, his breath warm against my cheek. "I'm too heavy for you."

I ducked my head against his shoulder and held fast. "I don't care."

Some of the tension drained from his muscles as he relaxed into me, and I breathed deeply, inhaling the scent of him. Sweat clung to our skin, sealing us together. I loved it.

Too soon, he nuzzled the side of my neck, then dropped a kiss on my throat before peeling himself away. "Be right back."

I watched as he sauntered toward the door, his muscles rippling as he moved across the bedroom, from his broad shoulders down to his tight ass. A silly grin spread over my face, and I snuggled deeper into the pillow and blankets that already smelled like him.

Barely more than a minute later he climbed back into bed next to me and pulled me close, then nipped the shell of my ear. "Sleep well, trouble."

A pang of hurt ricocheted through my heart, dimming the happiness from only a few moments before. Facing away from him in the near dark gave me the courage to speak. "Why do you call me that?"

There was a long beat of silence before his breath tickled the back of my neck as he spoke. "What?"

"Trouble."

"Have I ever told you"—he rolled me to my back and stared down at me—"that I was always getting into scrapes as a kid?"

I shook my head, brows dipping low. "I don't think so?"

"Well, I was. If it was dangerous, it had my name written all over it. I've always been addicted to trouble." My cheeks heated as he propped himself up on an elbow and swept his thumb over my lower lip. "And you, pretty girl, are the best kind of trouble there is."

My heart skipped a beat at his words, but I still made a face, not entirely convinced. "That doesn't really sound like a good thing."

"It is, believe me. I've never met anyone who keeps me on my toes the way you do, who pushes me until I'm ready to snap, then brings me back down with one sweet smile."

A tiny smile curved my mouth. "If you say so."

"Just take my word for it." He framed my face with one huge hand and pressed his lips to mine. Just as passionate our feverish kisses earlier, the gentle sweep of his lips over mine stole my heart. He pulled back and stared down at me in the darkness, his thumb slowly stroking over my cheek. He dipped his head and kissed me once more before gently rolling me to my side.

Sliding one arm under my pillow, he pulled me so my back pressed to his front and splayed one huge hand over my belly. Happiness curled through me as I scooted backward, plastering myself as close to him as physically possible. I was glad to see that he hadn't put clothes on, either, and I snuggled closer, wanting to feel every inch of him as I closed my eyes and drifted off.

It was dark when I next awoke, and a shiver racked my body. I groped blindly for the sheet, which had somehow ended up down around our waists. I rolled over, instinctually seeking out Vince's heat. He'd rolled to his back at some point, and one arm was tossed casually over his head while he slept.

I burrowed as close as humanly possible, and he stirred at my movements. He rolled his head my way. "You good?"

His voice was sleepy and raspy, and I turned my nose against his chest, loving the feel and smell of him. I rubbed my cheek against his skin as I shivered again. "I'm cold," I complained. "It's freezing in here."

"Mmm..." He hummed a little sound as he wrapped his arm around me, pulling me close. "I turned the air down earlier."

I lifted my head and peered blearily at him. "To what— arctic blast?"

He chuckled, low and sexy, and those gorgeous eyes slitted open to meet mine in the moonlight. "C'mere, babe. I'll keep you warm."

CHAPTER
TWENTY-SEVEN

VINCE

I rolled, taking her with me until I was firmly settled between her lean thighs where they gripped my hips. Yanking the covers up, I cocooned us in our own little world, then cradled her head in my hands and brushed my lips over hers.

The kiss was soft and sweet, tender and perfect. Our coupling earlier had been frenzied and frantic, as if we were afraid the other would suddenly call a halt.

Jana was fucking incredible. She hid so many layers of herself deep down, and I had a feeling I'd only begun to scratch the surface of the passionate woman I held in my arms. This time, there was no need to rush. I could take my time, taste and explore every delicious inch of her.

I couldn't see her in the dark, but I could feel her gaze on mine. She slid her hands over my shoulders, pulling me back down and bringing us even closer. I kissed her shoulder, her collarbone, up and over her throat. I found her mouth again, and she nipped playfully at my lower lip.

I growled and thrust my tongue inside her mouth at the

same time I rolled my hips, mimicking the thrusting motion. We both froze as the head of my cock found her hot center and slipped an inch inside.

The silky heat of her was like nothing I'd ever experienced. I fought my instinct to drive hard and deep, wallow in the perfection of the feeling.

Jana's fingers tensed, curling into the back of my neck, and I lifted my head. The covers slipped down to my shoulders, exposing her beautiful face to my view in the moonlight, and I met her gaze.

Her tongue darted out nervously, then her teeth sank into her lower lip as she watched me watching her.

With my thumbs, I gently stroked her temples. "You okay with this?"

She nodded a little. "I..." She swallowed hard but didn't break contact. "I get the shot. If, you know..."

She felt so damn good, but I wouldn't come inside her like this—not yet. "Just one more minute," I promised. Then I'd put on a condom. And hate every second of it.

I rocked forward, and she sucked in a breath as I slid all the way in with one smooth motion. "Holy Christ, baby." Fully seated inside her, I dipped my head and lightly bit her neck, then soothed the spot with my tongue. "You feel so good."

Her hands slid down my back, and I could feel her muscles tensing around me. Arching upward she lifted her hips, silently encouraging me to move. Slipping one hand under her ass, I ground into her, loving the feel of her silky heat. I never wanted to leave the shelter of her sweet, sexy body.

I'd lied to her before, when I called her superficial and self-centered. She was everything I'd ever dreamed of, more than I could ever ask for. I'd known there was something extraordinary between us the moment my lips touched hers, and if that kiss hadn't told me everything I needed to know, this sealed the deal for me.

I'd never felt like this with a woman before, and I had a sneaking suspicion I never would again. This, whatever I had with Jana, was something people searched for their whole lives. I wanted her every way, every single day; a lifetime wouldn't be enough.

It was too soon for any declaration of love, but neither was I going to give her up—not for a long damn time. I didn't know what our return to the real world would bring, but I would fight every damn day to keep her by my side. It wouldn't be easy, especially not in her world, but I knew I would do anything for her.

Jana and I had experienced the absolute worst of each other at the beginning of our relationship—now we were experiencing the best. I wanted more of her than she'd ever given anyone else, and I would endeavor to make each day better than the last.

Jana still stared up at me, a mixture of emotion in her pretty blue eyes. I released her bottom and moved my hand to her chin, making sure she was paying attention to every word when I spoke. "I meant what I said."

Twin lines of confusion appeared in the space between her brows, but she didn't voice her curiosity. I traced her lower lip with my thumb. "You're mine, Jana. And I'm yours."

I didn't wait for her to say anything, just pulled back and thrust in, hard and deep. She clutched at me as I pounded into her. It was rough and hard and feral, and I knew she didn't understand... but she would. I was marking her, making sure she would feel me on every inch of her each time she moved, forget every other man she'd ever been with, all of those memories replaced by the things we did together.

I pumped three more times, long and slow and deep, reveling in the feel of her. God, I couldn't stand the torture of feeling her body grip mine without being able to come deep inside her. I let out a sigh of regret as I slowly withdrew.

Jana's face twisted into an expression of dismay, and I knew my face reflected her thoughts. I immediately missed the heat of her as soon as my cock pulled free of her slick channel. No matter how much I wanted to fill her up, make her mine, I wouldn't risk it. We'd gone too far already, and I would never jeopardize her like that.

I stretched an arm out and swiped a condom from the nightstand, then rolled it on before levering myself over her again. Her hands automatically wound around my shoulders, reaching for me and pulling me close. I bent my arms, laying part of my weight on her, and she let out a soft little sound.

I loved the way she reached impatiently for me, as if she'd gone years without touching me instead of mere seconds. I loved the way her body curled into me, her flesh drawn to mine like a magnet to steel. Grasping the base of my shaft, I directed the head to her opening once more and pushed until I was fully sheathed inside her.

I kissed her, flicking my tongue across hers, tasting the faint hint of the toothpaste she'd used before bed. I rolled my hips, pressing my knees into the mattress for leverage as I drove into her. One hand left my shoulders and wandered down my back until she gripped my ass, encouraging—or, in Jana's case, demanding—I move faster.

A sense of urgency tugged at me, and I picked up the pace. Sliding my hand under her ass, I fucked her hard, every muscle in my body burning with exertion until a bead of sweat slipped down my temple. I could feel her inner muscles tightening, contracting around me, but I wasn't ready for her to come yet.

Jana held on as I rolled to my back, pulling her atop me. I grasped her hips and thrust upward, urging her to move. "Come on, country girl. Show me what you've got."

Bracing her hands on my chest, she began to move, tentatively at first, then faster as she fell into a rhythm. A growl bubbled up my throat as her motion forced me deeper into her. Her tits swung gently in front of my face as she lifted up and down, and she let out a little hum of pleasure as I caught the tip of one between my lips.

Her ass cheeks filled my palms, and I kneaded them as she rode me, my tongue curling around her tight little nipple. Her inner walls squeezed my cock, letting me know she was almost there. I thrust roughly upward, pressing down at the same time, forcing myself deep until I bumped her G-spot.

Tugging one tight peak between my teeth, I skated one hand up the curve of her waist and tweaked the other. The mixture of pleasure and pain pushed her over the edge, and she came on a broken cry, her body tensing before she slumped over me.

She let out a little sound of discontent as I pulled free of her and gently maneuvered her off me. "On your belly."

Throwing a disgruntled look over her shoulder at me, she moved into position—but not nearly fast enough. I swatted her ass and yanked on one foot until she lay prone in the middle of the bed.

"Hey!"

I grasped her hair in a ponytail and pulled, causing her back to arch. She tried to shift, but I straddled her legs, forcing them together until they were almost closed. I leaned forward and bit her earlobe, and a shiver rolled through her body. "My turn."

My cock lay in the crease of her ass, and I used my free hand to spread her cheeks until her opening was exposed to me. I fitted the head between her slit and shoved inside. "Fuck, babe."

Like this, with her legs pressed together, she felt tighter than ever, and fire licked up my stomach at the sensation. I was so damn close, but I wanted to draw it out, make every second count. Moving my hand around her hips, I searched for the tiny bundle of nerves between her legs. She gasped when I pinched it between my thumb and forefinger, and her hips bucked wildly.

I claimed her mouth in a brutal kiss, fucking her from behind and rubbing the sensitive nub until she writhed and twisted beneath me. I pressed down harder as my balls tightened with my impending release, and I was rewarded a second later as she ripped her mouth from mine and let out a keening cry.

Her pussy strangled my cock as she came, hurtling me toward the edge. I let go with a growl and ripples of heat and pleasure cascaded over my body as I emptied myself inside her. For a long moment, I remained that way, partially draped over her. My muscles trembled as I fought to hold my weight up and keep from crushing her.

Completely sated, I braced myself on a shaky forearm, then rolled us to our sides, still buried deep inside her. Our breathing slowly returned to normal, and I finally pulled free, removing the condom and tossing it in the wastebasket.

She rolled toward me as I came back to her, and she tucked her nose into the crook of my neck, curling into me as she started to drift off. I knew she was tired, but I wasn't done with her yet. Tangling my fingers in her hair, I tipped her head up and stared down at her pretty face. Her eyes popped open, and she stared at me in silent question.

"This—" I gave a gentle tug to her hair. I wanted to make sure she understood. "This is serious, you and me."

She gave a little nod, but I knew she wasn't quite certain what I was saying. Hell, I wasn't entirely sure, either. I just knew I needed to get the words out, because I would regret it if I didn't.

"It's gonna be hard as hell when we get home, but I don't care." I felt her fingers curl into the flesh of my back as I continued. "You occupy my every thought, every moment of every day. I want to be with you—I want to make this work."

She blinked rapidly, and I couldn't tell if the faint sheen there was from the moonlight or tears. "Me, too."

I studied her for a long moment. "Good." Releasing my hold on her hair, I kissed her once, long and slow, praying she could feel every emotion I couldn't yet put into words. A long moment later, I broke the connection and tucked her head against my shoulder. "Sleep."

She nestled in close, and I could feel the heat of her breath on my neck as she gradually drifted off. I wasn't sure how we'd make it work, but I would make damn certain it did. Because I wanted her right here—just like this—every night. I was starting to believe that an eternity wouldn't be enough.

CHAPTER
TWENTY-EIGHT

JANA

I was aware of the bright sunlight streaming through the doors before I even opened my eyes, and I snuggled deeper into the welcoming heat surrounding me.

Memory came flooding back as a feathery soft sensation moved slowly up and down my arm, and my eyes flew open. I was greeted by the sight of Vince's muscular pecs, the dark ink dancing as his chest rose and fell on deep, steady breaths.

"Hey."

His voice was raspy and soft, and I lifted my gaze slowly to his. "Hey."

The fingers making circles on my arm slid upward to my cheek. "Sleep okay?"

I nodded but didn't speak.

"Good."

I watched him as his fingers gently swept over my forehead, down the bridge of my nose, over my chin. I closed my eyes to the sensation as he touched every inch of me, tracing my features like he was committing every dip and curve to memory. I mentally did the same. I would remember the feel of him, the way he looked, his masculine scent, until the day I died.

My eyelids popped open as he traced a path down my sternum to the valley of my breasts.

"You're so beautiful." With the back of one knuckle, he brushed my right nipple.

Self-consciously, I brought my arm up between us, shimmying backward to put some distance between us.

Vince watched me curiously. "What's wrong?"

"Nothing." I shook my head, but his hand shot out, wrapping around my waist, and I let out a gasp as he tugged me toward him.

"Don't lie to me." His gaze dropped to my breasts for a moment, then back up to mine. His hand moved to touch my breast again, but I fended him off.

His eyebrow ratcheted upward, and I let out a sigh. "I just... I don't like my breasts."

"Why?"

There was no judgment in his tone, only curiosity, but it didn't stop the heat of mortification from creeping into my cheeks. "They're too big."

He studied me. "You don't want them anymore?"

I let out a mirthless laugh. "I never wanted them in the first place."

His brows drew together. "Then why did you get them?"

This time, he loosened his hold as I put some space between us, knowing I needed it. "It wasn't my decision to make." His eyes darkened as the implication sank in, but he didn't say a word as I continued. "I was a late bloomer. My first agent, Earl, said I would never make it if I looked like a little boy. And, at seventeen, I still hadn't sprouted. So Mama signed off on the surgery, and..." I shrugged like it didn't still hurt then laughed. "I surprised the hell out of everyone when I grew two cup sizes after the augmentation."

A muscle in his jaw ticked, and he was silent for a long moment. Finally, he propped himself up on an elbow as he stared down at me. "Can't you have a reduction done?"

I shook my head. "I could, but I don't want to. I hate being put under. I don't like the feel of it, the way I lose whole periods of time. I know it's dumb, but—"

"It's not dumb. I know exactly what you mean. It's the same reason you hate those pills."

I couldn't believe he'd listened to me. I swallowed down the tears that threatened at the back of my throat. "Yeah. Just like the pills."

He reached out to tuck a strand of hair behind my ears. "Do they bother you?"

"Physically? No." I hesitated for a moment. "It's just... I know a lot of people judge me because of the way I look."

He pushed to a sitting position. "Idiots."

"You did the same thing," I said softly. So much had happened between us since then, but the reminder sent a little pang of hurt shooting through my chest.

He must have read it in my eyes, because he moved before I could stop him, kneeling between my legs and placing his hands on the mattress on either side of my shoulders, caging me in with his huge body. "I was wrong. About all of it."

"I'm sure," I said derisively, staring at his chest instead of meeting his eyes. "Don't most men love big breasts?"

"Most," he agreed, leaning forward and kissing me. My heart fluttered as his lips teased mine, the kiss painstakingly tender and sweet. He moved to one cheek, then the other, and my eyes closed as he left a trail of kisses over my face before working his way down my throat.

I felt the scrape of stubble as his chin brushed my sternum, and I cracked my eyes open, watching warily as he cupped my breasts in his huge hands, causing them to plump and swell. I swallowed hard, battling the insecurity sweeping up my spine. His thumbs brushed the pink peaks, and they tightened and strained under his ministrations.

"But I love yours"—he dipped his head and kissed first one, then the other—"because they're part of you."

His words caught me completely off guard, and I couldn't stop the tears from springing to my eyes. I snapped my eyelids shut, but I knew Vince had seen, because one hand cradled my face a second later.

"Jana."

His tone demanded I look at him, and I somehow summoned the courage to meet his gaze through the sheen of moisture.

His thumb stroked my cheek and he leaned so close our noses almost brushed. "You are perfect. Don't ever doubt that."

His words, coming out barely more than a whisper, made me melt. I threw my arms around his wide shoulders and pulled him down, burying my face in his neck. He slowly relaxed his weight until he lay completely on top of me, pressing me into the mattress.

I was surprised—not to mention a little disappointed—when he pulled back a minute later and dropped a brief kiss on my lips. "Come on, trouble. I'm starving."

He rolled off the bed, and I sat up, unable to help the pout that pulled at my lips. I was starving, too, damn it—just not for food. Reluctantly, I slid from the bed and dressed, pulling on the closest things at hand, which happened to be the camisole and shorts I'd set out to sleep in last night but never had a chance to wear. A smile split my face as my gaze landed on the red dress pooled on the floor.

Vince caught me around the waist as I moved toward the door, and he pulled me in close. One large hand framed my face, tilting my chin up to meet his gaze. He searched my eyes for a long moment, then dipped his head and claimed my mouth. This kiss spoke of dominance and possession, and I felt myself lean into him.

There was no turning back from this. At some point over the past couple of weeks, I'd given him a huge part of my heart that I would never get back. I only hoped that he would be true to his word and not break it.

Because I knew it would never be whole again if he did.

CHAPTER
TWENTY-NINE

VINCE

I sat sprawled on the couch, legs propped on the coffee table in front of me. Jana was spread out beside me, her feet in my lap. I glanced down and smiled. Tonight's fuzzy socks had pink and blue stripes and came halfway up to her knees.

From the corner of my eye, I watched her, her attention glued to the TV. I couldn't believe how much things had changed in just the past forty-eight hours. The reserve and distance between us had melted away, and we'd spent every minute of the day together, talking about everything and nothing.

I'd cared for her before, but I felt even more possessive of her after learning how she'd overcome the adversity of the way she'd grown up. My family was my support system. I couldn't imagine coming from a single-parent home, let alone one who was drugged out of her mind half the time.

Jana was so much stronger than I'd given her credit for, and I loved that she never let it slow her down or hold her back. She'd set a course for herself in life, shed the skin of her past, and moved on. She would never play the victim.

Though I knew she was insecure about her background, she put on a brave face and persevered. She'd made a name for herself in country music, completely reinventing herself into a strong, smart, independent woman. She didn't need me to protect her from the assholes of the world, but I wanted to shelter her anyway. It was ingrained in me to take care of the ones I loved... And she was slowly worming her way into that category.

Jana caught me watching her and wiggled one fuzzy-socked foot near my groin. I grabbed it and growled a warning at her. "Trouble..."

"What?" She pouted prettily at me, affecting her most innocent expression. The slumbrous bedroom eyes totally ruined the effect, and I felt myself swelling until I was painfully hard.

Jana's eyes dropped to the bulge evident against the thin material of my shorts. "You were looking awfully lonely over there."

She bit her lip as I pressed my thumb against the arch of her foot and smirked down at her. "Is that right?"

"I just thought—"

Her words were interrupted by the vibrating of my phone on the table, and we both turned to look at it. For a moment, we only stared. A call at this time of night would either be good news or bad—there was no in between.

Jana tried to pull her foot away as I leaned forward to pick it up, but I held fast, not wanting to break the connection between us. Con's name lit the screen, and I tapped the button to answer. "What's up?"

"How's everything down there?"

"So far, so good." Holding the phone between my shoulder and ear, I stretched out an arm and swiped the remote off the table. Jana tried to tug her foot away one more time, and she let out a soft protest as I yanked her closer to me. "How are things going on your end?"

"They brought Adam Sorenson in for questioning yesterday. The kid admitted to sending her notes, but denies anything threatening. They're running analysis of the handwriting now, so we'll know more soon. He did lawyer up, and he managed to make bond. First offense, and all."

Anger burned through me. It didn't surprise me, but I didn't like it. "Someone keeping an eye on him?"

"Yeah, I've got Sullivan doing random checks to make sure he doesn't try anything stupid. Apparently, they found more paraphernalia in his home that appeared to be stolen."

Asshole. "Tell me they're charging him."

"Larceny, at least. Maybe harassment. They've got her car in impound, but so far they haven't been able to find any evidence of him tampering with her brakes. They printed the bleeder valve but came up empty."

"Have any of those assholes ever heard of gloves?" I snapped.

"Yeah, yeah," he replied. "I know where you're going. But you can't make evidence just appear out of thin air. They need something concrete tying him to her accident in order to slap him with attempted murder. Otherwise..."

Con trailed off, and I snorted. "So, what happens next?"

"If they don't find any evidence?" He sighed. "He does a few months and is back out."

I growled. "That's bullshit!" I could feel Jana's gaze on me, but I ignored it.

"Preaching to the choir," he replied. "I don't make the rules. But at least Phelps said it seemed to scare the kid straight. Aside from pulling the lawyer in, he gave them the info they were looking for."

That wasn't much of a consolation. The kid could be lying

through his teeth. "So, six months and he'll be back to doing the same shit?"

I heard a harried sigh on the other end of the line. "One thing at a time. His arraignment is set for beginning of next week."

"Great," I grumbled.

"Anyway, that's why I was calling. Since the PD are pretty certain they've nailed their guy, you'll be able to come home the day after tomorrow. The studio wants her back here, but they plan to keep you on at her place for awhile until everything settles."

It made sense, but I dreaded our time here coming to an end. "I'll let her know."

"I'll email you the details."

Not waiting for anything else, I ended the call and tossed the phone onto the cushion next to me, then tipped my head back and stared at the ceiling.

"Everything okay?"

Jana's soft voice pulled me from my reverie, and I rolled my head to the side to look at her. "Yep. We go back in two days."

"Oh."

Yeah. I felt the same way. This time when she pulled away, I let her go. She pushed herself to a sitting position, perched on the edge of the couch, and sent a worried look my way. "So... what does that mean?"

"I'll stay on at your place until everything's settled."

Her tongue darted out and swiped nervously over her lower lip, and she let out a shaky breath. "Then what will you do? I mean... after?"

"My job, or us?"

She flicked her eyes my way, then dropped them back to her hands. "Us, I guess."

I reached out and turned her face toward mine. "We figure it out day by day."

Her gaze slid away again, and I pulled her into my lap. "Hey." I waited for her to meet my stare. "That's not me blowing you off. This is going to be a huge adjustment for both of us, so we'll just have to figure it out as we go. You'll start touring again in a couple months, and I probably won't be able to travel with you most of the time."

"You would come?"

Those big blue eyes drilled into me, and a vise tightened around my chest. I was quickly beginning to realize that I would do just about anything for this woman. "If I can get away from work for a bit, sure."

"But... will Con mind?"

I didn't honestly give a shit what he thought. "I'd prefer to stay out of the spotlight, but we can deal with one issue at a time."

She bit her lip. "I don't think he likes me very much."

"Too bad." I wasn't about to let go of her, not unless she chose to walk away. Hell, maybe not even then. I wasn't one to give up easily; I'd rather stay and fight it out than throw in the towel when things got tough. "I didn't say it was gonna be easy."

"I know." Her shoulders dropped. "I just don't want to put you in an awkward position."

"Don't you worry about me. One thing at a time," I reminded her. "Let's get home first, get settled, and figure out a routine from there."

"But—"

Technically, in the eyes of God and the law, we were married. Unless something crazy happened, I had absolutely zero intention of annulling the marriage. She was mine, damn it, and I was going to fight for her. I threw all my cards on the table. "I'm all in if you are."

Her giant blue eyes flared wide at my words. "Okay."

I stared at her, assessing her response. "Before you agree to anything, just know that I'm not letting you go. So, tell me—are you in?"

"Yes," she breathed. A smile broke over her face as she wound her arms around my neck. "I'm so in."

"Good." I stood, pulling her to my chest. Everything else could wait, but right now, I needed my woman in my arms—right where she belonged.

CHAPTER
THIRTY

JANA

When I woke, Vince was gone. The sounds of bustling from the direction of the main room reached my ears, and a smile lifted my lips. Rolling from the bed I changed into shorts and a tank top, then headed down the hall to the bathroom. Once I was done, I padded toward the kitchen to find him. I stopped at the end of the short hallway, stunned. Beach paraphernalia littered the floor of the living room, and Vince threw me a grin.

"What's this?" My gaze flicked over the colorful umbrella, beach chairs, and towels.

"It's our last day here," he replied with a nonchalant shrug. "I thought we could spend it at the beach."

"Really?" It sounded almost too good to be true.

As if reading my mind, Vince nodded and smiled. "I just got off the phone with Dane, who's keeping an eye on our guy back home. We're good to go out now."

A huge smile lit my face, and I bounced up onto the balls of my feet. "I'll go get changed!"

I turned and bolted back down the hall toward the bedroom, and quickly yanked on the first swimsuit I came to, which happened to be the red one Vince was so enamored of. Once I was ready, I headed back to the living room, where I found Vince sitting on the couch, an indulgent smile on his face. I threw him a repentant smile and moved between the vee of his legs. "I forgot to say good morning."

His hands moved to my hips, then slipped around to cup the cheeks of my bottom. "It is now."

Synchronized, we leaned toward one another, our lips meeting in a hot kiss. His mouth moved over mine, slow and seductive. There was no rush, just the tantalizing prospect of fulfillment and desire as his tongue moved over mine. He released me with a soft groan and patted my butt. "Unless you want to end up back in that bed, we better get moving."

It was tempting, but I wasn't going to pass up my opportunity to spend a day at the beach, just being myself. For the first time since we arrived, I didn't have to hide away in the house or conceal my identity. We could go out and enjoy the sights and each other.

I slid off his lap and grabbed his hand. "Can we have a picnic on the beach?"

He shrugged. "Whatever you want. We'll leave the food here so it stays cold then come back and get it at lunchtime."

I moved toward the beach stuff and hoisted the umbrella over my shoulder. "Where did you find all this stuff?"

"In the shed on the side of the house." He scooped up the two chairs, then flung the towels over his shoulder. "There was a note in the welcome package that said we could use anything available."

I stretched up on my toes and kissed him once more. "Thank you for doing this."

His hands were full, but he somehow invaded my space,

made me feel like he was wrapped around every inch of me. "Anything for you, trouble."

I smiled at the nickname. I was still worried about what would happen once we got home and back to our real lives, but I pushed the thoughts away as I moved toward the door and held it open for Vince. I locked up, then we headed down to the beach, scouting the perfect spot as we walked. We settled about halfway between the shore and the house so that the water wouldn't disturb our things when high tide came in.

Once we'd put the chairs in place, Vince slipped the house key from my fingers and put it in a zippered pocket of his swim shorts, then held out a hand. "Come in with me?"

"Sure." I tucked my fingers into his, and we headed down toward the ocean.

We waded into the cool, shallow water, and I sucked in a breath. Even in the bright sunlight, it didn't feel any warmer than it had the day we'd arrived. Goosebumps rose over my skin as I shuffled my feet the way Vince instructed, venturing deeper into the ocean until I was in up to my waist. Vince wasted no time ducking beneath the waves. He came back up, water sluicing over his muscles, the refraction of the droplets in the sunlight making his tattoos stand out even more.

Tearing my eyes away from him, I pointed to a spot further out where a handful of people stood and walked around. "What's that?"

Vince followed my gaze. "A sandbar."

"I didn't realize they had those here."

He eyed me. "You've seen one before?"

I nodded. "I used to play in the crick behind our house when I was little."

"Crick?" A teasing smile lifted the corners of his mouth, and I dropped my eyes away, cheeks burning.

I hated when my backwoods upbringing reared its ugly

head around Vince. He made me feel inadequate on the best of days, let alone when I slipped and said something supremely stupid like that.

Vince was older, and he seemed infinitely more mature and worldly than I would ever be. He'd traveled in the military to other countries and immersed himself in the various peoples and cultures. Though I traveled, too, I was barely allowed to leave the hotel, let alone do anything touristy.

I cleared my throat. "Creek," I corrected myself. "Gram always used to call it the crick, so it kind of just stuck."

"I wasn't laughing at you." He brushed a strand of hair off my cheek and tucked it behind my ear. "I've just never heard anyone else use that term before."

I tipped my head. "You've heard of it?"

"Sure." He nodded. "We grew up close to the Slippery Rock, and a lot of locals called it a crick, too."

I smiled, my insecurities melting away. "Good to know I'm not the only one."

"Nope." He gestured with his chin to the sandbar. "Want to swim out there?"

For the next couple of hours, we swam and frolicked in the surf, splashing and teasing each other between kisses. Around lunchtime, we staggered out of the water, exhausted. We collapsed on our towels and lay in the warm sun.

Once we were mostly dry, Vince brushed the backs of his fingers over my arm. "You hungry?"

I pushed from my chair. "Famished."

A trip back to the house yielded a cooler full of sandwiches, crackers and cheese, and bottled water, and we carried it back to our chairs where we ate picnic-style under the umbrella.

Full and sated, we collapsed back in our chairs and relaxed, watching the beachgoers around us. Vince turned to me. "Did you have fun here?"

I smiled back. "I did."

His expression turned serious. "I know it hasn't always been easy between us, but I'm glad this happened."

"Me, too," I agreed, already feeling my cheeks heat. "I mean, I'm sure you'd have preferred to skip the whole marriage thing, but—"

"No." He pushed his shades to the top of his head and regarded me. "I wouldn't change a thing. It's been unconventional, for sure, but..." He shook his head. "I like it."

My heart fluttered at his words, overshadowing the negative thoughts that kept creeping in. I knew going in that being married would complicate things in the long run, I just hadn't figured out how much. Could we actually make this work? The more time we spent together, the more I hoped the answer to that particular question was yes.

"It's been a long day," Vince said from my left, and I rolled my head toward him.

"It is. I'm kind of tired already."

His eyes darkened. "How about a nap?"

"Is that a code word for sex?"

He cracked a grin. "Bet your ass it is."

Like I was going to say no to that. I stood and gathered our things, then took his hand and happily allowed him to lead me inside.

CHAPTER
THIRTY-ONE

VINCE

I breathed deeply, pulling in the scent of the ocean air and Jana's unique scent lilting on the breeze. Her shoulder bumped mine as we walked, and I looped an arm around her waist, resting my hand on the curve of her hip.

She smiled up at me, hair whipping around her face, eyes alight with joy. I'd always thought her beautiful, but these past few days had revealed a beauty far deeper than skin. She was the most amazing woman I'd ever met, both inside and out.

I could leave here, carry out the terms of the original agreement and divorce her six months from now with no one the wiser. Except... I didn't want to. I would never regret the events that brought us together, because I never would have gotten to know her otherwise. This woman pushed me beyond the edge of reason, beyond control. And I fucking loved every minute of it. I wanted all of her, every day, every way.

Was it crazy that I already thought of her as my wife even though we'd only been together less than two weeks? Probably, but I didn't give a damn. I'd never done anything by half-measures, and I wasn't about to now. I think I knew the moment she asked me to marry her what my answer would be. I'd resisted initially, trying to find another solution for her sake. She was worried about me, but the truth was, I never would have married her if I didn't think this could work.

I hadn't said a word to her yet about how I felt. She had enough on her plate. All I could do was be there for her and show her I wasn't going anywhere. Slowly, I'd win her trust and make her see that this was more than just a fling.

Dusk was just beginning to fall as we stepped onto the pier. Side by side, we ambled toward the end, past another couple who barely noticed our presence. Jana and I shared a secret little smile as we passed, and I pressed my fingers into the flesh of her hip, pulling her even closer.

When we reached the end of the pier, Jana leaned her elbows on the railing and gazed out at the sky, a dark lapis now that the sun had dipped below the horizon. I placed my hands on either side of her and pressed against her back, holding her in place with my body.

She tilted her face up to mine, her teeth buried in her lower lip. "Can I ask you a silly question?"

"Of course."

"I was just wondering..." She pulled her phone from her back pocket and met my gaze again. "Can I take a picture with you? You know, to remember..."

"To remember our honeymoon?" I watched a slight blush spread over her cheeks, and I grinned. "You realize this is our first picture together?"

"Technically, it's our second," she said with a small smile, referring to our doctored engagement photo.

"Our first real photo together," I amended. As a general rule of thumb, it wasn't something I kept track of. I didn't give a shit about pictures—normally. But everything about

Jana was different. My mind drew back to the photo Abby had taken, to the look in Jana's eyes. I wanted a lifetime of moments just like those.

"Here." I took the phone from her fingers, made sure the flash was turned on, then held it out in front of us. I kissed her temple just as I snapped the photo, then passed the phone back to her.

She smiled when she saw it, then tucked her phone away again. "Thank you."

I dipped my head and spoke next to her ear so she could hear me over the breeze. "Was the beach everything you thought it would be?"

She tipped her head up to me. "It's so much better than I dreamed."

"It's a helluva view."

"It is," she agreed as she turned in my arms. "But that's not what made it great."

Her eyes dropped to my lips, and I moved in closer. "Yeah?"

She nodded. "It wouldn't have been the same without you."

I studied her face. From the very beginning, she'd intrigued me. She was headstrong and exasperating, smart and incredible. We'd had our difficulties, and just like any other couple, I was sure there would be more rough patches ahead. But there was no one I'd rather be with than Jana. I slid my hand around the back of her neck. "I really like you."

Long lashes swept down over her eyes as she blinked up at me. "I really like you, too."

I slanted my mouth over hers, claiming, possessing. My mind and heart finally seemed to be on the same page, and I had no intention of slowing down or pulling back now. From here on out, it was full steam ahead. I wanted her, and she wanted me; that was all that mattered. We would work out all the other details later.

Several long minutes later, we broke the kiss and I took her hand. "We should get back so we can pack."

We turned to leave, and I was momentarily brought up short by the darkness. "Strange."

Both lights at the entrance of the pier were off, and we moved by the light of the thin crescent moon. A prickling sensation raced up the back of my neck, and I paused at the end of the pier, looking around for the source of discomfort. Something glinted in the sand at my feet, and I released Jana's hand so I could stoop down for a closer look.

Pulling out my phone, I used the flashlight function to light the area. Fragments of opaque white glass stuck up from the sand, and I lifted my gaze to the lamp attached to the pier. Standing, I stretched my phone upward to get a closer look. The base of the bulb was still screwed into the fixture, but the glass had been shattered.

"Probably some kids," Jana commented, picking up on what I was doing.

"Maybe," I said softly as I crossed to the other side. A rock lay next to the broken glass of the second bulb, and my gut clenched with dread. I stowed my phone in my back pocket and laced my fingers through hers. "Come on."

Jana was probably right. More than likely, it was a harmless prank by some kids. My head swiveled left and right the whole way back to the house, unable to kick the unease swirling in my stomach. I held the gate for her as we stepped onto the patio, and I handed over the key. "I'll get the stuff put away, then I'll be in."

I should have handled the pool stuff earlier, but Jana and I had fallen into bed after lunch and hadn't resurfaced until dinnertime. The storage shed was in the corner of the yard, so I could keep an eye on her while I got the stuff put away.

"TV and chill?" She tossed me a teasing smile, and I hardened.

"Definitely."

I grabbed our towels, all the while watching as she moved toward the door. I breathed a soft sigh of relief as she unlocked it and stepped inside, then closed the door behind her. Moving quickly, I grabbed the folding chairs and umbrella and stowed them in the shed. I snapped the combination lock into place, and a whisper of sound had my ears perking up. I turned a second too late, and pain exploded across my scalp as the object connected with my skull.

I tried to yell out as I fell, but my mouth refused to work. My last thought was of Jana, vulnerable and unprotected, before everything went black.

CHAPTER
THIRTY-TWO

JANA

I headed inside, a huge smile on my face that I just couldn't shake—and I didn't want to. Things between Vince and me were better than ever, and I could no longer ignore the fact that I was falling for him.

I was still worried about what would happen once we got home, though. We were legally married, but he could decide anytime that I wasn't good enough, or that he didn't want to be part of my lifestyle.

Everything in my life had finally begun to fall into place, and I felt like I was waiting for the other shoe to drop. I loved my career, but I was starting to love Vince just as much. I couldn't imagine life without him. Nothing ever went this well for me, and I didn't want to have to choose between the two.

I'd thought more than once about abandoning the spotlight, maybe transitioning to voice coach or songwriter. My contract stated I would have to complete next year's tour, but after that... Who knew what would happen by then? Like

Vince said, we would see what happened and reevaluate when the time came. As long as he was with me, I could figure out the rest later.

I closed the door behind me but left it unlocked for Vince to come in once he was done. We had left the lamp on before we went for our walk, and I allowed the soft yellow light to guide me down the hall to the bedroom. I tossed my sweater on the bed, and the sound of the sliding door opening and then closing drifted toward my ears. A smile curled my lips as I headed back out to find Vince.

I hoped tonight would be a replay of last night. A few minutes of TV, followed by hours of lovemaking. And talking —I'd never enjoyed talking to another person as much as I liked talking with Vince. I felt like I could share anything without him judging me.

He was the only person aside from Maggie that I'd ever told about my mother and my upbringing back in Kentucky. I didn't know how I'd ever gotten lucky enough to catch Vince's eye, but I didn't want to let him go.

As soon as I exited the hallway, a movement from the right caught my attention, and less than a second later, a huge palm clapped over my mouth as an arm banded around my middle like steel. I instinctively froze at the menacing voice.

"Don't fucking move."

Despite the training I'd done with Vince, my mind went blank, and I couldn't force my muscles to move. A combination of fear and helplessness washed over me and I fought to clear my head. Where was Vince? Was he okay? My phone was in my back pocket, but I couldn't use it until I got away from the man. I needed to get free and find Vince so we could get away, call for help.

I couldn't believe the asshole had found me here. Anger rose up, propelling me into action, and I fought wildly to escape my attacker's hold. I elbowed him in the stomach and was rewarded with a low grunt of pain. I heard Vince's voice in the back of my mind, reminding me of how to evade someone. *Soft spots, Jana,* he'd told me time and again.

Throwing my other fist downward, I aimed for the man's groin. He moved just in time, and the side of my hand connected with his upper thigh. I immediately kicked backward with my other foot and felt my heel connect with the man's knee. He let out a harsh curse and his hold around my waist loosened, his hand dropping away from my face as he stumbled.

It was enough to get free, and I bolted across the room. "Vince!"

Shit. Where the hell was he?

Just as I grabbed for the door handle that led to the patio, I was yanked back roughly by my hair. Pain exploded across my scalp, and I let out a stifled shriek. I fought against him, kicking over a chair as he dragged me toward the living room.

Half-turning, I threw myself against him as hard as I could, punching and kicking anywhere I could reach. The man and I collapsed to the side in a heap, knocking the end table over and sending the lamp to the floor with a crash. The light was extinguished, and for a split second, we both froze.

My lungs heaved with exertion, but I refused to give up. Trapped underneath him on my back, I fought like a wet cat, scratching at his face, trying to jab him in the eyes. A string of muffled curses met my ears, and I blinked in surprise when the overhead light flipped on.

"What the hell is going on here?"

I swiveled my head toward the very familiar, very feminine voice. Relief coursed through me as the woman came into view. "Maggie! Help me!"

She didn't spare me a glance, just glared at the man. "What the hell is taking so long? You said you had this under control."

What the fuck? I could only stare at her, trying to understand what the hell was happening. Just as her words registered, the man delivered an open-palmed slap to the side of my head. My skull connected with the floor, sending a shower of stars dancing in front of my eyes and pain slicing across my face.

"Didn't expect her to put up such a fight," the man said as he deftly caught the roll of duct tape Maggie tossed to him.

I tried to fight back, but I was no match for the heavy weight on top of me. The man quickly bound my hands, and I frantically searched my mind for something—anything—to save me. I'd tried everything Vince had taught me—except my last resort. Opening my mouth and relaxing my throat, I screamed, long and loud.

"Christ!" A heavy fist connected with my head again, and I went limp as the room dipped and swirled before my eyes. The man slapped a layer of duct tape over my mouth, then lifted me in his arms.

"Hurry the hell up." Maggie yanked open the front door, and I glared at her through my swollen eyes as we passed. The man tossed me in the backseat, then crawled in behind me and slammed the door shut.

Maggie hopped in the driver seat, and I glanced through the rearview window at the house. I tore my gaze away, my heart jumping into my throat as the engine cranked and the car lurched into gear, then sped forward.

Where the hell were they taking me? And why? Even though it had felt like a lifetime, I knew it couldn't have been more than four or five minutes that we'd spent wrestling on the floor inside. What worried me was that Vince hadn't come to my aid—and I couldn't begin to contemplate what that meant.

CHAPTER
THIRTY-THREE

VINCE

I came to, and a soft groan met my ears. Belatedly, I realized it had come from me. The ground beneath me felt hard and rough, and my head ached like a bitch.

Bracing my hands on the brick patio, I levered myself up and pushed to my knees. I gingerly touched the back of my head and found my fingers sticky with blood when I pulled them away. What the hell had happened?

My mind felt foggy, still in a daze, and I lifted my eyes to the small bungalow. I remembered that Jana and I had gone for a walk after dinner. I told her to go back inside while I grabbed the towels and stuff we'd left out earlier in the day. She'd stepped into the house, and then…

Shit. Someone must've sneaked up on me in the dark. They'd obviously hit me hard enough to draw blood and apparently knock me out. I'd hoped it was for only a few seconds, but I couldn't tell. Focusing on my surroundings, I lurched to my feet and took an unsteady step toward the house. What I heard from inside made my blood run cold. Voices—plural.

Shaking off the pain, I launched myself toward the patio door and threw it open. "Jana?"

My frantic question was met with no response, and I quickly took in the destruction of the room. One of the dining chairs was kicked over, and the end table next to the couch had been toppled, the lamp shattered in a dozen pieces on the tile floor.

From outside, a car engine started, and I bolted toward the front door. "Jana!"

I flung it open and stumbled out just in time to see the red of the tail lights fading into the dark as it rounded the turn. I yanked the phone from my back pocket. Not bothering with 911, I called the chief of police. As soon as he answered, I launched in with no preamble. "My name is Vince Incarnato, and someone just abducted Jana Malone from the rental we've been staying in. We can't let her off this island."

I knew Con had been in contact with the local police in case the worst happened, and I prayed that they would respond quickly.

Chief Rutland swore softly. "How long ago?"

"Just now." I started to rake one hand through my hair, then grimaced at the pain and dropped it back to my side. "They were in a small sedan, maybe a Honda or Toyota."

"Let me get the bridges shut down, and I'll call you back. Is this a good number?"

"Yes," I replied tersely.

The chief didn't respond as he hung up, presumably to dispatch patrolmen to lock down the island. I tapped the first number on my speed dial, then waited for Con to answer.

"What's up, Ink?"

"He's got her," I said, my voice breaking as a strange

emotion strangled my throat. "The bastard knocked me out and took her."

Perpetually calm, Con jumped right into protocol. "Have you been in contact with the police?"

"Just hung up with them."

"Good."

"I'll reach out to Phelps over here and see what's going on with Adam Sorenson."

"Thanks—wait! Her phone!" I didn't know why it hadn't occurred to me before. Probably because my mind was still muddled from the blow to my head. "She had her phone on her tonight."

"Is it still on?"

"I don't know." I couldn't help the sudden spark of hope that filled my chest. "We went for a walk on the beach right before this all happened, and I know it was on then because she was taking pictures. If it's still on her..."

"Might be a long shot, but I'll see if Doyle can work some magic."

Jason Doyle was a tech wizard Con had managed to snatch up when the man left the FBI field office in Chicago a few months ago. I prayed that the signal was active and that he would be able to trace her whereabouts—at least in the general vicinity. Anything was better than nothing.

I hung up feeling slightly more optimistic than I had a few minutes ago, and I stomped toward the kitchen. Grabbing a handful of paper towels from the holder, I slapped them against the back of my head. The flow of blood from the wound seemed to have slowed, but I was still feeling light-headed.

I strode through the house, trying to stay away from the scene of the struggle as much as possible while still taking in every detail. I couldn't fucking believe I'd let this happen. It was the second time Jana had been hurt on my watch, and I berated myself for not catching it sooner. Memories of that most recent letter came back to me, and my gut twisted with dread. If he got her alone, made it past the police, he could take her anywhere secluded to carry out his awful plan.

I should've been paying attention out by the pool; I should've heard the asshole coming. Instead, I'd been so wrapped up in thoughts of Jana that I hadn't been able to focus on anything else.

I gave my head a rueful shake. I would never forgive myself if we didn't bring her back safely. She'd come to mean so much to me in such a short period of time, but I still sometimes had difficulty reconciling my emotions. What I did know was that I couldn't let her go. I had to find her. The alternative was not an option.

I didn't know exactly what had transpired when she'd entered the house, but I assumed that the man had knocked me out, then gone after Jana. Would she have had time to change? I made for the bedroom and flipped on the light, my gaze sweeping over the room. The bed was still unmade, the covers flipped back and the pillows askew from our romp this afternoon.

My heart clenched, but I forced myself to focus. I didn't see her phone anywhere—not on the bed, not on the nightstand or dresser. I found her purse on the floor and rooted through it but came up empty. I hoped that meant she'd still had it on her when she was abducted. If we could even get one triangulation, a hint of where they were headed...

My phone rang, tearing me from my thoughts, and I answered without looking at the screen. "Yeah?"

Chief Rutland's voice came across the line. "I've got checkpoints at both bridges, and a third on the main road headed to Longboat Key. If they haven't made it out yet, they're not going to."

Relief and dread mingled in my chest, making it hard to

breathe. "What do we do now?" I had to do something. I couldn't just sit around and wait.

"I'm almost to your place now," Rutland replied. "We'll talk in person."

Almost as soon as I hung up, the sound of a car engine registered, and it slowed to a stop in front of the house, then cut off. I threw open the door just as Rutland was climbing out of the cruiser. I tipped my head toward the living room. "Come on in."

His gaze flicked over me, still holding the paper towels to my head, before dropping to the battered furniture strewn over the living room. He skirted the damage and headed toward the kitchen. I followed just a step behind him, and he searched for a light switch, then flipped it on and turned to me. "You hurt?"

I pulled the towels away from my head and made a face at the blood I found there. "I'm sure it'll be fine. Head wounds tend to bleed like a bitch anyway."

Rutland's lips pressed together in a firm line as he made a circular motion with his finger. "Turn." I tossed the towels on the counter and did as he asked. He made a low humming sound in the back of his throat. "Might need stitches for that one."

I threw a scowl over my shoulder at him. "I'm not going to waste time in some hospital getting stitches while my girl is gone."

Rutland inspected me shrewdly. "Tell me what happened."

I heaved a breath and told him everything I could remember. "I was still out on the patio when Jana went inside. I was locking the cabinet on the side of the house when someone must've snuck up on me and bashed me in the back of the head. The next thing I remember was waking up and hearing voices from inside. By the time I made it into the house, they were already getting in the car."

I told him what she'd been wearing and my speculations about her phone. "She might still have it on her. One of our guys is working on tracing it if it's still active."

Rutland was already pulling his phone from his back pocket. He relayed the information I had just imparted, then requested a medic be sent to the house. I slanted a look at him. "Tell me what I can do."

Not bothering with false hope or worthless platitudes, Rutland gave a slight shake of his head. "Give it some time. My guys are checking every car leaving the island and watching for anything that looks suspicious."

I growled low in my throat. "That doesn't really help."

"There's no magic formula to these," he replied.

He was a straight shooter, I would give him that. Although I knew he was telling the truth, I fucking hated the answer. My girl was out there somewhere—and I would tear this island apart to find her if I had to.

CHAPTER
THIRTY-FOUR

JANA

Maggie whipped the car around a turn, and I was thrown sideways under the force of the acceleration. The man, Carl, roughly gripped my biceps to yank me upright. I wriggled in place till I was sitting and tried to pull away from him, but his hold was too strong.

Maggie drove within the speed limit, careful not to draw undue attention to us. I could see her reflection in the rearview mirror, and I glared at her. She'd been my best friend, the closest thing I had to a sister, for nearly two years when we'd sung backup for Christina Tucker together. I couldn't begin to imagine what had possessed her to do this.

A set of flashing red and blue lights through the windshield caught my attention, and my heart gave a hard thump in my chest. *The police.* From the driver seat, Maggie swore.

"Relax," Carl spoke up. "Just drive normal."

The officer sped by, headed in the opposite direction, and despair settled over me. Deep down, I'd been hoping that

Vince had called the police and they were already on the way to save me. Less than twenty seconds later, another car whizzed by.

"Carl?" There was no mistaking the worry in her voice this time.

"Follow them," Carl directed.

Maggie's head whipped around to look at him. "Are you crazy?"

"Do it." His tone was hard and commanding, and Maggie reluctantly slowed the car, then turned at the next intersection. My heart thumped erratically as we circled back around and fell in behind the police, who were now far in front of us.

Red and blue lights pierced the dark night sky, heralding their position. As we got closer, I could see several police cruisers blocking off the road to the south end of the island that led to Long Boat Key, as well as the bridge back to the mainland.

"They're shutting down the island," Carl said softly. "Turn right up here and head back to the house."

Maggie did as he said, but I watched her fingers clench around the steering wheel. I could tell she was nervous, worried about being caught. Maybe I could use that to my advantage. Carl was definitely the one in charge here. I would have to isolate Maggie and see if I could talk some sense into her.

I watched our surroundings as Maggie wound her way through the side streets before turning back onto the main drag and heading toward the very tip of the island. A few minutes later, she turned left toward the beach and pulled to a stop along the side of what appeared to be a small condo complex.

The only light came from a street lamp on the corner; there seemed to be no life within any of the units. Judging from the shape of the building, I guessed there to be at least three condos. With the windows dark, it was hard to tell. They were either uninhabited during this slow season, or the occupants were out enjoying themselves. I prayed they were just out and would be returning soon.

Carl threw open the door, then grabbed my arm and hauled me out behind him. I didn't have time to move my feet, and I fell from the car, landing on my hands and knees on the rough pavement. My cry of pain was muffled behind the duct tape covering my mouth, and he picked me up like a toddler and set me on my feet. One hand fisted in the back of my shirt, he marched me forward, toward the door on the right side of the complex.

Maggie unlocked the door, and Carl led me through the dark condo. I stumbled a couple of times, bumping into furniture, and Carl roughly jerked me around until we reached a room at the very back of the unit. Lit only by the faint glow of the streetlight filtering through a small, frosted glass window, I could tell that it was a bathroom.

"Don't move."

I automatically stiffened as I felt Carl's hands landed on my hips and swept over my backside. My heart fell as he plucked the phone from my back pocket, then stepped away. Damn. I was hoping he would be too focused on everything else to think of checking for a phone. Now that I couldn't call for help, I'd have to come up with another plan.

"Get in." Following his directions, I clumsily stepped into the bathtub with its tiled surround. "Sit."

My body screamed at me to fight back, but there was nothing I could do. There was no way for me to escape—not without the use of my hands.

"Now!"

I jumped and did as he instructed. He pulled the roll of duct tape from his sweatshirt pocket and bound my feet together. He grabbed my hair and directed my gaze to his. Fear gripped me as his dead eyes stared into mine. "Don't try anything stupid."

He seemed to be waiting for a response, so I nodded using the limited range of motion with my hair still held in his firm grasp. He searched my face for another long moment, gave a curt nod and released me, then pushed to his feet and left. A sigh filtered through my nose, and I briefly closed my eyes, grateful that he hadn't tried to hurt me—yet. That at least bought me some time.

With him now gone, I took a look around. There was no paraphernalia on the shelves of the shower, nor was there anything on the vanity. It looked completely bare, as if they had either just arrived or were planning to leave. My heart kicked into overdrive at the realization. Best case scenario, they would try to ransom me. But as soon as the thought crossed my mind, I knew that wasn't the case.

Dread settled in my gut. I'd already seen their faces—they would have to get rid of me so I couldn't identify them. I didn't know how deeply involved Maggie was, so I discarded my earlier idea of trying to appeal to her sense of reason. That left only one option—escape.

Since it was dark, I hadn't been able to make out most of the condo when we came in. From the layout, I assumed it was small, maybe one or two bedrooms, just like the house Vince and I were staying in. My gaze drifted toward the small window on the wall to my left.

Rectangular in shape, maybe a foot and a half tall by three feet wide, it opened by sliding the pane sideways. There was a lock in the middle, but no screen that I could see. It was incredibly narrow for a normal person, but if I contorted myself just right, I might be able to slip through. I would have to go out face first, since there was no stool or anything to climb up on inside. Doing so ran the risk of me falling on my head outside, but I would have to gamble it.

I wiggled experimentally, testing the tape around my wrists and ankles. Vince had taught me self-defense, but we hadn't discussed escaping bonds. I'd heard once that duct tape would break fairly easily, but I'd never tried it. No time like the present.

Out in the man living area, I heard the soft jingle of a commercial on TV, and I mentally crossed my fingers, hoping it would drown out any noise I was about to make. Keeping one ear tuned to the outer room, I quietly placed my hands on the edge of the tub and maneuvered my feet into position beneath me.

My feet were bare, and I prayed they wouldn't slide out from under me when I tried to stand. Slowly contracting my muscles, I levered myself to my feet, inch by agonizing inch.

Hands and feet bound tight, I debated my next option. The floor of the bathtub was fairly slick, and I didn't want to risk falling down in here and cracking my head. There was a little more room to move around beside the vanity and toilet, but that meant I would have to get over the edge of the tub. A towel bar was anchored to the wall to my left, but it was too far away to grab.

Praying for the best, I sat on the edge of the tub and tested my balance. Leaning my back against the tiled wall, I slowly lifted my feet until they rested on the edge of the tub. My stomach muscles ached from the effort, and I took a short break. Shifting my weight, I rolled so that my left shoulder was against the wall then dropped my feet to the floor. My bare flesh landed with a soft slap, and I froze, listening for the tell-tale sounds of someone coming.

Thirty seconds passed with no indication that either one of them had heard, and I breathed a sigh of relief. Now I just had to get out of the duct tape and hope that the window opened. Shuffling toward the middle of the room, I drew back on what I'd read. If I lifted my hands over my head and pulled them down quickly on either side of my legs, it should put enough pressure on the tape to break.

Steeling myself, I lifted my hands up in the air, then breathed out and brought them down quickly. My wrist bone glanced off my kneecap, and I bit back a cry of pain as the tape tugged on my skin. I was rewarded at least with a tiny ripping sound, so I tried again.

Lifting my hands over my head a second time, I threw them downward, angling my arms out to the side at the last minute. For a moment, I didn't think it had worked. Then I felt the feathery caress of duct tape tickle my palm, and I realized with a giddy sense of glee that my hands were free. It had made a God-awful noise though, and I listened once again for Maggie and Carl to come running.

Nothing happened, and my heart began to beat frantically with a combination of hope and adrenaline. I sat down and quickly began to unravel the tape around my ankles, then yanked the tape off my face with a soft cry. My lips and cheeks stung, and tears popped into my eyes, but I brushed them off and began to attack the window.

I flipped the lock up and yanked as hard as I could to slide it open. For a second, it resisted. Then finally, blessedly, the swollen wood slid open an inch. Propelled by determination and fear, I muscled it the rest of the way open and popped my hands on the lip.

I braced my toes on the wall and managed to get my torso up and through the opening. The rough wood scraped my shoulder, but I gritted my teeth and pushed on. Outside, the familiar calls of frogs and insects met my ears, along with the sound of laughter from a few streets over.

I wiggled myself most of the way through, but my hips got stuck just as I heard footsteps squeaking along the tile floor of the condo, each one growing louder as the person neared the bathroom. All of a sudden, the door flew open and the lights came on.

"Goddamn it!"

I kicked my feet wildly, trying to push myself the rest of the way through the window. But Carl was too fast, too strong. He grabbed me and yanked me backward, scraping my stomach and chest as he dragged me back into the bathroom.

"Help!" I screamed. "Over here!" Vince's words came back to me, and I switched tactics. "Fire! Help, fire!"

Carl's hand connected with the side of my face, and I stumbled to the floor. He slammed the window shut and locked it, then grabbed my hair and yanked. My feet slipped on the cool tile floor as I tried to keep up with him while he dragged me toward the living room. I let out a grunt of pain when he dropped me to the floor, then backhanded me again.

Stars danced in front of my eyes, and spittle splattered over my cheeks as he leaned close and spoke. "Stupid little bitch. I'm going to make you regret that."

CHAPTER
THIRTY-FIVE

I prowled around the living area like a caged panther and ran my fingers through my hair for what seemed like the hundredth time since Rutland and the medic had left ten minutes ago. The wound on the back of my head had been cleaned, but I'd refused to go to the hospital as they'd suggested.

I tried to stay out of the way as a few officers milled around the small house, lifting prints and analyzing the scene. A sick sense of helplessness rose up as my gaze landed once more on the overturned furniture and broken lamp. Every second that passed without word of Jana was pure agony, and I was ready to scream.

My phone rang, and I snatched it from my back pocket, already sliding my thumb over the screen before the caller's name registered. "Yeah?" I barked out.

"Sorenson is a no-go," Con replied.

I let out a swift curse. "Are you sure?"

"Positive. Sullivan's got him under surveillance, and he says the guy hasn't left his house all afternoon."

Fuck. Who the hell else could it be?

"I've reached out to Phelps to see if he has any new information," Con said. "He did tell me that analysis on the handwriting came back, and they've officially ruled out Sorensen writing the three threatening letters."

My heart hit the floor around my feet. "So we're definitely looking for someone else then."

"Looks that way," Con replied grimly. "His prints were found on the love letters, and all seven of those were postmarked from the same place. The other three letters show no trace of fingerprints, partial or otherwise, and each was postmarked from a different location."

I thought on that for a second. Someone was definitely trying to cover their tracks.

"We need to figure out who else may have a grudge against her," Con continued. "Any ideas?"

I frowned at the question. Looking at it objectively, I had to admit that there were probably several people out there who despised Jana on principle, whether they were in the music industry or just part of the general populace. It was irrational for a normal person to hold that much of a grudge against Jana just for being popular and successful, but stranger things had happened. Jealousy and inferiority fueled all kinds of negative feelings which could bubble to the surface.

"Not off the top of my head. Anything on social media?" I questioned.

"Nothing out of the ordinary that Doyle has found," he replied. "But that's kind of like searching for a needle in a haystack. Her assistant handles all of her stuff, right?"

I nodded. "I believe so."

"Let's reach out to her and see if she's seen or heard

anything strange and go from there. She may even know someone who might wish Ms. Malone harm."

"I can't imagine. I think the police have already questioned her."

"Never know," Con said. "Sometimes people think of things after the fact."

"Fair enough. I'll try to get a hold of her and get some answers."

I hoped Maggie would be able to help as I clicked over to my contacts and dialed her number. I waited impatiently as it rang several times, then rolled over to voicemail. The hair on the back of my neck stood on end, and unease slithered through me. It wasn't like Maggie to not answer her phone. In fact, I don't think I'd ever seen her without it in hand. Unease quickly turned to alarm as my second phone call went unanswered.

I dialed a third time, grimacing as it too went to voicemail. Shit. What if something had happened to her, too? Disconnecting the call, I tapped Con's number, and he answered on the second ring. "What'd you find out?"

"I can't get a hold of Maggie. Can we get someone over there to check on her?"

There was a beat of silence on his end. "Are you sure we should be chasing that right now?"

Anger engulfed me. "If someone thought Maggie knew where Jana was, what's to say they didn't go after her, too?"

"All right, I'll get someone on it," Con promised. "Keep trying her and see if she's just tied up."

I made a face. It was a poor choice of words, considering the mental images flashing through my brain. "I can't fucking sit here with nothing to do. Tell me how we can find Jana."

"I don't know, Ink." Con's voice was uncharacteristically softened by sympathy. "Rutland will take care of it. I spoke with him just before you called back. He's got the island locked down, so no one's getting in or out without being checked over. They've got guys on patrol, too. They'll find her."

"Right." I ended the call and dropped my chin to my chest. I wished I could be as confident as he sounded. But this was Jana we were talking about. My girl was missing, and I needed to find her before that crazy fuck hurt her.

I swore I would find whoever was responsible for this— then I'd bring all kinds of hell down on them.

CHAPTER
THIRTY-SIX

JANA

I glared at Carl as he tightened the duct tape around my waist, securing me to the chair. My hands were bound again, behind me this time, and my ankles were duct taped to each leg of the chair.

"There." He stood and threw a look over his shoulder at Maggie, who sat on the couch, one leg crossed over the other, watching us impassively. "I'll be back in a couple minutes."

He disappeared out the front door, and I willed Maggie to look at me. Finally, she did. I cursed behind the tape covering my mouth, and she let out a cold laugh. "Poor Jana. Can't sweet talk your way out of this, can you?"

What the hell are you talking about? Why are you doing this? I screamed the words from behind my gag, but Maggie just glared at me, her foot bouncing impatiently in the air.

"Is that supposed to make me feel bad for you?" She stared at me for a long moment before hopping to her feet and shoving her face in front of mine. "After everything you've done, you deserve this and so much worse."

My eyes widened in question. What the hell did I ever do to her? I voiced the question in my mind, but my words were muffled once again behind the tape. Maggie's eyes dropped to my mouth, and she grabbed a corner, then ripped it off with no finesse.

I jerked back, pain exploding over my face. *Damn it*. The first time had sucked, and the second time wasn't any better. "Why are you doing this?" I choked out through numb lips.

Maggie grabbed an oak chair from the table beside us and spun it around, straddling the seat so she was facing me. "Your life, everything you've done over the past two years"—her eyes bored into mine—"that should be me. I was on track to be Magnolia Way's next top star before you showed up."

"What are you talking about?" I asked. "You said you wanted out, that you—"

"I lied," she snapped. "The second they looked at you, listened to you sing, they threw my ass right out the door."

"I—If I'd known—" The music industry was cutthroat; she knew that. I wasn't honestly sure there was anything I could have done differently. It wasn't as if I were the one to turn her down.

"As if that wasn't bad enough," she snapped, "then you had to steal Jackson, too."

I gaped at her. "Jackson Meyers?"

"He was mine!" She screamed, her index finger jabbing inches from my face. "You took everything from me!"

I shook my head. "Maggie, I swear—I never wanted—"

"Don't give me that," she barked. "I despised you the moment I laid eyes on you. So pretty and perfect, exactly what they wanted. I lost everything because of you." She glared at me. "We'll see how much you like it when I take away everything that matters most to you."

My stomach revolted at the thought. I couldn't believe that Maggie, the woman I'd considered my closest friend for the past two years, was capable of something so heinous. I glared at her. "How could you do this? We were friends!"

"We were never friends," she scoffed.

Her revelation stunned me. "You offered to be my assistant. Said you still want to be involved!"

She left out a peal of laughter. "So I could be close to you, you idiot. I had to use any opportunity available to me to make your life miserable."

"Don't be stupid," I warned. "You're going to get caught, and you're going to take that guy"—I used my head to gesture toward the door—"down with you."

"Oh, no. He's looking forward to this just as much as I am." She smirked. "Funny how fate has a way of sending people your way exactly when you need them."

I racked my brain, trying to figure out if I knew the man but came up blank. He looked familiar, but I couldn't place him. Dismissing it for the moment, I changed tacks.

"So, what? You kill me. Then what happens?" I lifted a brow at her. "You've been out of the game too long. Do you really think Magnolia Way will pick you up again? They won't want to invest that kind of time and money in you. They didn't want to do it the first time. What makes you think they'll do it now?"

I knew I had hit her where it hurt the most, because her eyes darkened with fury, and she let out a hiss. "You evil bitch."

I laughed. "Awfully ironic, coming from you. You're the one willing to commit murder because you weren't talented enough."

"I swear—" Her hand flew out and wrapped around my throat, her nails digging into my skin. I winced and tried to jerk back, but my body was hampered, tied to the chair. "I won't miss having you gone," she snapped. "Being your fucking gopher, keeping track of your phone calls and appointments. I deserve so much more than this."

Releasing me, she sat back in her chair and rolled her neck from side to side, like she was trying to relieve the tension from her muscles. She drew a deep breath, and centered her gaze on me again. "But none of that matters now. Since you decided to take everything away from me, I found a way to get it back."

The way she said it sent a little chill down my spine. "What do you mean?"

A vicious smile lifted one corner of her mouth. "Does Carl look familiar to you?"

I hadn't paid much attention before, but now I drew his face into focus, paying attention to each detail of his face. She was right; there was something familiar about his blue eyes. What was it? "I know him," I whispered. I could feel it in my bones.

Maggie made a little sound in the back of her throat. "You don't know him, exactly. But he knows you—rather, he knew of you. Ever hear of the six degrees of separation?"

I nodded slowly, warily, and she continued. "After that whole ordeal with Jackson, I found myself at a bar one night, debating what to do. I was so furious with you, and I couldn't help but vent to the man next to me. Turns out Carl"—a huge smile stretched over her face—"spent some time in Kentucky a couple decades ago."

I felt like I was floundering. I would have been a kid; how the hell would I have known him back then? Cold suddenly settled over me as memories of Mama's men came flashing back in rapid succession. Dozens of nameless faces that I rarely paid attention to.

"Shame that your mom was such a slut." Maggie tsked. "She really should've made sure you knew who your daddy was."

The implication slammed into me like a lightning bolt, throwing me back in the chair and temporarily stealing my breath. "What are you saying?"

"I'm saying," she spoke slowly, "it was incredibly fortunate that you never changed your will. With your mother in jail, guess who has access to your life insurance payout?"

I blinked several times, my mind working furiously. The last time Mama and I had spoken, she had told me she was no longer seeing Burt. Instead, she was back with my father. *Carl.* "Did he...?"

"Set her up? Like it was hard to have her arrested." Maggie rolled her eyes. "Why would the cops believe her, given her history?"

Anger burned through me. "And my car? That was you, too?"

"You made it so easy." She shook her head almost bemusedly. "You were too lazy to use actual keys for your house, so they just sat in the drawer. You know"—she sat forward, her intense stare pinning me in place—"I kept them for almost a week, just to see if you'd notice. You never did." She shook her head as she stared at me. "I mean, really. How stupid are you?"

A combination of rage and humiliation curled in my gut, turning my body hot. "You know Vince won't let it go until justice has been served. They'll find you."

"They'll find someone." Maggie shrugged again, completely unconcerned. "With that idiot sending the stupid love notes, I figured that was as good a way as any to get rid of you for once and for all." She let out a little laugh. "I thought those recipes were a nice touch, didn't you?"

My stomach twisted in disgust. It only proved how absolutely insane she was. "You hate me this much—to kill me and risk going to jail?"

"Yes—and we won't be going to jail." She waved a hand in

the air. "They'll look at the man who sent you notes, just like we intended. They'll arrest him, and that will be that."

They would send an innocent man to jail? Of course they would, I thought bitterly. They planned to kill me for money; they wouldn't hesitate to take down anyone in their way. "How the hell will you explain being here?" Something else occurred to me at that moment, too. "And how did you know where I was?"

"Well, that's an easy one. You called me."

"So?" What the hell did that matter?

"So..." She dragged out the word. "I've had one of those tracker apps on your phone for months now. When you finally turned your phone back on..."

She trailed off, and angry tears stung my eyes. In turning to her for advice, I'd unwittingly led her straight to us. "I hope you enjoy it while it lasts," I snapped. "Money isn't everything."

"No, it's not." Maggie tipped her head to one side. "But it sure as hell makes life a little better."

"You're—" Fear ricocheted through me as I heard the scrape of heavy feet against the pavement outside. Maggie slapped the tape over my mouth once more, then moved toward the kitchen just as the door swung open.

Carl stepped inside, and I couldn't tear my eyes away as he closed the door behind him and met my gaze. I still couldn't believe this man was my father. Now that I looked at him— really looked at him—I saw the similarities. The same blue eyes, the same basic facial structure. I'd never before realized how little I resembled Mama. Maybe that was why she'd despised me so much. It had to be hell on her to have a little girl who looked exactly like the man who'd skipped out on her.

Tears clouded my vision. It was ironic, almost. I'd spent a good portion of my life wondering about my father; this was the first and last time I would ever see him. I knew he had absolutely no emotional connection to me whatsoever, but how the hell could any parent do this to their child—and for money?

I'd cut Mama off because of her greed and self-sabotaging ways. But Carl—the father I'd never known—felt zero compunction killing me for a hundred thousand dollars. I wanted to demand answers, but the tape over my mouth prevented me from doing so.

His cold eyes jumped between Maggie and me, then back to her. "Everything good here?"

I twisted my head to look at Maggie as she held up a bottle of cleaning fluid. "Yep. Just getting rid of the fingerprints."

Fury streamed through my veins at the injustice of it all. I'd finally found a man who truly cared about me. I'd found something with him I'd been searching for my whole life— acceptance, understanding. Love. I'd wasted so much time in the beginning trying to seal him out of my heart for fear of being hurt. Now I would never have the opportunity to tell him how much he meant to me.

I glared at Maggie through watery eyes as she swabbed the duct tape covering my hands, ankles, and mouth, obliterating any lingering evidence. My eyes widened as Carl stepped forward, a dark gleam in his eyes.

"We gotta move before the police show up."

Maggie's gaze snapped to his, her fear barely concealed in her honey-colored eyes. "They're here?"

"Close." Carl gestured to me. "Someone must have called about her screaming her head off. They're questioning the neighbors a couple streets over."

Maggie hopped to her feet, then ran to the door and shoved her head outside. A moment later, she tipped her chin toward Carl. "All clear."

He braced one hand behind my back, the other behind my knees, then lifted me against his chest. My arms ached from being bound behind me, and Carl had taped my ankles together again. We stepped outside, and my heart leaped with hope as I saw the red and blue lights flashing through the palm fronds dancing in the breeze. God, help was close—so close. If I could just somehow get them to hear me, see me...

The strobing lights were extinguished along with my hopes as Carl tightened his hold then slipped around the building and deeper into the dark. "All right, girl. Let's get this over with."

CHAPTER
THIRTY-SEVEN

VINCE

The sound of sirens met my ears, and I glanced out the window as at least two police cruisers flew past on the main road, their red and blue lights piercing the dark sky.

My heart kicked up in my chest, and a mixture of hope and fear swirled in my stomach. Had they found Jana? Sitting here, just waiting for something to happen, went against every fiber of my being. I needed to be out there. I needed to find my girl and bring her home safe.

I didn't bother to lock the door behind me as I burst out of the house and jogged down the sidewalk, following the red and blue lights up ahead. My phone rang, and I dug it from my back pocket as I slowed to a walk.

Con's name filled the screen, and I tapped my phone to connect the call. "Yeah?"

Con didn't bother to beat around the bush. "We have a problem, Ink."

"What did you find? Is Maggie okay?"

A heavy sigh filled the phone. "We haven't been able to

locate her. Her home is dark, and her car appears to be missing."

"Have the police put out a BOLO?" My heart clenched, and I picked up my pace, still following the police cruisers. The lights seemed to be stationary now, maybe half a mile ahead. I wasn't sure exactly what I was doing; all I knew was I couldn't sit in that damn silent, empty house any longer wondering where the fuck Jana was and if she was okay.

"Not much they can do at this point," he replied. "They spoke with Harvey, who said he was last in contact with her yesterday morning. If she doesn't respond within another 24 hours, we can review our options. But until then..."

"That's bullshit!" I exploded. "Maggie's missing and my wife was kidnapped. By tomorrow it could be too fucking late."

Silence fell before Con spoke. "This is more than a job to you, isn't it?"

"She was never a job," I choked out. "Con... I've gotta find her."

"We will." His voice was firm and so much more optimistic than I was at the moment. "We'll do everything we can," he reiterated. "That's why I called you. Jason pulled up Jana's phone and was going through some of her recent messages and phone log. There was a call made from Jana's phone to Maggie's four days ago, and the call lasted just under six minutes."

I let out another curse. Had someone managed to intercept the call? Or maybe Jana had slipped and mentioned to Maggie where she was. I seriously doubted that was the case, but Maggie was her closest friend. I could see how she might confide in her, especially as tumultuous as our relationship was at that point. It was more imperative than ever that we find Maggie. "What do we do now?"

"Since the PD's hands are tied, we'll have to keep trying

her. Jana takes precedence at the moment, so I'm not pulling him off that."

"No, no, of course not," I agreed.

He paused for a beat. "Ink, I need you to listen when I tell you this."

My feet halted of their own accord, feeling as if they'd turned to cement in my shoes. "What?"

"There was a ping off one of the towers down there just a few minutes ago."

My heart slammed against my ribcage as my gaze darted toward the red and blue lights up ahead. "Where?"

"Northern part of the island. We contacted Rutland, and his guys are tracing it now."

My heart rate doubled as I watched the lights strobe against the sky. Had they found her?

"Don't get your hopes up," Con said softly. "Even if they find the phone..."

There was a good chance they wouldn't find her with it. Or if they did... Helplessness rose up, thickening in my throat, threatening to choke me. I had to be strong for her; I had to believe that we would find her.

"I know."

"I'll keep you posted," Con said.

I disconnected the call and forced myself to think as I stowed my phone in my back pocket. Most everyone knew that, given the right resources, any phone could be traced as long as it was active. If Jana's abductor had found her phone, he almost certainly would have disposed of it. Likely—but not a certainty. I needed to know exactly what Rutland's men had found.

Shoving away my macabre thoughts, I allowed anger to well up in their place, hot and fierce. I embraced it as I kicked into a run again, and my muscles burned as I pushed myself harder and faster in the direction of the red and blue lights.

The sound of an engine on the main road caught my attention, and I watched a third set of lights whiz past. I cut across to the main drag, and two police cruisers came into view parked outside a small beach plaza housing a series of small, touristy shops. I slowed to a walk a block away, drawing in lungfuls of the humid evening air.

Rutland glanced my way and did a double take when he recognized me. "What the hell are you doing?"

"I know you're looking for her phone," I confessed. "I just... I have to know."

His gaze was hard as he stared at me, and I could see the sympathy and understanding in the dark depths. "You know I can't tell you anything," he said.

"I know, I know." I raked my hands through my hair, hissing in a breath as my fingers tugged at my forgotten wound. "I just... I don't know what to do."

He took a step closer. "We're working on getting a search party organized right now. Maybe you can head down to the station and help them out. We'll need any information you can provide. Photographs, the clothing she was last seen wearing, anything that might help us find her."

I knew he was just doing his job, but I'd already told him everything I knew. "Is there anything I can do?"

Rutland threw a quick look at his patrolmen, then propped his hands on his hips and regarded me for a moment. He opened his mouth to speak, but a fire engine, lights flashing and sirens blaring, raced past us. A chill crept down my spine as the huge truck slowed about half a mile up and turned right, heading toward the beach. I met Rutland's gaze. "What's going on?"

He opened his mouth to speak, probably to try to dissuade me again, but I cut him off. "Please, Chief."

He blew a harsh breath through his nose. "We got a call from a neighbor a couple minutes ago saying she thought she heard a woman call for help." He took one look at my face, and his brows lowered. "But I can't be sure, because the caller also said she thought the woman yelled about a fire."

"That's her!" I practically yelled. That was exactly what I had told Jana to do in case of an emergency.

"Listen—"

"Trust me on this," I insisted. "It's her. We've got to find her."

Rutland looked torn, but he finally nodded reluctantly. "I'll see if I can get a few more officers over there to question the residents." He threw me a dark look. "Don't make me regret telling you—and don't do anything stupid."

I shook my head. "I would never do anything to jeopardize her safety. I just want her back."

Didn't mean I was just going to sit around and wait, though. I turned and headed back in the direction of the bungalow Jana and I had been staying in. Once I was far enough away and Rutland's attention had been diverted, I bled into the shadows and looped around, heading toward the beach. I followed the flashing red and blue lights and watched as several patrolmen moved from house to house, knocking on doors.

I crossed a side street in front of what appeared to be a small condo complex. Two sets of windows were dark; the third unit glowed brightly, as if someone had left every light on inside. Suddenly, the door swung open and two patrolmen stepped out.

I started to walk past, but the Texas license plate caught my eye. It wasn't out of the ordinary for rental cars to have plates from out of state, but still... My gaze lifted to the make and model of the car, then darted toward the complex. In the open doorway of the condo, a woman stood backlit from the lamp in the living room behind her. Prickles ran over my skin, and I took several steps closer.

"Thank you for your time, ma'am," the officer said.

"Oh, it's no problem at all. Wish I could help." The Southern drawl was soft and familiar—very familiar.

My eyes snapped to the woman's face. "Maggie?"

Her eyes grew wide as they met mine, and she quickly closed the door behind her as she disappeared inside. The two officers lunged at me as I raced forward. "Stop right there!"

I lifted my hands in a defenseless gesture. "That's her! That's my wife's assistant!"

"Sir, I'm going to need you to come with us."

"Call Rutland," I demanded. "I'm Jana Malone's husband. That woman in the room"—I tipped my chin toward the condo they had just exited—"that's Maggie Clelland. She works for my wife. The police back in Texas said she's missing, but she's here. She knows something! I know she does."

The two officers exchanged a quick look, and one finally lowered his hand to his radio. "Chief, we've got something you'll want to hear."

CHAPTER
THIRTY-EIGHT

JANA

The condo was located on the corner one street from the beach, and my mind raced as Carl carried me across the pavement. As we moved, I pushed my tongue against the tape, trying to push it off. It had begun to loosen from when Maggie had yanked it off earlier, and tears of frustration welled when it refused to come free.

The long leaves of palm fronds whipped against my face as we cut through the trees, and I felt the change in tempo as he sank into the soft sand. I refused to go down like this. I had too much to live for—especially now. If I could just get this tape off and get someone's attention... Summoning every bit of energy I had, I bucked wildly in his arms, squirming to get free.

Carl fumbled me for a moment before losing his grip. "Shit!"

We tumbled to the ground, and I landed face-first in the sand. The duct tape covering my mouth muffled my cry when something sharp cut into my forehead. Forcing myself to move, I rolled to my back and kicked upward at Carl, aiming for his groin. My feet connected, and he let out a grunt as he bent over and covered himself.

I kicked upward again, this time aiming for his face, but he jerked out of the way just in time. He threw himself backward, landing on his ass in the sand, a mixture of anger and astonishment on his face. "Stupid bitch!"

I rolled my shoulder against my face, trying to lift the edge of the duct tape but he was on his feet again before I could pull it free. He lunged forward, batting my feet away and pressing them to the ground, then settled on my thighs so I couldn't move. I winced as he delivered a stinging slap to my cheek. "I fucking swear to God. You're making it easier to kill you, you know that?"

He hauled me to my feet. Still bound with duct tape, I stumbled and fell to my knees again before he grabbed me around the waist and yanked me against his side. "I felt bad at first when Maggie suggested it, but damn…" He stooped down and threw me over his shoulder in a fireman's carry. "I'm kind of looking forward to it now."

It took a second for the words to sink in. This was Maggie's idea? After the way she'd spoken earlier, the bitter resentment she harbored toward me, it shouldn't have surprised me, but it did. It hurt to know that the woman I'd considered my closest friend for the past few years had orchestrated this.

A trickle of blood dripped into my eye as Carl shifted me. Blinking away the sweat and blood obscuring my vision, I tried to place our surroundings, but everything was almost impossibly dark. The moon peeked out from behind a cloud, and the pier rose up in front of us as he cut across the sand. His shoulder dug into my stomach, and I felt bile rise up in my throat with every jolting step. I closed my eyes and forced it down.

Carl's heavy tread clomped against the wooden planks of the pier, and my eyes flew open. Panic seized my chest. Oh, my God. He was going to throw me in the ocean. I struggled in earnest, kicking my feet and throwing my body side to side. Suspended over his shoulder, he had better leverage this time. He clamped one arm tightly around the back of my legs and grabbed my hair with the other hand, effectively curling me around his torso and subduing my movement.

My heart raced and I pleaded incoherently from behind the duct tape for him to let me go. Before I'd worked out a plan in my head, we'd reached the end of the pier. Carl dropped me unceremoniously to my feet, and I stared up at him, tears streaming down my cheeks. I prayed he would take the tape off my mouth to at least let me speak. Instead, he slipped his hands under my armpits and lifted me until I was sitting on the railing.

"You're something else, you know that? So talented. Must've got that from my side." He chuckled a little. "God knows your mama was never good for much."

I glared at him, and he let out a soft exhalation as he stepped backwards. For a glorious moment, hope bloomed in my chest. Maybe he would leave me here, give him a chance to get away before the authorities found him.

"Sorry, Jana girl." He almost looked remorseful as he shook his head. "But we really need that money."

My optimism was extinguished as he grasped my bound ankles and lifted, toppling me backward over the railing. My scream came out muted, barely more than a squeak as I hurtled through the air. It felt like I was falling forever before my body hit the water and cold sliced through me.

All of a sudden, it was all around me, pulling me under, wrapping me in cold, inky darkness. I became acutely aware of a stinging sensation as the salty water flooded the wound on my face. Unable to use my arms, I bucked wildly, trying to propel myself toward the surface. I couldn't see a thing, and I hadn't had a chance to drag in a breath before I'd gone under. My chest felt tight, and my throat began to burn with the desperate need for oxygen. Then the fear set in.

I thrashed and kicked, trying to get my feet under me, but the water curled around me, distorting my surroundings as it dragged me toward the bottom. I knew I was supposed to allow my body to go limp so my mind could get its bearings, and it took every ounce of willpower to relax my muscles and stop fighting the pull of gravity.

I drifted slowly downward before landing shoulder-first with a gentle thump, sending up a hazy swirl of sand as my body displaced the silt layering the bottom of the ocean. My eyes burned, clouded by salt water and fatigue, and I fought to shift my weight so I could get my knees under me. The sand shifted, throwing me off-balance, and I collapsed to my back, completely devoid of energy.

The last of my oxygen escaped my nostrils, rising in tiny bubbles to the surface, and my eyes followed their path. A shaft of silvery light danced above me, and I imagined the moon reflecting off the dark surface. Then, suddenly, it was gone.

A sharp barb pierced my heart as I thought of Vince—of everything we'd been through, of everything we'd never have the chance to experience. Sending up one last prayer to keep him safe, my eyes drifted closed, and water rushed into my lungs, ending my fight.

CHAPTER
THIRTY-NINE

VINCE

Anger boiled up in my veins as I regarded Chief Rutland. We stood on the sidewalk at the corner of the condo unit where Maggie was ensconced inside. "Please," I practically begged. "There's no reason for her to be here."

Rutland shook his head. "She invited my men in, allowed them to search the property. Why would she do that if she had something to hide?"

"I don't know!" Nothing about this made sense.

"Let my guys do their job," he said firmly. "We found Ms. Malone's phone in the Dumpster next to the ice cream parlor, and we've got feet on the ground questioning everyone in the neighborhood. We're doing what we can."

Turning on a heel, I stormed away from the small rental house, raking my hands through my hair. The bitch knew something—she had to. Fury engulfed me, threatening to take over, and I forced myself to think clearly. Maggie was here— but why? What would prompt her to come all the way to the beach unless she somehow meant Jana harm?

I stopped in the middle of the road and glanced back at the condo complex, my mind spinning with possibilities. I didn't know what had been used to knock me out—I hadn't wasted the time to go searching for the weapon. Regardless, any woman was capable of a well-placed hit to the back of the head. But could she overpower Jana?

I seriously doubted it, especially with the recent self-defense moves we'd been working on. Maggie was a small woman, just slightly taller than Jana. There had been obvious signs of struggle, but I couldn't imagine Jana willingly getting into a vehicle with her. There had to be someone else involved.

I laced my hands together on the top of my head and tipped my face up to the moon, then closed my eyes. The island was closed. Maggie was here, which was a good indication that Jana was still here somewhere. But where?

My ears perked up at a soft sound that carried on the light breeze. Little more than a squeak, it jolted me into action. A splash followed, sending chills down my spine. It was louder than the waves crashing gently against the shore and seemed to come from farther out. It also sounded large.

I started walking, unsure exactly of where I was going until I broke through the palm trees and stepped onto the soft sand. There was no light to speak of whatsoever, and it took a moment for my eyes to adjust. My gaze swept the vista in front of me and it finally sank in. *The pier*.

In the moonlight, my eyes picked up a lone figure striding quickly back down the dock in my direction. The memory of the broken light bulbs flashed before my eyes, and I was running before I even thought about what I was doing.

"Rutland!" I screamed over my shoulder. "Get down here!"

The man on the pier snapped his head toward me. In the moonlight, I could only make out the pale white of his face as

I charged toward him. He broke into a run, and I tackled him as soon as he reached the end of the pier. Pinning him to the ground, I stared down at him. A cold, calculating look filled his eyes—and I knew.

"You motherfucker!" Slamming my fist into his face, I growled at him. "What'd you do to her?"

The man's face twisted into a sneer as his eyebrow split open and thick, dark blood oozed out. "I don't know who you're talking about."

"Bullshit." I landed another hard punch to his nose, and blood spurted over his lips and chin. "Where the fuck is she?"

He turned his head and spat out a mouthful of blood. "Fuck you."

I shook him hard, and the back of his head hit the worn wood of the pier with a solid *thunk*. "I swear to God, if you don't tell me where she is—"

A slow smile spread over his mouth, exposing his blood-stained teeth, looking nearly black in the darkness. "Bitch is gone."

The splash I'd heard suddenly registered, and ice settled in my veins. Smashing my fist into his face one more time, I rolled off him and sprinted to the end of the pier. My lungs heaved from exertion, and I threw myself against the railing, scanning frantically for her.

"Jana!"

A few feet from the post of the pier, a few bubbles surfaced and rippled across the water. Without thinking, I launched myself up onto the railing and dove into the water. Salt burned my eyes as I twisted my head left and right, looking for her in the dark, murky depths. Suddenly, a flash of white below me drew my attention.

I dove downward, stretching for the tangle of fabric far below me. My lungs began to ache as I cut through the water. Finally, my fingers touched the billowing white fabric that rose around her like a cloud. I grabbed up Jana's body in my arms and pushed against the sea floor, shooting us toward the surface.

I gasped in a breath as soon as we broke free of the water, but Jana remained limp in my arms. Her head lolled backward, and I noticed the duct tape hanging loosely from a corner of her mouth.

"Fuck!" Using my legs to tread water, I pounded her roughly on the back, hoping it would jolt her lungs into action. "Come on, trouble. Don't give up on me now."

Positioning us so her head was above water, I kicked forcefully toward the shore. "Help!"

Several policemen waded into the water and pulled Jana's lifeless body from my arms. Just a few feet away, I rested on my hands and knees, eyes burning as I watched them perform chest compressions. The sound of running feet approached, and a medic slid into place next to her, taking over. What felt like hours passed as I watched them pump air into her lungs with no reward.

"Come on, baby. Fight for me!" Tears mingled with the water running down my cheeks, and my heart twisted in my chest. The searing pain of the wound on the back of my head was nothing compared to the sight of Jana lying there, pale and still, as if the life had leached from her body.

Suddenly, with a horrific gagging sound, Jana spit up a mouthful of water. The medic turned her on her side as she coughed and sputtered, ridding her lungs of the vile fluid.

Spurred by hope, I scrambled closer and placed a hand on the medic's shoulder, my gaze fixed on Jana. The woman studied me for a long moment. She must have read the urgency in my eyes, because she settled Jana on her back, then, apparently satisfied that she was well enough for the moment, scooted out of my way.

I practically threw myself over Jana and pulled her against

me. She was so weak she couldn't move or speak, but I didn't care. I ran my hands over every inch I could touch, from her perfect, gorgeous face, down her back and hips. "Thank God…"

I buried my head against her chest, my lips moving over her cold, wet skin. "Christ, baby, you scared the life out of me. I was so fucking worried about you."

A shiver racked her body, and she coughed several more times. I tipped my head up to look at her, and a pair of bright blue eyes met mine. Her hand lifted, curling into the sodden fabric of my shirt and held on for dear life.

"I don't know what I'd have done if…" My voice broke as I trailed off. "Thank fuck you're okay."

"Sir…" Off to the side, the medic's voice slowly penetrated the blood rushing through my ears. "I need to check you both over."

I wrapped my fingers around Jana's where they grasped my shirt and nodded, my eyes still locked on hers. "Her first. Make sure she's okay."

I gave her hand a little squeeze to let her know I wasn't going anywhere, then released her so the woman could finish her work. Everything had happened so quickly, and I finally took a moment to look around. My eyes were drawn to the pier, looking for the man I'd knocked out on the way to find Jana, but he was gone.

I swept my gaze over the dim beach before it fell on Chief Rutland. He stood off to the side, watching as two patrolmen slapped a pair of handcuffs on a man. I couldn't make out his features in the moonlight, but I was positive it was the same guy from the pier. They hauled him to his feet, then escorted him up the beach, presumably to take him into custody.

Rutland's gaze swung to mine, and I staggered to my feet. He held out a hand as I approached. "Well done. We couldn't have done it without your help."

I bit back the angry retort that sprang to my lips as I shook his hand. Had they listened to me and questioned Maggie, maybe this wouldn't have happened. Or maybe, I thought as my anger slipped away, it would have been too late. If we'd gone in to talk with Maggie, I never would have heard the noises on the beach that led me to her. We certainly would have been pulling up a body instead of my wife who was finally safe.

"Thank you for your help." I dropped my hand to my side, then tipped my head in the direction of the condo where Maggie was staying. "What's happening with Maggie?"

Rutland rested his hands on his duty belt. "My men are bringing her in as we speak."

After everything Jana had been through, I was going to make damn sure she never had to worry about her safety again. "What about the guy? Did he admit to anything?"

"Not yet." Chief Rutland shook his head. "His story is that Maggie was the mastermind."

"The asshole threw her in the fucking ocean and left her to drown." The thought still had the power to make my blood run both hot and cold.

"I know, I know." Rutland held up his hands in supplication. "And we'll get both your statements so we can do our best to put both of them away."

I scowled. That wasn't good enough, but I knew he was doing everything he could. Despite his feelings on the matter, he was bound by the law. "I want a restraining order against both of them—same goes for Jana."

I threw a look at the woman in question who the EMS were currently loading onto a stretcher, then turned back to Rutland. "Where's the closest hospital?"

"Right over the bridge in Bradenton." He tipped his chin at me. "Make sure they check that wound."

I gave a noncommittal nod as I dug my phone out of my

back pocket, grimacing as I hit the home button. After my swim in the ocean, I didn't expect it to work. Miraculously, the waterproof cover I used actually seemed to have protected it, because the screen lit up immediately.

I glanced at Rutland. "I'll touch base with Con and let him know what happened."

"No need." He waved me off. "I'll take care of it, make sure you guys are good to get home as soon as you're released."

"Thanks."

Every muscle in my body protesting, I made my way up the beach behind the medics. Once they'd loaded her in the back of the ambulance, the medic who'd cared for Jana nodded to me, and I shot her an appreciative smile as I hopped in.

Jana's eyes met mine, squinting against the brightly lit interior of the truck. I took her hand in mine as I leaned in close to her ear. "Good thing I'm gonna be around from now on. Someone's gotta keep you out of trouble."

A tiny smile lifted the corners of her mouth at my gentle tease, and I brushed my lips over her temple. "I'll never let anyone take you from me. You're mine, Jana Incarnato."

CHAPTER
FORTY

JANA

"Babe?"

"Back here," I yelled from the bedroom. I grabbed the last pair of socks from the bottom of the laundry basket and shoved them into the dresser, then closed the drawer with a smile. I loved seeing my clothes next to his, the way he'd welcomed me wholly into his life. I loved being surrounded by his things, being surrounded by him. Though it'd only been a few weeks, we'd fallen into a comfortable rhythm.

After the ordeal with my father and Maggie, I'd spent a day in the ICU in Bradenton before we flew back home. The studio had cut ties with Maggie, who'd claimed innocence initially. She hadn't been able to make bail, so she was still in Florida awaiting sentencing. My father had several prior offenses, and he'd been denied any chance at bail. He was currently being charged for attempted murder and would likely be put away for a long time.

In my statement to the police, I'd explained their plan to kill me, then swindle my mother out of the life insurance payout she would have received on my behalf. An officer spoke with my mother to corroborate the events that had transpired prior to her arrest almost a little over a month ago.

Apparently, Carl had swept back into her life like a white knight, luring her away from Burt. My father had convinced her to move in with him and, since my mother never had any money of her own, he'd made several small deposits into her account to win her over. While she thought Carl had been helping her out, she'd unwittingly given him access to her account information and checkbook. He would have easily been able to drain the account with her none the wiser.

Vince appeared in the doorway, and his eyes immediately landed on me. He strode forward and pulled me into his arms. "Good news."

"Yeah?" I stretched up on my toes for a kiss, luxuriating in the slow sweetness of his lips on mine, the way his hands slid over my back.

Vince broke the kiss and smiled at me. "Maggie pled guilty."

My brows shot up. "Seriously?"

"It was the smart thing for her to do." He lifted one shoulder. "Her lawyer managed to talk her into spilling everything and getting a plea deal."

Unease sat heavily in my stomach. "So she's still going to jail, right?"

"She'll do some time." Vince's gaze turned wary, and he let out a little sigh. "She's been charged as an accessory to attempted murder along with several other things, but they cut down on the sentence because she's cooperating."

I leaned away. "Tell me how that's a good thing. Because the way I see it, she'll be back out in no time."

"I know, babe." He pulled me back to him. "But we've got restraining orders—"

"Great," I mumbled sarcastically. "I've got a piece of paper to protect me."

"Come on, now." Vince stroked my hair. "They've done what they could."

I couldn't hide the disappointment I knew shone on my face. I wanted justice; I wanted them to be punished for what they'd done—not only to me, but to everyone else they'd hurt in the process. It wasn't fair.

"I don't like it, either," he continued, his soothing voice rumbling next to my ear. "But it's what we've got to work with, so we need to take it."

"I know. It still sucks."

"It does," he agreed. "But I'd like to believe that Maggie wouldn't be stupid enough to try something like this again. She knows she won't be as lucky a second time."

That was true, at least. "What about my father?"

"With his history, he'll be doing some serious time. You won't have to worry about him again."

"Good." I curled in closer to Vince, reveling in his heat and strength. I wanted to put that time behind us and move forward.

"Besides, you know I'll never let anyone hurt you."

I tipped my head up and looked at him. His expression was earnest, and it made me melt a little inside. Since Vince was no longer required to work security for me, we'd both returned to work once we arrived home. But Vince was more protective than ever. He was constantly checking in to make sure I'd gotten to and from the studio okay each day, and he hated when his jobs for QSG took him away from me at night.

He stared down at me. "Do you know what today is?"

"Um..." I searched my mind but came up empty. "Thursday?"

"That, too." He chuckled, then turned serious again. "Today marks exactly one month that we've been married."

I blinked. "You kept track?"

"You didn't?"

He laughed when my mouth flopped open then snapped shut again as I floundered for a response, and I lightly slapped his chest. "Whatever. So, what'd you get me?"

"It's always about you, isn't it?" His tone was teasing as he slipped his hands lower until they cupped my bottom. "I was thinking something more... mutually satisfying."

"By all means." I grabbed his shirt and stepped backward, tugging him toward the bed. "Show me what you had in mind."

He grabbed my hips and lifted me, then lay me back against the cool fabric of the comforter as he settled himself over me. I was already reaching for him when he grabbed my hands, stilling my movements. My gaze jumped to his, and my breath caught at the emotion I saw swirling there.

"You're beautiful." He released my hand and stroked my hair, then cupped my face. "I don't tell you that enough."

"You do—"

His thumb swept over my mouth, silencing me. "I don't tell you how much I look forward to seeing you each day. How happy you make me." His chest rose and fell. "How much I love you."

It was the first time either of us had uttered those words, and tears sprang to my eyes as happiness spread through my body. "Really?"

"How could you ever doubt it?" His lips lowered to mine, and he kissed me soft and slow. I slid my fingers through the short strands of hair at the back of his neck as he thrust his tongue against mine.

A long minute later, I surfaced from my haze of pleasure

and met his gaze. "I've wanted to tell you forever—I love you, too."

He grinned, pulling me with him as he rolled to his back. "Show me."

EPILOGUE

VINCE

SIX MONTHS LATER

Buttery morning sunlight spilled through the window behind Jana, turning her hair to spun gold and bathing her in an ethereal glow. She was absolutely gorgeous, inside and out, so much that it hurt to look at her sometimes. I had no idea how I'd ever gotten so lucky, but I knew one thing—I was never going to let her go.

I watched as her eyelashes fluttered against her cheek, those gorgeous, big blue eyes blinking open and meeting mine, as if she could feel me watching her.

I swept a strand of hair off her face and tucked it behind her ear. "Good morning, beautiful."

Jana shifted her head on the pillow to look at me, a sexy, sleepy smile playing at the corners of her mouth. "Merry Christmas."

It was a very merry Christmas, and I couldn't wait to share it with her. "You ready for breakfast?"

"Mhmm. In a minute." She burrowed her head into the crook of my neck, tangling her legs with mine, and I pulled her into my arms, the way I did each morning. The queen-sized bed we were currently curled up in was smaller than the king we typically shared at home, but I wasn't going to complain.

Yesterday afternoon we'd flown into Pittsburgh to spend Christmas with my family, and they'd insisted we stay with them instead of a hotel. It was the first time Jana had met my parents, who'd immediately welcomed her into the fold. My mom was beyond thrilled to meet her and already loved her as much as I did.

Last night, once we were alone in our room, Jana had broken down and cried. I didn't completely understand her reaction, but I knew the tumultuous relationship with her mother had done a number on her. Jana was part of my life for good, and I would do everything in my power to never let anything hurt her again.

A little over a month ago, Jana had moved her things into my house and we'd listed her two-bedroom home for rent. Sharing a bedroom at my place left two other rooms open— rooms that I hoped would be filled soon. My mom had hinted at grandkids on the phone, but I'd warned her not to say anything in front of Jana. Though we both wanted kids eventually, I knew it would be tricky with Jana's career, and I promised myself I wouldn't pressure her.

I swept one hand down her back and patted her butt. "Come on, sweetheart."

She let out a little groan before peeling herself away, a sexy little pout taking up residence on her pretty face. I caught her and dragged her back to me, one hand tangled in the hair at the back of her head. "Hotel tomorrow night, then you're all mine."

I kissed her once—hard—then let her go. My cock twitched as I watched her slide from the bed, lean muscles rippling as she lifted her hands over her head and stretched. With our busy schedules prior to the holiday, it'd been several days since we'd had a chance to have sex. My parents probably wouldn't care, but I preferred to be in a hotel where we could be alone—especially as vocal as Jana could be sometimes.

Several hours later, we'd eaten and were gathered in the living room to exchange presents. My brothers and their families would be coming in tomorrow to celebrate, which gave us some one-on-one time with my parents. I passed Jana a brightly colored package, and her cheeks glowed with happiness as she pulled out a pair of fuzzy socks and clutched them to her chest.

"I love them! Thank you." She leaned over and kissed my cheek, then turned her attention to my dad, who was doing his best to distract her with talk of his new tool set.

I pulled up the camera function and slipped my phone to my mom. She met my gaze, a huge smile on her face. "I was worried at first, but now that we've met her…"

I knew exactly how she felt. My parents were initially concerned and slightly disappointed to hear that I'd eloped with Jana before I even bothered to introduce them. I'd eventually told them it was a whirlwind romance, and that I'd known the moment I met her that I loved her and had to have her. Looking back, I think that was the truth. We'd both tried so hard to conceal our true emotions and failed miserably. Thank God.

Mom passed me an ornament with Jana's name inscribed on it, then pulled me into a hug. "I'm happy for you."

"Me, too." I softly kissed her cheek, then turned back to my wife. I laid a gentle hand on Jana's shoulder to get her attention, and my dad shot me a knowing look as Mom sank down on the couch next to him.

"Hey, babe. One last thing." She looked up at me with curious eyes as I passed her the ornament. "Now that you're officially part of the family, you get your own ornament."

She reached out and tentatively touched the silver Treble Clef, her bright eyes jumping between my parents and me. "I... Really?"

"Absolutely," my mother encouraged with a smile. "Go put it on the tree."

A huge grin split Jana's face as she slipped it from my fingers and headed for the tree in the corner. I followed right behind and pointed out a spot high up right in front. "How about there?"

As she stretched up to hang the ornament on the branch, I dropped to a knee. She turned, and her eyes widened at the sight of me. "Vince...?"

"It's occurred to me that you never received an official proposal." Her eyes sparkled with unshed tears as she stared down at me. "We told everyone that we got engaged at Christmas when I took you home to meet my family." I opened my arms wide. "Now it's the truth."

One tear escaped and slipped down her cheek. "I can't believe you did this."

She still wore the ring I'd given her during our fake proposal, so I didn't have anything to give her, except myself. I stood and pulled her into my arms. "Never doubt that I want to be with you. You deserve the absolute best, baby, and I want to spend the rest of my life giving it to you. We're already married, but I want you to know that I'm in this because I want to be—because I love you more than anything."

A stifled sob caught in her throat, eliminating her words as she threw herself against my chest. I caught her, wrapping my arms around her waist and lifting her off her toes as I hugged her tight. "Don't cry, beautiful. You know I can't stand those tears."

She spoke against my chest, but the words came out muffled, and I let out a little chuckle. "Didn't catch that."

My mom and dad had made themselves scarce, and I kissed Jana's forehead.

She lifted her head to meet my gaze. I lowered her until her feet were flat on the floor, then swept a stray tear from her cheek. Her mouth trembled, and I fought a smile as she sniffed loudly. "You didn't have to do this."

I cupped her chin and lifted her gaze to mine. "I wanted to. You deserve it." Her mouth trembled in a shaky smile, and I slid my fingers through her hair, cupping the back of her head. "Everything about our relationship was unconventional, but I wouldn't change it for the world."

"I love you." She looped her arms around my waist and tipped her head up to me. I pulled her close as she leaned into me. Her teeth cut into her lower lip as she studied me. "I have something for you, too."

"Oh?" I followed behind as she made her way up the stairs to the guest room where we were staying.

She stopped just inside the room, and I closed the door behind us. A strange feeling gripped me as she turned to face me, looking incredibly unsure of herself. "I... I didn't want to do this in front of your parents."

I stiffened, my entire body going rigid. I was pretty certain that no good conversation had ever started with something like that. It meant she was worried how I would react. It put me on edge, and I stared silently at her as she continued. Her eyes darted around the room, unable to make contact with mine for more than a second or so.

"I just..."

She wrung her hands together nervously, and I fought to keep my tone level. "Whatever it is, sweetheart, you can talk to me."

Her lips rolled together, and her chest rose and fell on a

deep breath before she spun on a heel and crossed the room. She bent and riffled through her suitcase for a moment before pulling out a small rectangle, clutching it to her chest as she turned to face me. "I..." She faltered and started over. "I wasn't sure what you would say, so..."

I eyed her quizzically. She was worried that I wouldn't like her gift? My gaze fell to the item, which, from the back, looked like a small photo frame. I held out my hand. "Let me see."

She swallowed hard and took a step forward, then extended the object to me, facedown. I slipped it from her shaky fingers and flipped it around. My brows drew together at the blurry black and white image.

"Wh—" The air left my lungs as the small typed letters in the upper left-hand corner registered.

Baby Incarnato.

I lifted my gaze to Jana, who looked like she might cry. "Is this real?"

She wrapped her arms around her stomach—the still-flat stomach that housed our tiny baby—and nodded. "I know we haven't really talked about it, but..." She shrugged helplessly.

"Jana..." My voice started to break, and I cleared my throat as I stepped forward and pulled her to me. "This is the best Christmas present ever."

"Really?" She stared up at me.

"Really."

She looked thrown. "You never said anything."

"I didn't want to pressure you." I grinned at her and pressed one hand to her middle. "This is fucking incredible." I held out the frame and looked at it again. "How far along are you?"

"About eight weeks." She placed her hand over mine where it rested on her belly. "I had the ultrasound taken the day before we left. I was going to wait until we got back home, but..."

"This was perfect." I wrapped my arms around her and kissed her, long and slow. We would have dozens of Christmases in our future, and I looked forward to every single one with Jana and as many babies as we were blessed with. I pulled back and grinned down at her. "I was happy before, but this? This is only the beginning."

If you loved Vince and Jana's story, you won't want to miss the next book in the Quentin Security Series! When Abby unearths a dark secret tied to her family's past, only her brother's best friend can protect her from a killer determined to silence her forever. Turn the page for a sneak peek of Tempting the Devil!

TEMPTING THE DEVIL

PROLOGUE

ABBY

The figure moved forward, closing the distance between us. "Sitting here all by yourself, little one?"

I nodded up at the deep voice, unable to form words. The man's face was blurry, and I couldn't quite pull it into focus as he moved in front of me.

"You're a good girl, aren't you, Abilene?"

I nodded, a strange sensation taking root deep in my belly. I couldn't quite explain it, but it was the same kind of feeling I'd had once after eating too many cookies. A little sick, a little afraid of what would happen if I were caught.

The bulky figure took a seat on the coffee table in front of me. "I seem to be missing some money, Abilene. Had twenty dollars right on the kitchen counter and now it's gone. You wouldn't know anything about that, now would you?"

I shook my head, fear and something else rising up in my

throat, stealing my words as he leaned closer. His features remained obscured, fuzzy but somehow still familiar.

"I think you took it, Abby." Again, I shook my head vehemently, but he cut me off as I tried to speak. "It's okay, I understand. I'll keep your secret."

One huge hand settled on my knee. "No one has to know."

The hand slid up my thigh, and the butterflies in my belly kicked into full flight.

"Such a pretty little thing..."

CHAPTER ONE

ABBY

My feet felt heavy as I trudged through the hotel that had served as a home to me for the past two nights. My brother had offered to let me stay with him, but I'd declined.

Con had already done enough for me, and I didn't need to add to his burden. He was absorbed in his business, and he'd already taken the time out of his busy schedule to move my things into Violet's place, even enlisting the help of his friend and employee, Cole.

The hotel bar came into sight, and I pushed down the guilt that threatened to swallow me whole. God, I was so tired. Tired of the guilt. Tired of feeling sad and out of control.

The last couple of weeks felt like a rollercoaster of activity and emotion. Even now that I was finally off the ride, the world around me was still spinning violently. After the past few days, I just needed a little bit of time to myself and a drink or two to take my mind off of things.

Everything had happened so quickly. Two weeks ago I'd left college in Connecticut to move in with my guardian,

Violet. Dallas was home for me, and I'd gone to live with Violet while Con opted to enter the Marines after our parents passed away. Aside from my brother, she was the only other person I had to call family.

I should've known something was off, but I was so busy with moving and getting settled that I'd ignored all the signs. Violet seemed to be more forgetful than usual, but I hadn't thought much of it—until the day of the fire.

On Monday morning, I left Violet in the sunroom where she enjoyed drinking her coffee and working on her crossword puzzles. I shopped for groceries then stopped by the drugstore to pick up Violet's prescriptions, completely oblivious to the turmoil unfolding back home.

I would never forget the sight that greeted me when I turned onto the street. Fire trucks had gathered in front of the house, creating a barrier around the burning house, and thick black smoke billowed up from the old brick ranch.

A sobbing Violet greeted me by the ambulance. Though she wasn't hurt, it was glaringly obvious; she couldn't be left alone. While I was gone, Violet had apparently decided to make breakfast. From what we concluded, she'd forgotten about the pan on the stove and the bacon she'd been frying caught fire.

Violet threw water on it to put it out, succeeding only in helping the fire to spread. Thank goodness a neighbor two doors down had heard Violet yelling for help. He'd called the fire department and they'd arrived minutes later.

Most of the kitchen was toast—no pun intended—but at least the house had been salvaged. The fire had spread from the kitchen into the surrounding living and dining rooms, scorching the walls and floors. My brother had hired a company to clean the house and renovate the kitchen so we wouldn't have to wait for the insurance check to come through. We would eventually need to replace the flooring in all the rooms, but for now it just needed to be clean and livable.

Two days after the fire, Violet moved into an assisted living facility. She'd apparently been making plans for several months, but I was blindsided by her choice. I couldn't deny her request, and I'd spent the past few days helping to get her settled. I was exhausted mentally, and I couldn't bear to be at home right now.

Though I wanted to turn him down, I couldn't refuse Con's offer to put me up in the hotel. Since I hadn't been able to get to work either, I was a little low on funds. I was scheduled to start this past week working for my brother's security company, but with everything going on he'd pushed my start date to next Monday. I was actually looking forward to it, hoping like hell it would give me something else to focus on.

I stepped into the hotel bar and threw a quick glance around. Since it was Friday night, most of the tables were occupied, either with travelers wanting to relax and unwind or locals who'd come to grab a nightcap before heading home for the evening. Sliding onto the tall leather barstool, I allowed my gaze to rove the room.

Most of the men were older, overweight, slouched over their drinks, still dressed sloppily in wrinkled suits and ties. Coming down here was a stupid mistake. I should have called my friend Jamie and asked her to come meet me, but I knew she was going out with Brandon tonight, and I didn't want to interrupt their date.

My attention was drawn to the bartender who leaned against the bar in front of me. "What can I get you?"

"Um..." I'd never been a big partier in college, preferring to focus instead on my studies. I'd had big plans back then, none of which had included moving back home the moment I graduated. Shaking off the thought, I forced a smile to my face as I passed him my credit card. "I'll have an apple martini, please."

He moved away with a nod and began to gather up the things he needed to make it. I was always impressed by bartenders' abilities to memorize and make so many different drinks, and I watched fixedly as he shook the liquid, then strained it into a glass before sliding it my way.

"Thank you."

He returned my card, and I added a tip to the receipt before signing it and passing it back to him. I lifted the drink to my lips and took a sip, then settled back in my seat as the sweet liquor exploded over my tongue.

I could feel a set of eyes on me, and I glanced around again. An older man, dressed in a wrinkled collared shirt with a light brown stain in the region of his breast pocket, stared at me like he wanted to devour me.

It was bad manners to meet someone's eyes without acknowledging them, but I forced down the urge to flash him a polite smile. I wasn't here to encourage anyone. Studiously avoiding him, I turned my back and tuned out the older gentleman to my right.

My gaze slid over the sea of faces seated sporadically around the room. I was scanning the back wall when I suddenly froze, stunned by the sight of the gorgeous man tucked away in a corner booth. My insides tingled as heat raced through me, and I shifted on my barstool. Focused on the plate of food in front of him, the man didn't seem to be aware of my presence. Story of my life.

Suddenly, as if feeling my eyes on him, his gaze lifted. I immediately ducked my head, my heart thundering in my chest as I stared at the green liquid sloshing precariously in my glass. I forced my hand to steady as I drew in a deep breath.

Holy shit, he'd almost caught me ogling him. Heat crept into my cheeks, and I flicked a glance up through my lashes to see if he'd noticed me. My chest tightened a little with disappointment when I found his attention once more focused on the plate in front of him.

I turned my body a bit, keeping him in my peripheral vision as I sipped on my own drink. I took the opportunity to look him over as he drank deeply, his Adam's apple bobbing with the motion. The sleeves of his black button up shirt were rolled up, exposing corded, veiny forearms that my fingers itched to touch. Chiseled jaw, dark hair that was cut close to the sides but left longer on top. Broad shoulders and thick biceps.

I couldn't see the color of his eyes from here, only the dark look in them, warning everyone else away. Sitting all alone in the corner booth, he practically had the words *fuck off* stamped across his forehead.

A rail-thin blonde approached, and her hip bumped into his table. Her giggle lilted on the air, and my insides tightened with something like jealousy as it reached me. How ridiculous was that? I didn't know this man at all. *But you'd like to*, my subconscious spoke up. That was true enough. I couldn't tear my gaze away as I watched the interaction between the man and the blonde across the room.

He offered her a tight smile, then redirected his gaze to the glass in his hand. But the blonde didn't get the memo. Drink balanced in one hand, she leaned toward him and ran her fingers over his arm. Even from here, I could see him tense. It took guts to hit on a guy who looked like that, so I gave the girl props. But he obviously wasn't having any of it, and he was too nice to tell her to pound salt.

I watched in rapt fascination as the woman jerked away from him and made an agitated gesture with her hand. Her movements became wilder, more pronounced. She was obviously giving him hell for something. The man started to shake his head, but the woman's voice grew louder and louder.

The man in the booth looked incredibly uncomfortable as people around them turned to watch the show unfold.

I bit my lip, then made a split decision. I didn't know this man or what had transpired between him and the beautiful woman next to him, but I felt compelled to intervene. Adjusting my purse over my shoulder, I slid from my barstool and made a beeline toward the booth.

Halfway across the room, my steps faltered. What the hell was I doing? My gaze flitted around, looking for the bathroom so I could change my course and escape inside where no one would be the wiser. But the door I sought was nowhere in sight, and I dimly remembered passing it on my way into the bar. Damn it.

Drawing in a deep breath, I steeled myself as I continued along my trajectory, straight toward the man seated in the booth and the leggy woman next to him. The closer I got, the more my stomach twisted. Oh, God, this was a terrible idea.

"You just left me!" the woman practically wailed. "I thought I meant something to you!"

A lover's quarrel. Even worse. I couldn't tell why, precisely, but I felt bad for both of them. I felt bad for the woman who obviously believed she and the man had shared something special, only to have him leave. But I felt bad for him, too. She was making an unholy scene—and no one deserved that, regardless of the situation.

My eyes flew back to the man in the booth. He was doing a good job of keeping his emotions in check, but I saw the hard lines of his face, the tight clenching of his jaw as she railed at him. I swallowed hard as I stepped up next to the woman.

My head barely came up to her shoulder, and not for the first time since I left my spot across the bar, I was swamped with a sense of insecurity. The man's eyes flicked to where I stood next to the beautiful blonde, and I could practically read the question in their depths.

Who are you, and what the hell are you doing?

Instead of responding, I cleared my throat and brushed lightly against the woman, silently prodding her to move. Still wrapped up in her ongoing tirade, the woman didn't even notice me.

"You asshole! I can't believe you," she fumed. "You promised you would—"

I tapped her on the shoulder. "Excuse me."

"What?" The woman whipped toward me, eyes wide and slightly crazed looking.

"I, um..." I swallowed hard and tried again, forcing myself not to cower under her intense glare. "I think you're mistaken."

Her wide blue eyes flew toward the man in the booth, then back to mine, still filled with a mixture of hurt and anger. "About what?"

I smiled, praying that neither could see my unease. "I think you have the wrong guy."

"No." She shook her head and pointed a finger his way. "He—"

"Trust me." I drew a deep breath. "He's my boyfriend."

ALSO BY MORGAN JAMES

QUENTIN SECURITY SERIES

Twisted Devil – Jason and Chloe

The Devil You Know – Blake and Victoria

Devil in the Details – Xander and Lydia

Devil in Disguise – Gavin and Kate

Heart of a Devil – Vince and Jana

Tempting the Devil – Clay and Abby

Devilish Intent – Con and Grace

Quentin Security Box Set One (Books 1-3)

Quentin Security Box Set Two (Books 4-6)

*Each book is a standalone within the series

RESCUE & REDEMPTION SERIES

Friendly Fire – Grayson and Claire

Cruel Vendetta – Drew and Emery

Silent Treatment – Finn and Harper

Reckless Pursuit – Aiden and Izzy

Dangerous Desires – Vaughn and Sienna

Rescue & Redemption Box Set One (books 1-3)

RETRIBUTION SERIES

Unrequited Love – Jack and Mia, Book One

Undeniable Love – Jack and Mia, Book Two

Unbreakable Love – Jack and Mia, Book Three

Pretty Little Lies – Eric and Jules, Book One

Beautiful Deception – Eric and Jules, Book Two

Sinful Illusions – Fox and Eva, Book One

Sinful Sacrament – Fox and Eva, Book Two

Retribution Series Box Set 1

Retribution Series Box Set 2

Retribution Series Box Set 3

The Complete Retribution Series

STANDALONES

Death Do Us Part

Escape

BAD BILLIONAIRES

(Radish Exclusive)

Depraved

Ravished

Consumed

ABOUT THE AUTHOR

Morgan James is a USA Today bestselling author of contemporary and romantic suspense novels. She spent most of her childhood with her nose buried in a book, and she loves all things romantic, dark, and dirty. She currently resides in Ohio and is living happily ever after with her own alpha hero and their two kids.